Also Available from Bloom Books

Roomhate

**THE RULES OF DATING
(COWRITTEN WITH VI KEELAND)**
The Rules of Dating
The Rules of Dating My Best Friend's Sister
The Rules of Dating My One-Night Stand
The Rules of Dating a Younger Man

ROOMHATE

PENELOPE WARD

Bloom *books*

Published by Bloom Books, an imprint of Sourcebooks
P.O. Box 4410, Naperville, Illinois 60567-4410
(630) 961-3900
sourcebooks.com

Originally self-published in 2016 by Penelope Ward.

Cataloging-in-Publication data is on file with the Library of Congress.

Printed and bound in the United States of America.
WOZ 10 9 8 7 6 5 4 3 2 1

CHAPTER 1

A car nearly hit me as I practically floated across the street in a daze after leaving the attorney's office. All these years, I'd tried so hard not to think about him. Now, he was all I could think about.

Justin.

Oh my God.

Justin.

Flashes of him invaded my mind: his dark blond hair, his laughter, the strum of his guitar, the deep sadness and disappointment in his gorgeous eyes the last time I saw him nine years ago.

I was never supposed to face him again, let alone own a house with him. And there wasn't a chance in hell that Justin Banks was going to agree to share a house with *me,* either. Whether we liked it or not, though, the beach house in Newport was ours now. Not mine. Not his. *Ours.* Fifty-fifty.

What the hell was Nana thinking?

I'd always known she cared deeply about him, but there was no way I could have predicted the extent of her generosity. Justin wasn't even related to us, but she'd always thought of him as her grandson.

I picked up my phone and scrolled down to my friend Tracy's name. When she picked up, I let out a sigh of relief.

"Where are you?" I asked.

"On the East Side. Why?"

"Can you meet up? I really need to talk to someone."

"Are you okay?"

My mind went blank before slowly filling again with fragmented thoughts of Justin. My chest tightened. He hated me. I'd avoided him for so long, but I was going to have to face him now.

Tracy's voice snapped me out of my thoughts. "Amelia? Are you still there?"

"Yeah. Everything's fine. Uh…where are you again?"

"Meet me at the falafel place on Thayer Street. We'll have an early dinner and talk about whatever is going on."

"Okay. See you in ten."

Tracy was a fairly new friend, so she knew little about my childhood or teen years. We taught together at a local charter school in Providence. I had taken today off to meet with my grandmother's attorney.

The smell of cumin and dried mint saturated the air inside of the Middle Eastern fast-food restaurant when I walked in a few minutes later. Tracy waved from a corner booth, a Styrofoam container of tahini-covered chicken kabobs and rice already planted in front of her.

"You're not gonna get anything to eat?" she asked with her mouth full. A dollop of yogurt sauce coated the side of her mouth.

"No. I'm not hungry. Maybe I'll take something to go on the way out. I just needed to talk."

"What the hell is going on?"

My throat felt parched. "Actually, I need something to drink first. Hang on." The room felt like it was swaying as I made my way to the refrigerator by the counter.

After returning from purchasing a bottle of water, I sat down and let out a deep breath. "I got some pretty crazy news today at the lawyer's office."

"Okay..."

"So, obviously you know I went there because my grand-mother passed away a month ago."

"Yes..."

"Well, I was just meeting with the attorney to go over her estate. Turns out she left me all of her jewelry...and half of her summer house on Aquidneck Island."

"What? The beautiful house in that picture on your desk?"

"Yeah. That's the one. We'd always go there in the summer when I was younger, but in recent years, she rented it out. The property was in her family for generations. It's older, but it's beautiful and overlooks the water."

"Amelia, that's amazing. Why do you seem so upset?"

"Well...she left the other half to a guy named Justin Banks."

"Who is that?"

The only person I've ever loved.

"He was a boy I grew up with. My Nana took care of him while his parents worked. Justin's house was on one side, mine was on the other, and Nana's was in the middle."

"So, he was kind of like a brother to you?"

I wish.

"We were close for many years."

3

"From the look on your face, I get the feeling that something changed?"

"You'd be right."

"What happened?"

There was no way I could handle rehashing it all. Today had already been too much for me to absorb. I would give her a shorter version.

"Basically, I found out he was keeping something from me. And I freaked out. I'd rather not get into it. But let's just say I was fifteen at the time and having a really hard time handling my hormones and my issues with my mother. I made a rash decision to move away and live with my dad." Swallowing the pain, I said, "I left everything behind in Providence and moved to New Hampshire."

Thankfully, Tracy didn't pry as to what the secret was. That wasn't the issue I needed to talk about today.

"So, you basically ran away from it all rather than dealing with it."

"Yeah. Ran away from my problems…and from Justin."

"You haven't spoken to him since?"

"After I left, there were several months where there was no contact. I felt so guilty about the way I handled things. I did eventually try to see him and apologize once I came to my senses, but by then it was too late. He didn't want to see me or talk to me. I can't say I blamed him. He moved on, fell in with a different crowd, and then eventually moved to New York soon after graduating high school. We just completely lost touch, but he stayed in contact with Nana, apparently. She was like a second mother to him."

"Do you know whatever happened to him?"

"I haven't looked him up. I've always been too scared to find out."

"Well, we need to take care of that right now." She put down her fork and dug inside her purse for her phone.

"Whoa…what are you doing?"

"You know I'm a self-proclaimed professional stalker." Tracy smiled. "I'm looking him up on Facebook. Justin Banks, you said his name was? And he lives in New York City?"

Covering my eyes, I said, "I can't look. I won't look. There are likely hundreds of guys named Justin Banks out there anyway. You probably won't find him."

"What does he look like?"

"The last time I saw him, he was sixteen, so I'm sure he doesn't look the same. He has dirty blond hair, though."

He was really cute. I can still see his face like it was yesterday. I could never forget it.

Tracy was reading aloud information for the different Justin Bankses popping up on Facebook. Nothing stood out until she said, "Justin Banks, New York, New York, musician at Just in Time Acoustic Guitar."

My heart dropped, and to my surprise, I could feel tears trying to fight their way through my eyelids. The emotions rising to the surface so fast were unsettling. It was as if he'd come back from the dead. "What did you just say? Works where?"

"Just in Time Acoustic Guitar? Is that him?"

The words wouldn't come out, so I stayed silent, pondering the name; it was the same one he'd always used as a kid playing guitar on our street corner.

Just in Time.

"That's him," I finally conceded.

"Oh my God, Amelia."

My heart started to pound faster. "What?"

"This guy is…"

"What? Tell me," I practically yelled before downing the rest of my water.

"He's…gorgeous. Absolutely freaking gorgeous."

Covering my face, I said, "Jesus. Please don't tell me that."

"Take a look."

"I can't."

Before I could refuse again, Tracy shoved the phone in front of my face. It shook in my hands as I took it.

Sweet Jesus.

Why did I even look?

From what I could see in the profile photo, he was beautiful—just like I remembered, but at the same time, really different. Grown-up. He was wearing a gray beanie and had a fair amount of chin scruff that he had never been able to grow when I'd known him. He was leaning into a guitar and looked like he was about to sing into a microphone. The look on his face was intense and gave me the chills. When I went to click on the other photos, it wouldn't let me in because his profile was set to private.

Tracy reached out for the phone. "He's a musician?"

"I guess so," I said, handing it back to her.

He used to write songs for me.

"Are you going to contact him?"

"No."

"Why not?"

"I guess I don't even know what to say to him. Whatever is meant to happen will happen. I'll have to talk to him eventually, but I'm not gonna be the one to make the first move."

"How exactly is this housing arrangement going to work, anyway?"

"Well, the attorney gave me a set of keys and told me that

another set was sent to Justin. Both of our names will be on the deed. Nana also set aside some money to be used for house repairs and maintenance to the property during the off-season. I'm assuming he's been made aware of all of the same info."

"You don't want to sell the house, right?"

"No way. There are too many memories, and it meant so much to Nana. I'm going to use it this summer and then maybe eventually rent it out if he agrees to it."

"So, you have no idea how he plans to use his half? You're just going to show up there in a few weeks, and if he's there, he's there, and if he's not, he's not?"

"Pretty much."

"Oh, this is going to be interesting."

———

Fourteen Years Earlier

The boy that Nana started watching this summer was sitting outside of her house. There was no way I could let him see me looking the way I did right now. I just wanted to watch him without him knowing I was there.

There was little I knew about him. His name was Justin. He was about ten years old like me, maybe eleven. He'd just moved here to Rhode Island from Cincinnati. His parents had money; they had to if they could afford the large Victorian house they bought next door to Nana's. They both worked in downtown Providence and paid Nana to watch Justin after school.

Peeking through the curtains of my bedroom window, I could finally see what he looked like. He had shaggy dark blond hair and was apparently trying to teach himself how to play the guitar. I must have stood there at the window for almost an hour watching him strumming the strings.

Out of nowhere, a sneeze escaped me. His head whipped up toward the window. Our eyes met for a few seconds before I immediately ducked. My heart was pounding because now he knew I'd been watching him.

"Hey. Where did you go?" I could hear him ask.

I stayed crouched down and silent.

"Amelia...I know you're there."

He knew my name?

"Why are you hiding from me?"

Slowly standing up with my back facing the window, I finally answered, "I have a lazy eye."

"A lazy eye? Is that like a wandering eye?"

"What's a wandering eye?"

"I'm not sure. My mom always says my dad has a wandering eye."

"A lazy eye means I'm cross-eyed."

"Like cockeyed?" He laughed. "No way. That's so cool. Lemme see!"

"You think it's cool to have an eyeball that goes inward?"

"Yeah. I would love that! Like, you could look at people, and they wouldn't even know you were staring at them."

He was starting to make me giggle.

"Well, mine is not that bad...yet."

"Come on. Turn around. I want to see it."

"No."

"Please?"

Unsure of what came over me, I decided to let him see me. I couldn't avoid it forever.

When I turned around, he flinched. "What happened to your other eye?"

"It's still there." I pointed to my right eye. "This is just a patch over it."

"Why do they make it the same color as your skin? From here, it looked like you had no eye. Scared the crap out of me for a second."

"My eye doctor is going to make me wear this four days a week. Today is the first day. Now you see why I didn't want you to see me!"

"It's nothing to be ashamed of. It just startled me at first because I didn't know what was coming. So, your cockeye is under there? I want to see it."

"No, actually, the covered eye is my good one. The doctor says that if I don't use my good eye, the lazy eye will strengthen and straighten out over time."

"Oh…I get it. So, can you come outside now? Since you don't have to hide from me anymore?"

"No. I don't want anyone else to see me."

"What are you gonna do when you have to go back to school tomorrow?"

"I don't know."

"So, you're just gonna stay inside all day?"

"For now. Yes."

Justin didn't say anything. He just dropped his guitar, stood up, and ran over to his house.

Maybe I really had scared him off after all.

Five minutes later, he came running back toward his spot in front of Nana's. When he looked up into my window again, I could hardly believe my eyes. (Well, eye.) Covering his own right eye was a gigantic black patch. He looked like a pirate. He sat down, lifted his guitar, and started strumming. To my surprise, he then began to sing a song. It was a take on "Brown Eyed Girl," except he'd switched the lyrics to "One

Eyed Girl." That was when I figured out that Justin Banks was equal parts insane and adorable.

After he finished singing, he took a black Sharpie marker out of his pocket.

"I'll color yours in too. Will you come outside now?"

A feeling warmer than I'd ever known filled my heart. That was the exact moment Justin Banks became my best friend. That was also the same day he first graced me with a nickname that would follow me through our teenage years: Patch.

CHAPTER 2

It was definitely the calm before the storm; I just didn't know it yet.

The property was in good shape because the neighbor, Cheri, who was also Nana's good friend, had been looking after it. Three days into my stay at Nana's summer house—my summer house—I was knocking on wood that the peace and quiet would continue. No word from Justin. No word from anyone. Just me, myself, and my books as I enjoyed a tranquil start to summer amidst the salty ocean air that surrounded me on the island.

Never in my life had I been more appreciative of this kind of peace. It was just over a month ago that it felt like my world had ended when Nana died. But I'd also just discovered that Adam, my boyfriend of two years, had been cheating on me. The night I found out, we'd just had sex when he went to the bathroom to dispose of the condom and take a shower. He'd left his phone on the bedside table, and that was when I saw all of the messages from some girl named Ashlyn.

He normally always took his phone everywhere, even to the bathroom, but that night he'd slipped. I later looked her up on Facebook and saw that half of the pictures she posted were of the two of them. Over the six months prior, I'd been feeling that something was off with him. That had been my final confirmation. Just before I left for the summer house, I found out that Adam moved to Boston to live with her.

So, this was a major time of transition for me. At twenty-four, I was single again and starting a new life in Newport for the summer. My teaching job in Providence afforded me summers off. My hope was to find a temporary job for the season, but for now, I just wanted to enjoy a few weeks of relaxation.

My day would start with coffee on the upper deck that overlooked Easton's Beach. Listening to the seagulls, I would peruse Facebook, read my *In Style* magazine, or simply meditate. I'd then soak in the tub upstairs for as long as I pleased before getting dressed and starting my day, and by that, I mean curling up on the couch with my book.

By midafternoon, I'd make lunch and bring it back out to the upper deck. Before nightfall, I would drive down to Thames Street in Newport and browse the shops, looking at blown glass, trinkets, and nautical artwork. Then, I'd stop for gelato or coffee.

The day typically wound down with a trip down to the dock for some freshly caught lobster or quahogs. I'd take them home in a bag and steam them in a pot outside in the yard. Then, I'd sit down to dinner with a bottle of chilled white wine while enjoying the sunset over the Atlantic.

This was the life.

My routine stayed the same for a few days until my rude awakening hit.

Returning from downtown Newport with my bag of crustaceans one night, I noticed that the front door to the house was wide open. Had I forgotten to lock it? Was it the wind?

My heartbeat accelerated when I entered the kitchen to find a tall, leggy chick with cropped platinum-blond hair. She looked like a young Mia Farrow and was stocking the cabinets.

I cleared my throat. "Hello?"

She turned around before covering her chest. "Oh my God. You scared me." Walking over to me smiling, she held out her hand. "I'm Jade."

With fine features, high cheekbones, and that pixie cut, Jade could have been a model. I was the complete opposite with my long, dark hair and curvy figure.

"I'm Amelia. Who are you?"

"I'm Justin's girlfriend."

My stomach sank. "Oh…I see. Where is he?"

"He just went to the market and the liquor store."

"How long have you been here?"

"We just arrived about an hour ago."

"How long are you staying?"

"Not sure, really. We're just gonna see where the summer takes us. Neither of us were expecting this development… you know, the house."

"Yeah…I know." I looked down at the French-manicured toes peeking out of her heels. "Do you work?"

"I'm an actress, actually…on Broadway. Well, *off* Broadway for now. I'm in between jobs, but I'll probably be going back and forth to New York for auditions. What do you do?"

"I'm a middle school teacher. So, I get the summers off."

"Oh, that's really cool."

"Yeah. It's fun. Where does Justin work?"

"He works from home right now, selling software. He can work from anywhere. He also performs. You know he's a musician, right?"

"Actually, I don't know much about him anymore."

"What happened between you two, anyway? If you don't mind my asking…"

"He's never told you anything about me?"

"Just that you grew up together and that you're Mrs. H's granddaughter. Honestly, he never mentioned you at all until we got that letter from the attorney."

Even though that was expected, it made me sad. "That's no surprise."

"Why do you say that?"

"It's kind of a long story."

"Did you guys ever date?"

"No. It was nothing like that. We were just good friends, but we drifted apart after I moved away."

"I see. This whole thing is a little weird, right? I mean, inheriting a house like this out of nowhere?"

"Well, my grandmother was very generous. My mother is her only child, and Nana loved Justin like a son, so…"

"Your grandmother left the house to you and not your mother?"

"Mom and Nana had a bit of a falling-out some years ago. Thankfully, they made amends before she died, but things were never really the same again."

"I'm sorry to hear that."

"Thanks."

Jade opened her arms to pull me into a casual hug. "Well, I really hope we can be friends. It will be nice to have a girl around to shop with, check out the island."

"Yeah. That'd be nice."

"I hope you'll have dinner with us tonight?"

I wasn't ready to face him. I needed to make up a story and get out of here.

"Actually, probably not tonight. I'd better be leaving—"

"That's what you're good at, isn't it?" a deep voice I hardly recognized interrupted me from behind.

"What's that?" I asked, swallowing nervously and refusing to turn around to look at him.

"Leaving," he said, louder. "That's what you're good at."

My breathing was ragged, but it was when I turned around that I nearly lost it.

Holy fuck.

CHAPTER 3

Justin was standing in front of me, and I swear it was like the boy I'd left behind had been swallowed up by a lean mass of muscle. He looked so different from what I remembered nine years ago. The anger on his face was transparent and somehow made him even more incredibly hot. It just would have been better if it weren't directed toward me.

His skin was a beautiful shade of bronze that complemented the natural golden streaks in his dark blond hair. The smooth face I remembered was now rough and unshaven. A rope and barbed wire tattoo wrapped around his bicep. He was wearing camouflage cargo shorts with a tight, white ribbed tank that hugged his chiseled chest.

An indeterminate amount of time passed as I took him in. Even though I was too stunned to say anything, my heart was screaming. I knew deep down my reaction wasn't just because of my physical attraction to him. It was because despite all of the changes, one thing had stayed exactly the same. His eyes. They reflected the same hurt that I remembered from the very last time I had seen him.

His name finally managed to roll off my tongue. "Justin…"

"Amelia." The deep, throaty sound of his voice vibrated through me.

"I wasn't sure if you were ever going to show up."

"Why wouldn't I have?" he sneered.

"Well, I thought maybe you were avoiding me."

"You've overestimated your significance to me. Of course, I was going to come. This is half my house."

His words stung. "I didn't say it wasn't. It's just…I hadn't heard anything from you."

"Interesting how that goes."

Clearly uncomfortable with our sparring, Jade cleared her throat. "I was just asking Amelia if she wanted to have dinner with us tonight. Maybe you guys can catch up."

"Apparently, she already has plans."

I turned to him. "Why do you say that?"

"Oh, I don't know…because you're holding a bag that smells like dirty snatch?"

"It's fresh seafood."

"Doesn't smell very fresh to me."

"God. We haven't seen each other in nine years, and this is how you act?" I turned to Jade. "Is he always this rude?"

Before she could answer, he cracked, "I guess you bring it out in me."

"You think Nana would be happy right now with your attitude? Something tells me she didn't leave us this house so that we could fight with each other."

"She left us both this house because we each meant something to her. No one said we have to mean anything to each other. Anyway, if you cared so much about what Mrs. H thought, maybe you shouldn't have run away."

"That's a low blow."

17

"The truth hurts, I guess."

"I tried to contact you, Justin. I—"

"I'm not talking about this now, Amelia," he said, speaking through gritted teeth. "It's old news."

It was unnerving to hear him call me by my actual name. Aside from the very first day we'd met, he'd always called me Patch or Patchy. It felt like a slap in the face for some reason, like he was trying to emphasize how much we'd grown apart.

Justin went from hot to cold as he shut down, heading back outside to retrieve the groceries from his car, but not before slamming the door behind him.

I shuddered, looking over at Jade, whose eyes were moving from side to side in confusion.

"Well, that was a nice start," I joked.

"I don't know what to say. I've never seen him act like that toward anyone, to be honest. I'm really sorry."

"It's not your fault. Believe it or not, I probably deserve it."

The only thing worse than the rude reception he'd given me was him blatantly ignoring me during dinner and for the rest of that night. That hurt more than anything he could have ever said to me.

———

If I thought the evening was horrible, my lack of sleep assured that the next morning was even worse.

Apparently, Justin had found a way to use his anger—by taking it out on Jade. Let's just say playing guitar wasn't the only talent he'd fully developed over time. Jade's moaning in the middle of the night as Justin pounded into her had woken me up. The walls had literally shaken. It had been impossible to go back to sleep after that. I'd tossed and turned, my thoughts alternating between rehashing Justin's words from earlier to imagining what that scene in the other room actually looked like. Not that I should have been thinking about the latter, but I couldn't seem to help myself.

It was 7 a.m., and the house was quiet, so I assumed they were both catching up on sleep after their sexcapade. When I snuck downstairs to make some coffee, to my surprise, Justin was standing in the kitchen alone, staring out the spacious window overlooking the water. Coffee was percolating. His back was toward me, so he hadn't seen me standing there yet.

I used the opportunity to admire his stature and the flawless skin of his defined, shirtless back. Black gym pants hugged his beautifully round ass. I had never realized how incredible his ass was. My physical attraction to him really irked me under the circumstances, but that didn't stop me from checking him out. He had a rectangular-shaped tattoo in the middle of his back. Squinting, I unsuccessfully tried to figure out what it was. He startled me when he suddenly turned around and met me with an incendiary stare.

"Do you always ogle people when you think they can't see you?"

I swallowed the lump in my throat. "How did you know I was standing here?"

"I could see your reflection in the window, genius."

Shit.

"You didn't even flinch. I didn't think you noticed me."

"Clearly."

"Are you trying to make me hate you or something? Because you're doing a pretty damn good job."

Justin didn't answer my question. Instead, he just turned back toward the window.

"Why do you do that?" I asked.

"Do what?"

"Say things to piss me off, then shut down?"

He continued to speak to the window. "Would you rather I just continue to piss you off? I'm trying to get my anger in check with you, Amelia. You should be happy I know when to stop…unlike some people."

"Will you at least look at me when you're talking to me?"

He turned around and walked toward me slowly, then leaned his face in. I could feel his words on my lips when he asked, "Is this better? You'd rather me in your face like this?"

I could practically taste his breath. My entire body felt weak from the close contact, so I backed away.

"I didn't think so," he snarled.

I walked over to the refrigerator and opened it, pretending to look for something. It annoyed me that my peaceful mornings were a thing of the past.

"You always get up this early?" I asked.

"I'm a morning person."

"I can see that…so bright and cheery," I said, sarcastically. "Some of us need sleep, though."

"I slept just fine last night."

"Oh, I know…after you traumatized me. You must have passed out after all that screwing. Could you two have been any louder last night?"

"Well, excuse me. If I can't fuck in my own house, where do you expect me to do it?"

"I didn't say you couldn't do it. Just be more respectful."

"Define respect."

"Doing it quietly."

"Sorry. I don't fuck quietly."

As much as I hated that answer, I somehow felt that those words would be repeating in my head later tonight.

"Forget it. Clearly, you don't know the meaning of respect."

"Respect? Why should I respect you? Because you're not getting laid? Why don't you hook up with some salty dude down at the dock? Maybe then you won't care so much about other people's business."

"Salty dude?"

"Yeah. You know, the guys that live on the boats. The ones who sell you that nasty fish you were eating last night."

I just shook my head and rolled my eyes, refusing to dignify that comment with a response.

He surprised me when he suddenly lifted the carafe. "Want some coffee?"

"Now you're being nice?"

"No, I just figured you're sticking around for some reason. It must be the coffee."

"This is my kitchen."

He winked. "*Our* kitchen." Grabbing two mugs from the cabinet, he asked, "How do you take yours?"

"Cream and sugar."

"I'll take care of it while you go put on a bra."

I looked down at my boobs, which were hanging freely beneath my white T-shirt. Not expecting to run into him this early, I hadn't thought to put one on. Too embarrassed to acknowledge the fact that he'd noticed, I went back to my room and got dressed.

When I returned, he was back at the window, drinking his coffee.

"Is this better?" I asked, referring to my dress.

He turned around and gave me a once-over. "Define better. If better means I can't see your tits anymore…yes, it's better. If better means you *look* better, that's debatable."

"What's wrong with this?"

"It looks like you sewed it yourself."

"Actually, it's from one of the shops on the island. It is handmade."

"Out of a potato sack?"

"I don't think so."

Maybe?

He snickered. "Your coffee's on the counter, Raggedy Ann."

My inclination was to try to come up with a comeback, but then I realized that was probably what he wanted. I needed to kill him with kindness instead of showing my anger.

"Thank you. That was nice of you to make it for me."

Asshole.

I took a sip and immediately spit it out. "What did you put in this?"

Instead of answering me, he just started to crack up. His laughter resonated through the kitchen, and as much as I hated that it was at my expense, it was the first time he'd laughed. It took me back in time for a moment and served as the only real reminder that the smoking-hot asshole in front of me used to be my best friend.

"You don't like it?"

"It's a bit strong. What is it?"

"It's coffee fusion, actually."

"What does that even mean?"

Justin sauntered over to the cabinet and took out a can and a package. "It's my own recipe. Cuban coffee mixed with this one." He pointed to the black packaging that had a white skull and crossbones on it.

"What the hell is that?"

"It's coffee. I order it online. Nothing else is caffeinated enough for me."

"That's why you wanted to serve it to me, wasn't it? You knew I'd hate this...concoction."

Instead of answering, he simply let out that raspy laugh of his again, except this time, he was laughing way harder than before.

Jade entered the kitchen, wearing a long black T-shirt that must have been the one he wasn't wearing. "What's so funny?"

Justin's mischievous eyes peeked out from behind his mug. He snickered. "We were just having coffee."

Jade shook her head. "You didn't drink his mud, did you? I don't know how he likes that stuff."

I reminded myself of my plan to kill him with kindness. Taking another sip of the coffee, I nodded. "Actually, at first taste, it was pretty strong, but I actually think I really like it."

It was disgusting.

"You'd better be careful. That shit is potent. Justin is immune to it, but the one and only time I drank it, it kept me up for like four days."

Justin chuckled. "Apparently, *we* kept Amelia up last night."

Jade turned to me. "Oh, shit. I'm sorry."

Shrugging, I said, "It's no big deal. I got used to it after a while."

"Was that when you decided you wished you could join in?" he cracked.

Fuck him.

I was not going to respond to that.

The more I looked over at his smug expression, the more determined I became to finish the entire damn mug of coffee to spite him.

Jade chose to ignore Justin's earlier comment. "What do you say after breakfast we head to town, Amelia? I'd love it if you could show me around the island."

"All right. That would be nice."

She walked over to Justin and wrapped her arm around his waist. "You want to come with us, babe?"

"No. I have shit to do," Justin said before finishing off the last of his coffee and putting the cup in the sink.

"Okay. Just the girls, then."

The coffee had turned me into a jittery fool. As Jade and I walked around Newport that morning, she kept having to tell me to slow down. Apparently, in her heels, she couldn't keep up with me.

At one point later in the afternoon, we stopped to rest our legs. Jade and I sat on a wooden bench overlooking the dozens of docked sailboats as the sun shone over the water.

"So, how did you and Justin meet?" I asked.

"I was in the audience at this club called Hades in the city. Justin was performing there that night. He was eyeing me the whole time he was singing, and after the show, he came to find me. When he said he was thinking of me while he was singing the last song, I nearly died. We've been inseparable since."

My face felt hot. I wasn't willing to admit to myself that it was jealousy. The thought of them connecting so intimately while he was in the middle of performing made me uncomfortable for some reason. Maybe because it reminded me of the songs he'd used to write for me. You'd think nothing would bother me after having to endure their fucking last night.

"What kind of music does he play now?"

"Well, he does some covers of artists like Jack Johnson, but he also writes a lot of original stuff. He mostly plays clubs, but his manager has been trying to get him a music deal. Of course, the girls all go crazy over him. That part has taken some getting used to for me."

"I'm sure it's hard."

"Yeah. Big time." She tilted her head. "What about you? No boyfriend?"

"I just got out of a relationship."

I spent the next half hour rehashing to her what had happened with Adam. Jade was really easy to talk to, and I could tell it upset her to find out about Adam cheating on me.

"Well, better to find out these things now while you're still young than to waste a decade with someone like that," she said.

"You're very right."

"We'll have to find you someone this summer. I've seen a lot of hot guys walking around here today."

"Really? Because the only ones I've seen were holding each other's hands."

She laughed. "No. There were others."

"I'm really not looking to get into another relationship."

"Who said anything about that? You need to get laid, have some fun, especially after what that dick of an ex did to you. You deserve a hot summer fling, someone who knocks your socks off, someone you can't stop thinking about even when they're not around."

Sadly, it's your boyfriend that I can't get out of my head at the moment.

She meant well, so I just smiled and nodded even though I had no intention of sleeping with anyone this summer.

On our way home, we passed Sandy's on the Beach, a restaurant that was known for live music at night and really good food. A sign out front read, *Temporary Summer Help Wanted.* Since there was a university just over the bridge, a lot of the students went home in the summer, leaving some of the local restaurants in need of temporary waitstaff.

I stopped short in front of the entrance. "Do you mind if I go in and inquire about this?"

"Sure. I'd actually like to check it out too."

It turned out that Sandy's was desperate for summer help. Both Jade and I had waitressing experience, so we sat down and filled out applications. By the time we walked out of there, we each had a job. The manager basically told us we could work any night we wanted. The extra money and flexibility was impossible to pass up. Jade was particularly happy that the manager had told her it was no problem if she had to suddenly cancel a shift in the event she got called back to Manhattan for an audition. We were each going to start tomorrow.

That night, Jade thought we should celebrate our new jobs over dinner and drinks on the upper deck back at the house. It hadn't dawned on me how peaceful being away from Justin all day had been.

When we walked in the door, butterflies started to swarm in my stomach again as soon as I smelled his cologne. Justin was standing in the kitchen drinking a beer when Jade ran over to him and wrapped her arms around his neck. Justin was tall—over six feet—but Jade wasn't that much shorter than him. Next to them, I was basically a mouse.

God, he cleans up nice.

Justin had changed out of his camouflage shorts from earlier into dark jeans and a gray shirt with black stripes that hugged his chest. He'd done something to his hair that I couldn't pinpoint. Maybe washed it? Whatever it was, it brought out the blue in his eyes—eyes that were now gazing into Jade's.

She ran her fingers through his hair, then kissed him. "I missed you, babe. Guess what? We both got jobs at this restaurant on the beach."

"Did you tell them you could get called back to New York anytime?"

"The guy said it didn't matter. He said I could basically just work whenever I want."

"Really? That sounds a bit shady to me. But whatever. You sure he doesn't just want in your pants, Jade?"

"He said the same thing to me," I interrupted.

"Well, then it can't be that."

It took me a bit to realize that he'd just insulted me.

Jade intercepted before I could muster up a comeback. "It's mild out. I was telling Amelia we should all have dinner on the upstairs deck tonight. We could barbecue that steak I have marinating in the fridge."

I didn't have the heart to tell her I didn't like red meat, so I just kept quiet. Justin would probably think I was looking for an excuse not to have dinner with them.

Kill him with kindness.

"I'm not that great of a cook, but I can make a big salad," I said.

Justin smacked the counter. "Great. I'll start the grill while Amelia tosses her big salad."

He started to walk outside when I yelled after him.

"You know what Nana would say to you right now? She'd tell you to go wash your dirty mouth out with soap."

He turned around and lifted his brow. "Soap wouldn't cut it."

I supposed I should have been happy that he was talking to me as opposed to pretending I wasn't there. Maybe we were making progress?

After chopping up lettuce, carrots, red onion, tomatoes, and cucumbers, I dressed the salad with homemade honey mustard vinaigrette.

I carried it upstairs, where Justin and Jade were already

sitting down at the table. Jade had poured three glasses of Merlot, and Justin was sipping one as he looked over at the waves, which were rough tonight.

Once we started eating, Justin wouldn't look at me or make conversation. I filled my plate with salad and bread, and it took a while before anyone noticed that I wasn't eating anything else.

Jade's mouth was full when she said, "You didn't even touch the steak."

"I don't really like to eat meat."

Justin chuckled. "Is that why you can't find a man?"

I dropped my fork. "You're a prick. Seriously. I don't recognize you anymore. How were we ever best friends?"

"I used to ask myself that all the time before I stopped giving a shit."

I got up from the table and went downstairs. Leaning against the kitchen counter, I breathed in and out slowly to calm myself down.

Jade came up quietly behind me. "I really don't get what's going on between you two or why he refuses to talk about it. Are you sure you guys never dated?"

"I told you, Jade. It wasn't anything like that."

"Will you tell me what happened?"

"I think he should be the one to explain it to you. Honestly, I don't want to piss him off any more than I already have by overstepping my bounds. Besides, I can honestly say that if he's mad, it's because of the way I left…my running away. Anything that happened before that is irrelevant now. He's pissed because of how I handled it."

"Let's just go back upstairs and try to have a nice dinner."

Back on the upper deck, Justin was stone-faced, pouring more wine into his glass. A part of me wanted to slap him across the face, but another part felt guilty that I had caused so much anger in him. He said he didn't care, but I refused to believe he would be acting up like this if he didn't.

I touched his arm. "Will you just talk to me?"

He whipped his arm away. "I'm over it. I'm not talking about anything."

"Will you do it for Nana?"

His head flipped up, and his beautiful blue eyes darkened. "Stop fucking bringing her into this. Your grandmother was a wonderful woman. She was the mother I never had. She never turned her back on me like pretty much everyone else in my life. This house is a representation of Mrs. H, which is why I'm here. I'm not here because of you. You want me to talk, but what you don't seem to understand is that I don't have anything to say about what happened almost a decade ago. I've erased it all. It's too late, Amelia. I don't care if you and Jade hang out, all right? But don't bother trying to get through to me because we're not gonna be friends. You put me in a shit mood, and I don't want to spend this whole summer in a shit mood. We're roommates. Stop pretending there is something more to it. Stop pretending to like the goddamn coffee. Stop pretending everything is just great. Cut the shit and see things for what they are. We don't mean anything to each other." He got up and took his plate. "I'm done, Jade. I'll see you in the room."

Jade and I sat in silence, listening to nothing but the sound of the waves crashing beneath us.

"I'm so sorry, Amelia," she said.

"Please. Don't, okay? He's right. Sometimes, you can't fix things." Despite the complacent words that had come out of my mouth, a tear fell down my cheek.

———

29

Eleven Years Earlier

Mom had left to go out again. Lord knew where she went or with whom. I could never count on my mother, Patricia, for anything. There were only two people I could depend on in my life: Nana and Justin.

The one good thing about Mom leaving me alone most nights was that it allowed me to sneak out of the house and go wherever I wanted. Nana assumed my mother was home, so she couldn't stop me.

Justin and I were planning to meet in fifteen minutes. We were going to the mall to hang out with some of the other eighth graders from school. These kids were part of the cool crowd that Justin and I had been trying to break into. Because the two of us mainly hung out with each other, we weren't really associated with any one clique.

He was waiting at the corner with his hands in his pockets. I loved when he wore his baseball cap backward and the way the dirty blond strands of hair peeked out of the sides. I was starting to notice little things like that more and more lately. It was hard not to.

He walked toward me. "You ready to go?"
"Yeah."

Justin started to run. "We have to hurry up. The next bus is in five minutes."

I didn't know why the thought of hanging out with these kids was making me so nervous. Justin didn't seem nervous at all. He was more confident than me in general.

When we stepped inside the mall, the fluorescent lights were a sharp contrast to the dark winter outside. We were supposed to be meeting these kids at the food court, so we made our way to a map of the three-story building.

My heart was pounding as we approached the two boys and a girl who were standing outside of an Auntie Anne's pretzel stand. Justin could tell I was on edge.

"Don't be nervous, Patch."

The first thing out of Chandler's mouth was, "What the hell is that?"

"What?"

"Did you shit yourself, Amelia?"

My heart was now beating out of my chest as I looked down at myself. I knew that despite my nerves, I hadn't lost control of my bowels. One knew if that happened, right? No. This was not poop. I wasn't prepared for it because it was the first time I'd ever gotten my period. At thirteen, I was later than most of the other girls I knew. This was probably the worst timing imaginable.

Justin looked down, then up into my panicked eyes.

I mouthed to him, "It's blood."

Without hesitation, he gave me a quick nod as if to say that he had it covered.

"It's blood," he said.

"Blood? Ew…gross!" the other boy, Ethan, said.

"Amelia stabbed herself with my knife on the way here."

I'd been looking down, but I whipped my head up and looked over at my friend incredulously.

Chandler's eyes widened. "She stabbed herself?"

"Yeah." Justin smiled. To my surprise, he took a pocket-knife out of his jacket. "See this here? I carry it everywhere with me. It's a Swiss Army knife. Anyway, I was showing it to Amelia on the bus. I dared her to stab herself in the abdomen. Crazy girl that she is, she actually did it. So, anyway, she's got blood on her pants now."

"Are you joking?"

31

"Wish I was, dude."

The three of them looked at each other before Chandler said, "That's the coolest fucking thing I've ever heard!"

Ethan smacked my arm. "Seriously, Amelia. That's some epic shit right there."

Justin laughed. "Yeah, so we figured we'd come say hey since we were almost here anyway…but we should probably get her to the emergency room."

"Cool, man. Let us know how it goes."

"All right."

"What the heck did you just do?" I whispered as we walked away.

"Don't say anything. Just walk."

The cool night air hit us as we exited the rotating doors of the mall. We stood on the sidewalk and stared at each other for a moment before breaking into hysterical laughter.

"I can't believe you came up with that crazy story."

"Not that you should be ashamed of the truth, but I knew you were embarrassed. So, I wanted to do something. You were pulling on your hair like crazy."

"I was? I didn't even realize."

"Yeah. You do that when you're really nervous."

"I never knew you noticed that."

His eyes traveled down to my lips for a moment when he said, "I notice everything about you."

Feeling suddenly flushed, I changed the subject. "You carry a knife?"

"I always do. You know, in case something happens when we're out. I need to be able to protect you."

My heart that was beating for those jerks just a moment ago was now beating incessantly for an entirely different reason.

"I'd better get home."

"There's a drugstore right there. Why don't you go get something? Ask them if they have a bathroom you can use."

I went inside and used the money I had reserved for video games at the mall arcade to buy a box of maxi pads and some cheap granny underwear. I'd tackle tampons later when I had time to figure out how to use them.

When I emerged, Justin took off his hoodie and handed it to me. "Here, wrap this around your waist."

"Thank you."

"Where are we going now?" he asked.

"What do you mean? I have to get home! I have blood all over my pants."

"No one can see it with my jacket wrapped around you."

"I still don't feel comfortable."

"I really don't want to go back home tonight, Patch. I know where we can go...where we won't know anyone. It's a place I go by myself sometimes. Come on."

Justin led me down the sidewalks of Providence. After about ten minutes, we turned a corner and approached a small red building. I looked up at the illuminated sign.

"This is a movie theater?"

"Yup. They show the kind of movies that nobody knows about or that people don't talk about. The best part? They don't even care how old you are here."

"Are they bad movies?"

"No. Not like those naked kind of movies, the ones I told you my dad watches. No. These ones are like foreign with subtitles and stuff."

Justin bought two tickets and a popcorn for us to share. The theater smelled musty and was practically empty, which was perfect considering I didn't want to see anyone tonight. Even though the seats were sticky, this was just what I needed.

The movie was a French film with subtitles, called *L'Amour Vrai*. The cinematography was mesmerizing, and the plot was more serious than the comedies we normally watched. But it was perfect. Perfect not only because of what was on the big screen, but because of who was next to me. I lay my head on Justin's shoulder and thanked God for a friend who always knew exactly what I needed. There was also a twinge of something unidentifiable running through me.

That wasn't the last independent film Justin and I would watch together at the little red theater. That place became our secret hangout over the next couple of years. Indie movies became our thing. Going there wasn't about being seen at the big cinema or running into people from school. It was a place where we could both escape from reality without being watched, a place where we could be together and get lost in a different world at the same time.

The following afternoon, I listened from my window as Justin sat on Nana's stoop, playing a new song I'd never heard him perform before. It sounded like "I Touch Myself" by the Divinyls, but he'd changed it to "I Stab Myself."

Gotta love that kid.

CHAPTER 4

A couple of weeks passed, and things hadn't gotten any better between Justin and me. Rather than taunt me, he'd resigned himself to just ignoring me altogether.

The house had four bedrooms. Since I'd turned one of them into an exercise room, Justin used the other one as an office during the day. His muffled voice could often be heard from behind the door as he made work calls. Apparently, the company he worked for sold business solutions software.

Jade and I were working almost every night at Sandy's as well as the occasional afternoon. One day in particular, we were on break when we overheard the restaurant owner, Salvatore, complaining that the band who performed most nights had suddenly quit. Sandy's was probably the most popular spot on the entire island for live music. That was what it was known for, even more than the food. So this didn't bode well for business.

Jade's voice was low. "I wonder if Justin would be interested in playing here."

I'd been feeling kind of sick as it was this afternoon, but the mere mention of his name made my stomach feel even more unsettled.

"You think he would want to perform in a place like this?"

"Well, he's used to bigger venues, but it's not like he's doing anything else. He took the summer off, but I get the feeling he actually regrets it. He's been in a horrible mood since we got here. I think he's itching to play again. It might do him some good to get back in the game for a bit on a smaller scale. There wouldn't be any pressure. No one knows him out here."

The thought of getting to see Justin perform gave me goose bumps. On one hand, it would be amazing. On the other, I knew it would be painful for me to have to endure him here at night. Him actually agreeing to it probably wouldn't pan out, so I vowed not to obsess over it unless it became a reality.

"I'm gonna talk to Salvatore," Jade said.

I tried to change the subject. "Do you think you and Justin will get married?" Not sure why I asked that question. I'd been curious as to how serious they were, and it just came out.

Jade hesitated. "I don't know. I really love him. I hope so, if we can work out our differences."

"Differences? Like what?"

She took a sip of her water, then frowned. "Well, Justin doesn't want kids."

"What? He told you that?"

"Yeah. He says he feels it's irresponsible to bring children into the world unless you can be one hundred percent sure of your capabilities as a parent. He says he doesn't feel that his own parents should have ever had children, and he just doesn't think it's for him."

"Really…"

"Don't get me wrong. I don't want kids anytime soon. My career comes first right now, but someday I would like to have them. So, if he definitely doesn't want kids, then that could be a problem."

"He'll probably change his mind as he gets older. He's still so young."

She shook her head. "I don't know. It's really bad. He won't even have sex with me without a condom, even though I'm on the pill and we're monogamous. He refuses to take even the slightest chance. He's super paranoid."

Trying to block out the images of them having sex, I simply said, "Wow."

It made me really sad that Justin felt that way because of his parents. They were constantly working and had never paid enough attention to him when we were kids. His mother was always away on business trips. That was part of why Nana was so important to him. Truthfully, my mother shouldn't have had a child either. But her poor parenting didn't stop me from wanting to have a child of my own someday.

Jade took a closer look at my face. "Are you feeling all right?"

The stress of my reunion with Justin was finally catching up with me. My nerves were shot, and it was making me sick.

"Actually, I've been feeling ill all day. My stomach is upset, and I have a headache."

"Why don't you go home early? I'll cover your shift and let the manager know what's up."

"Are you sure?"

"Of course."

"I'll owe you, then."

"Believe me, there will come a time that I get called back to New York, and you'll make good on that."

"Okay," I said, getting up and unfastening the black smock tied around my back.

The entire walk home, despite vowing not to think about it, my thoughts once again turned to Justin and the fact that Jade was going to try to get him the gig at Sandy's. It had been years since I'd heard his singing voice. I wondered what it sounded like now that it was deeper and he had years of practice.

Justin's older black Range Rover was parked outside of the house. He was expecting Jade and I to both be at work. I had to pass through the kitchen to get upstairs to my room and hoped I wouldn't run into him without Jade here as a buffer.

Relief washed over me as I entered the empty kitchen. I grabbed a water bottle and some Advil for my headache and tiptoed up the stairs so that Justin didn't notice me.

The sound of heavy breathing coming from his bedroom stopped me in my tracks at the top of the stairwell. I could hear sheets rustling. My heart beat faster. He didn't think anyone would be home.

Oh my God.

He must have a girl in there.

Shit.

How could he do that to Jade?

I had to pass his room to get to mine anyway. Thank goodness Nana had this hallway carpeted. Covering my chest with my hand, I crept slowly toward his door, which was cracked open. I closed my eyes briefly to prepare myself for what I might witness when I peeked inside.

Nothing could have prepared me for the reality behind that door.

There was no girl.

Justin's eyes were tightly shut as he lay back on the bed—alone. His jeans were undone, halfway down his legs. His left hand was firmly wrapped around his enormous cock as he pressed down on his balls with his other hand.

Holy mother of...

Swallowing the saliva building in my mouth, I watched the movement of his hand as he stroked himself hard in a twisting motion. He'd gotten himself so aroused, you could hear the slick sound of the wetness as he pumped into his palm.

I knew that watching him was wrong. In fact, this was probably the lowest thing I'd ever done. But there was absolutely no way I could look away. No. Way. If this were going to be the reason I went to hell, then so be it. I'd never witnessed something so intense, never imagined that he could be deriving so much pleasure alone.

I wanted to see how this ended.

I *needed* to see how it ended.

Justin's mouth was agape, the tip of his tongue slowly sliding back and forth across his bottom lip as if it were seeking out the taste of something or someone.

I want it to be me.

My own body was shaking, my clit throbbing. The ache to be with him, to join him was immense. So enraptured in every move he made, I was no longer thinking about whether watching him was right or wrong.

Hypnotized.

He was fisting the sheets with one hand now while fucking his palm faster. With every movement, my muscles clenched tighter. I was wet, bewildered at my mind's complete surrender to my body.

The low, deep groans of pleasure that came out of his mouth were making it that much worse. I knew wholeheartedly that this—watching him pleasure himself—was the single biggest turn-on I had ever experienced. Getting off was normally such work for me. I needed my vibrator and porn and even then, sometimes it was impossible to relax enough to make myself come. Right now, I had to cross my legs to control the need building between them.

As he licked over his bottom lip again, my own tongue tingled as I imagined what his wet mouth would feel like against mine. As he pumped into his hand, I imagined that it was me wrapped around his cock. I had never wanted anyone as badly as I wanted him in that moment.

His dark golden hair was matted and messy as the back of his head pressed against the headboard. The clank of his belt buckle became more pronounced as he thrust his hips, his fist working harder to keep up. The intensity of his self-pleasure left me in total awe.

His breathing became even more ragged as his eyes rolled back. I swallowed hard and watched, mesmerized as streams of cum shot out from his large crown like a fountain. The grunts of pleasure escaping him as he orgasmed were just about the sexiest sounds I'd ever heard come out of a man's mouth.

My heart felt like it was pounding out of my chest. Watching this whole thing unfold had made me totally lose my sense of reality. I felt like I'd been experiencing every movement, every feeling right along with him, except I wasn't allowed to come. It was as if I'd seriously lost my mind in the process. That was the only thing that could possibly explain why my body had decided to betray me, letting out an involuntary sigh….*moan*? I wasn't sure what it was, but it caused Justin to jump back. His head whipped toward me, and his shocked eyes met mine for a brief second before I ran back down the stairs.

Humiliated.

Mortified.

Escaping out the front door and down to the water, I continued to run aimlessly on the sand. At one point, about a mile down the beach, I had to stop and catch my breath, even though I wanted to keep running. I'd gotten so wrapped up in Justin that I'd forgotten how sick I was this afternoon. It was all hitting me again as I stumbled over to the shoreline and vomited into the ocean.

I collapsed into the sand and must have sat there for over an hour. The sun was starting to go down, and the tide was coming in. It felt like everything was closing in on me. I knew I couldn't avoid going home forever.

What if he told Jade what I'd done?

That I had been watching him.

Oh God.

He was going to crucify me for this.

What excuse could I possibly give him that would explain why I had been hiding behind his door, watching him ejaculate like it was a Fourth of July fireworks performance?

I decided that I needed to get home before Jade did. Maybe I could convince him not to say anything. Brushing the sand off my thighs, I made my way back to the house.

Adrenaline rushed through me upon finding Justin standing in the kitchen, drinking out of a half-gallon of orange juice. I stood silently behind him and watched as he put the container back.

Justin turned around and finally noticed me standing there. His hair was wet, making it appear brown instead of blond. He must have taken a shower to wash away the awkwardness of our encounter. Looking painfully handsome in a brown distressed T-shirt that fit his chest like a glove, he just stared me down.

Here it comes.

I braced myself for his humiliating words, but he continued to look at me blankly without saying anything. He slowly walked toward me, and all of the muscles in my body tightened. He was going to get in my face and do it.

Shit.

Justin stood inches away from me. He smelled so effing good, like soap and cologne. I could feel the heat of his body, and my knees started to feel weak. He stared deeply into my eyes. It wasn't necessarily an angry glare, but it wasn't a happy or amused look either.

After several seconds of silence, he took a deep breath and said, "You smell like vomit."

Just as I opened my mouth to respond, he turned around and walked back toward the stairs before disappearing.

That was it?

I smelled like vomit?

He was going to let the whole thing go? Or was he just saving it for later when Jade came home? I would have to wait anxiously to find out.

————

Business at Sandy's had really suffered since losing The Ruckus—their headlining band. Salvatore had managed to fill the spot each night with mediocre local talent, but people were noticing the difference. The place would empty out much earlier than normal, and we weren't getting as many customers in general.

I knew that Jade had spoken to Justin about taking on a few nights, but last I'd heard, he wasn't interested. So, you could imagine my surprise when he turned up at Sandy's early one Friday evening with his guitar strap wrapped around him.

At first, I didn't realize it was him until he looked over at me. Butterflies swarmed in my stomach the moment I noticed him standing near the door, looking like he didn't know where to go. Since it was unseasonably cool out, he was wearing a navy hoodie and a beanie. God, he looked sexy in that hat. It always seemed to bring out his eyes. Really, he looked sexy in anything, but today, he was particularly hot because he also hadn't shaved in days.

Given how he'd treated me, my physical attraction to him never ceased to amaze me. It was easier to focus on the physical, I suppose. Justin's exterior, which was so different from what I remembered, helped distract from what I knew was inside. The truth was, as much as I wanted him physically, it didn't compare to the longing that remained for my old friend. Somewhere hidden beneath the brawn and beauty, I knew he was still in there, and that frustrated me.

As far as I knew, Justin had never mentioned the jerk-off encounter to Jade, nor had he tortured me about it. I didn't know why he'd decided to give me a pass on that, but I was eternally grateful.

Jade had gotten called out of town for an audition this morning. I'd assumed that he was going to go back with her.

I stopped wiping the table I'd been cleaning and walked over to him. "What are you doing here?"

He lifted his guitar from around his neck. "What does it look like I'm doing?"

"I thought you went to New York with Jade."

"She's not going to be gone very long. And I already committed to this...*gig.*" He said it almost scornfully.

"I thought you were against playing here. I overheard you telling Jade that you'd rather perform at a prison than a lowly beach hut."

"Yeah. Well, I guess she showed your boss some footage of me, and he made me an offer I couldn't refuse."

"How long will you be playing here?"

"I don't know. A few weeks. Until we leave."

"You're not staying the whole summer?"

"No. That was never the plan."

Disappointment set in. I should have been happy that he was leaving soon, but hearing that news had the opposite effect on me.

"Wow. Okay. Well…do you need me to show you around?"

"I'm good," he said before walking away from me, heading toward the back of the restaurant.

Justin disappeared for at least an hour. He was scheduled to perform at eight, so he had about twenty minutes to go before showtime.

My curiosity got the best of me as I went in search of him. The door to one of the back rooms was cracked open, and I could see him downing a bottle of beer and looking stressed. I wondered if he ever got nervous before a show. Even though he considered performing here a joke, he was still going to be putting himself out there.

His eyes darted to the side, and he noticed me standing there. We just stared at each other. It was ironic, but the only times I could ever feel the remnants of our old connection were in these fleeting moments of silent eye contact. Sometimes silence spoke the loudest.

I left him alone again, making my way back down the hall and into the restaurant to tend to the customers I'd been ignoring.

Things really started to get busy. Without Jade working tonight, we were short-staffed, and I was having a hard time keeping up with the orders. Sandy's had indoor and outdoor seating. Normally, I would only be working one section, but tonight I was going back and forth between the two.

It was nice out, so I knew they would have Justin performing outside. I kept glancing over to the small stage to see if he was there. It was past eight, and he hadn't made an appearance yet.

Sometime close to eight thirty, I was in the middle of serving a large party of ten when I first heard it: the chilling sound of a soulful voice that was not familiar in the least. He gave no introduction. No warning. He just started to sing out the first few words, followed by the strum of his guitar. The song that Justin had chosen to start with was a cover of "Ain't No Sunshine" by Bill Withers.

The crowd soon quieted down, and all eyes were on the stunning blond male specimen with the spotlight shining down on him. Despite the fact that I was carrying a large round tray of dirty dishes, I couldn't move. The vibration of his thick, smoky singing voice had completely paralyzed me, penetrating my body and soul.

Aside from the lone teardrop that had fallen the night he'd lost it on me during the steak dinner, I hadn't shed any more tears—until now. It was all too much. Hearing how different his voice sounded, how he'd trained it over the years, was a wake-up call as to how much I had missed. All of the hours of practice that must have gone into honing that beautiful voice, and I hadn't been there for any of it. The guilt, the emotions, the reality of a decade gone...everything started to pummel me at once. Not to mention the song—about a girl leaving. It probably had nothing to do with me, but in my mind, it sure as hell felt like it did.

You had to have true talent to perform solo acoustically. All eyes were on you and nothing else. There were no distractions to take away from a cracked voice or any other screw-ups.

Justin sang the song flawlessly. The vibration of his voice was like a deep massage to my entire being. My heart filled with pride. Whether he liked it or not, I was so damn proud of him.

At the same time, I felt a rush of antsy excitement, much like a teenager seeing a boy band in concert. Adrenaline was pumping through me. A part of me wanted to just shout, "This is my Justin! I knew him way back when." Another part of me wanted to rush the stage and wrap my arms around him.

The way his fingers worked the guitar effortlessly almost rivaled the sexiness of his voice. Women were starting to leave their tables, throwing money down at his feet.

Jesus.

Did they think he would start undressing or something if they gave him enough? I'd never seen anyone throw money around here like that before. They'd certainly never thrown dollar bills at The Ruckus. I guess that was just the type of effect Justin had on women.

By the third song, I needed a breather. Retreating to the bathroom, I splashed water on my face before returning outside to the tables just in time to hear him finally speak into the microphone in a low and sultry voice.

"I'm Justin Banks from New York City. I'll be here for the next few weeks. Thanks for coming out tonight."

Applause and a few whistles rang out. My focus on Justin had prevented me from tending to my customers. A few of them were waving me down, antsy for refills, so I took their orders and made my way over to the outdoor bar.

Justin took a sip of beer, then spoke through the mic again. "This next song is an original I recently wrote myself. Hope you like it." He strummed the guitar once and added, "It's called, 'She Likes to Watch.'"

My body stilled upon hearing the title, and it took a few seconds to register.

"This song goes out to all the sneaky little voyeurs out there. You know who you are."

The retaliation that I'd assumed he'd waived was in fact simply delayed and about to be dished out in all its glory. I refused to look over toward the stage. The bartender placed the drinks in front of me, and I forced my wobbly legs to move long enough to drop them off with their rightful owners before the song started.

She pretends to be a good girl,
Quiet and refined.
But Daddy always said,
Those are the worst kind.
Turns out he was right.
As I found out the other night...

She likes to watch.
Mmm hmm...she likes to watch.

You think you are alone,
Until you hear that little moan.

She likes to watch.
Mmm hmm...she likes to watch.

She'll catch you naked and exposed,
When you think the door is closed.
She's a princess and a voyeur,
Curiosity will destroy her.
Maybe therapy will heal ya,

It's not too late for you, Amelia.

She likes to watch.
Mmm hmm...she likes to watch.

And my kinky little friend,
Insists on staying till the end.

She likes to watch.
Mmm hmm...she likes to watch.

When the song eventually ended, the crowd went wild. They apparently loved the idea behind it. Did he really have to put my name in there? A part of me was mortified, but I had to admit, there was another part of me that was...relieved. Him writing the song was a little reminder of the way things used to be.

When I finally garnered the courage to look over at him, he flashed a mischievous smile before moving right into the next song. I was sure he could tell by the look on my face that he'd successfully managed to embarrass me.

Well played.

———

Back at the house that night, Justin retreated to his room without so much as one word to me. It felt a little strange knowing that we were alone for the first time without Jade. The feeling was short-lived, though.

At eleven the next morning, I was still in bed when I heard the front door open. I could hear the muffled sounds of Jade's and Justin's voices as she joined him in their bedroom. She must have left the city really early in the morning to come back here.

As much as I liked Jade, something was unsettling about her return. There was always an underlying jealousy that I couldn't help feeling. When the bed started creaking, nausea set in.

Damn.

She had been home all of three minutes before pouncing on him. I couldn't say I blamed her one bit, but I really didn't want to hear it. I covered my head with my pillow, shut my eyes, and reminded myself that they would both be gone in a few weeks.

Three weeks.

Around noon, I threw on a terry cloth sundress before joining Justin and Jade downstairs. The sun pouring into the kitchen was blinding.

Justin smirked and lifted the carafe. "Coffee?"

I flashed an exaggerated smile. "You know what? Yes. I would love some."

Determined to continue my façade about loving Justin's coffee, I refused to back down. Sadly, my body was becoming accustomed to the unusually high level of caffeine. The one morning I'd skipped it, regular coffee hadn't done the trick. I was becoming addicted to Justin's coffee fusion, and that really sucked.

"So, how was Sandy's last night?" Jade asked. "Did my baby rock the house?"

"He was amazing. Everyone loved him."

Justin's eyes met mine for a brief moment. I wanted him to know that I sincerely meant that.

He brushed it off. "It was fine. It'll give me something to do to pass the time here."

"What did you play?"

"I tried out a new song."

I swallowed.

"The one you played for me the other night?" she asked.

"No. A different one."

It dawned on me that Justin had probably chosen to perform "She Likes to Watch" last night in particular only because Jade hadn't been there. It still baffled me that he was keeping the whole incident to himself when he could have just told her and embarrassed the shit out of me.

He smiled at me. "Want a refill, Amelia?"

I smiled bigger. "Don't mind if I do. This stuff is really growing on me. Quite a surprise."

"Well, I know you love surprises."

I rolled my eyes at him. Thankfully, Jade had no way of knowing what he was referring to.

Serving me coffee continued to be a running joke. He thought I was drinking the mud to spite him. The joke was on him. He didn't realize I truly wanted it. The morning coffee exchange was the only real opportunity for normal communication with him anyway, so I took what I could get.

Jade raked her fingers through Justin's messy morning hair. "I noticed Olivia commented on your Instagram post last night."

Looking upset, he moved Jade's hand off of him. "Jade... don't."

I had to ask. "Who's Olivia?"

"Justin's ex. She works in the music industry and is really annoying. She comments on all his stuff, even though she knows he has a girlfriend. So disrespectful."

"I can't help that she comments on my shit," he growled.

I was sure there were many former girlfriends.

Olivia.

Huh.

Was I seriously jealous of someone else now too, when I had no right to be jealous at all? That was pretty pathetic. But my jealousy when it came to him was certainly nothing new.

My inability to handle these feelings was a big factor in my moving away, and it had ultimately changed the course of our lives.

———

Ten Years Earlier

"I don't like it when they start playing these games."

Justin whispered in my ear, "We don't have to stay here if you don't want to, Patch." His hot breath caused a shiver to run down my spine.

"It's okay," I said.

"You sure?"

"Yeah."

A group of kids from school were hanging out in Brian Bosley's basement. From time to time, Brian would suggest that we all start playing Truth or Spin. It was a combination of Truth or Dare and Spin the Bottle. Brian would select the "victims," as he called them. He would ask a question, and if the person pleaded the fifth, refusing to answer, Brian would spin the green Heineken bottle. The victim would then have to kiss whomever the bottle pointed toward. The kiss needed to last a full minute; that was the rule.

It was fun to watch as long as neither of us got called upon. Part of the deal in getting invited back to Brian's was to play along with his games. Somehow, neither Justin nor I had ever gotten picked to participate the last couple of times we had come here.

"Banks."

My heart dropped when I heard Justin's name.

"Yeah?"

"You're up."

"Shit," Justin muttered under his breath.

He flashed me a worried look before Brian posed the question.

"Question. Do you or do you not secretly want to bone Amelia?"

My best friend's face turned red. I didn't think I had ever seen it that color before. My heart was pounding. I couldn't believe Brian had asked him that, and I was truly scared of the answer, whichever way it went.

He shook his head. "Pass."

Brian sounded surprised at Justin's refusal. "Pass? Are you sure?"

"Pass."

"All right, then." Brian wasted no time bending down to spin the bottle. The glass spun around, scraping across the laminate basement floor before coming to a stop.

"Oh! Your not-so-lucky victim is…Sophie!"

Justin looked at me. The worry in his eyes was tangible, but he knew he had to go through with it.

"One minute," Brian reminded.

Sophie, who'd been sitting on the ground, slithered toward him. I watched, devastated, as Justin pressed his lips into hers. She opened her mouth wide and wrapped her hands around the back of his head, pulling him harder into her and practically eating his face. I had always known she liked him.

It felt like my heart was slowly breaking with every second that passed. That was the longest minute of my life. It was the first time the jealousy monster had reared its ugly head to that extent.

When the minute was up, Justin wiped his lips with the back of his hand and came back over to me. I wouldn't even look at him. I knew I shouldn't have been mad, but my feelings were out of my control.

"Are you okay?" he asked.

I continued to look down at my shoes. "Let's just go."

He followed me. "Patch...it's just a game."

"I don't want to talk about it."

We started the quiet and awkward walk home. I stopped suddenly in the middle of the sidewalk and turned to him. "Why didn't you just answer the question?"

He looked at me for the longest time before admitting, "I didn't know what to say."

"What do you mean?"

"If I said no, your feelings would have been hurt. If I said yes...then things would be weird between us. And I don't want that. Ever."

"Was she your first kiss?"

He hesitated, looking up at the dark sky, then whispered, "No."

I shook my head and started to walk ahead of him. It felt like I didn't know him anymore.

"Patch, come on. Don't do this."

Tears started falling. I was crying, and I couldn't even pinpoint exactly why. That was the first time I realized that I'd fallen in love with him. I loved Justin. More than a friend, more than anything. I was so mad at myself.

My biggest fear was losing him. It hit me that it was going to happen someday.

Maybe it was already happening.

CHAPTER 5

A week later, and Justin had practically become a local star in Newport overnight. The crowd at Sandy's was nearly double what it had been before he became the nightly entertainment. Of course, the newest patrons were primarily young women who had heard about the hot new headlining guitarist.

One late afternoon, Jade and I were just headed out the door to work when her cell phone rang. "Shit. Hold up. It's my agent," she said.

I waited in the doorway for her to take the call.

After a few seconds, her hands started trembling. "You're kidding. You're kidding!" Jumping up and down, she covered her mouth. "Oh my God. Oh my God! Yes, of course, I can." Finally, she let out a yelp of excitement. "Thank you, Andy. Thank you for letting me know! Oh my God. So, what's next? Okay. Okay. I'll call you tonight," she said before hanging up.

"What's going on?"

Jade let out a scream of joy and pulled me into a hug, her bony frame pressing against my ample chest.

"I got the part of understudy for a pretty big role in *The Phenomenals*…on Broadway! It was one of the two auditions I had last week. I thought it was a long shot. My agent wasn't even going to send me initially!" When she let out another loud squeal, Justin came downstairs.

"What the hell is going on down here?"

She ran toward him and threw herself into his arms. "Baby! I got understudy for the role of Veronica in *The Phenomenals*!"

"Are you kidding? Holy shit. That's fucking awesome!" He lifted her up in the air and spun her around.

Feeling awkward and like a third wheel, I cleared my throat and said, "Congratulations, Jade. I'm so happy for you."

Justin finally put her down. "When does this all go down?"

"They want me in New York in a couple of days."

He looked frazzled. "Aw, shit. All right…um…I wish I hadn't committed to that gig at Sandy's. I would have just gone back with you."

"It's okay. It's only a couple more weeks that you promised him, right? It'll go by fast."

"Yeah."

Jade smiled. "Be nice to Amelia."

———

From the moment Jade left, Justin made even more of an effort to stay in his room during the day, and he also ignored me at the restaurant. He never performed "She Likes to Watch" again.

Aside from intentionally joining him in the kitchen when I knew he was having his coffee, there was no other interaction. It seemed that Jade's departure was causing even more distance between us.

A few days later, I'd just gotten home from an afternoon shift at Sandy's when what sounded like wretched hurling coming from upstairs caught my attention. Without thinking it through, I ran up the steps to find Justin keeled over with his face inside the toilet.

"Oh my God, are you throwing up?"

"Nah. I'm giving cunnilingus to the toilet. What the fuck do you think?"

"Did you eat something bad?"

He shook his head before another volcano of puke erupted from within him. Looking away, I shut my eyes until he was finished.

"Can I get you any—"

"Just go, Amelia." He flushed the toilet.

There was something about a person being sick and helpless that made you see the child in them. Despite trying to act tough, Justin seemed virtually helpless in that moment.

"Are you sure I can't get you—"

"Leave!" My body shook as he screamed.

As another round of vomiting commenced, I reluctantly went back downstairs.

After several minutes, I could hear him returning to his bedroom. I stayed downstairs for about an hour. Things were unusually quiet. On a normal day, he'd be moving around in his room, so I knew he'd either fallen asleep or was lying down. Being the paranoid person that I was, I started to imagine that maybe he'd passed out from dehydration. He hadn't come down to get a drink of water. Given all that he'd thrown up, that was dangerous.

I sucked it up and marched up the stairs. Lightly knocking

on his door, I didn't bother to wait for him to respond before entering. "Justin?"

He was lying on his side, his head against the pillow, and his eyes were open. He just stared at me blankly, but his eyes seemed glassy.

"Are you okay?"

"No."

Without seeking permission, I approached and placed my hand on his forehead. It felt hot to the touch. "You're burning up. We need to take your temperature."

I ran to the bathroom and fished through the medicine cabinet for a thermometer before returning to Justin.

"Put this in your mouth."

He chuckled. "That's normally my line."

Rolling my eyes, I demanded, "Just do it." I was slightly relieved that he was actually joking around with me.

Amazingly, he didn't fight me on taking his temperature. The thermometer beeped, and it showed that he had a significant fever.

"It's one hundred and two point five. Were you supposed to play tonight?"

"Mmhmm," he moaned.

"I'm calling Salvatore, telling him you can't make it."

"Don't. I might see how I feel in an hour."

"There is no way you are going to be able to perform like this."

"I'll call him in an hour," he insisted.

Justin's phone buzzed, and he reached over to check it before placing it back on the nightstand.

"Was that Jade?"

"Yeah."

"Does she know you're sick?"

"Yes."

"Does she have rehearsal tonight?"

"No."

"Is she coming?"

"No. Why would she come all the way here because I have a fever?"

I didn't have an answer. I just knew that if my boyfriend were this sick, I would want to be with him. Maybe he'd downplayed it.

"What can I get you?"

"Nothing. Privacy. That's what you can get me."

"I'm getting you something to drink. I don't care what you say. You'll get dehydrated."

"Make it a stiff one if you're gonna continue playing nurse," he yelled after me.

I went downstairs and returned with a bottle of water, pills, and a small towel.

Handing him the bottle and two Tylenol, I said, "Here. Drink up." Justin swallowed the pills and took a sip before eyeing the washcloth.

"What the hell are you going to do with that thing?"

"It's a wet cloth." I placed it on his forehead. "It will bring down the fever."

He moved my hand off him. "I can take care of myself, Amelia."

Ignoring his comment, I simply said, "I'll call Salvatore. Get some sleep."

After another bout of vomiting, Justin turned in for the night. Even though I'd left some extra waters with him, I worried that maybe he wasn't drinking anything. So, I decided to check in on him one more time before I went to sleep.

He was awake and sitting up on the bed and looked really pale.

"How are you feeling?"

"Like shit."

"We should take your temperature again."

This time when I pulled the thermometer out of his mouth, my heart nearly stopped. "Oh my God. It says one hundred four point five. Justin, that's dangerous. We need to get you to the emergency room."

"I'm not going to the hospital."

"This is not up for debate."

Grabbing my phone, I immediately started searching the Internet for information on adult fevers. "It says here that a fever over one hundred and five can be deadly. You could get brain damage."

"That's a little extreme. Don't you think?"

"I don't care if it's extreme. You need to be seen."

"I'm not going."

"Then I'll stay here all night until you agree to go."

"Emergency rooms skeeve me out."

"Would you rather be dead?"

"Hmm. It's a toss-up between that and being stuck in this room with you yelling in my ear."

"That's real nice."

"Why are you involving yourself in this, Amelia?"

"I don't care how you feel about me, all right? I care about you. I always have, and I always will, and I don't want anything to happen to you."

After a long pause, he closed his eyes and let out a deep breath. "All right. I'll fucking go."

"Thank you."

Justin was shivering during the dark ride to Newport

59

Hospital. Before we left the house, I'd texted Jade and promised to keep her updated throughout the night.

When we arrived, we lucked out that the emergency room was pretty quiet. They took Justin right into one of the small curtained-off treatment areas in the back. No one—including Justin—protested me going back there with him.

They hooked him up to an IV and gave him Motrin. Over the course of an hour, they also ran a battery of blood tests.

A new doctor who had just come on shift entered the room.

"How are you feeling, Mr. Banks?" he asked.

"Like crap." Justin squinted to get a closer look at the doctor's hospital ID. "Is your name seriously Dr. Danger?"

The doctor rolled his eyes. "It's actually pronounced like hanger. Dang-er."

"Do they know what's going on with him, Doc?" I asked.

He held out his hand. "Call me Will. Please."

I took it. "Amelia."

He smiled, sort of giving me a flirtatious vibe. "Well, we think it's a combination of things going on here. An unidentifiable bacterial infection that caused a high fever and vomiting in addition to dehydration. We've ruled out more serious issues." He looked at Justin. "You're very lucky your girlfriend brought you in. Fevers of that level can be quite dangerous in adults."

Justin glanced over at me briefly before he turned to Dr. Danger again. "How long am I gonna be sick?"

"It's probably going to last a few days, but we'd like to keep you overnight for observation because of the severity of your fever and to get some more fluids and vitamins into you."

"I have to sleep here?"

"Yes. We'll move you into a more comfortable room."

Justin frowned. "Can I object?"

"I'm afraid not. I'm sure your girlfriend will keep you company."

"Oh. I'm not his girlfriend," I corrected. "His girlfriend is in New York."

"Sister?"

"No. We're just..." I hesitated. What were we? "We were friends years ago. Now we live together in a house we both inherited."

Dr. Danger looked utterly confused, then asked, "You're not dating each other, then?"

"No," Justin was quick to answer.

"No," I repeated.

"Do you live locally, Amelia?" Dr. Danger asked.

"Yes. I live about ten minutes down the road."

"I actually just moved here from Pennsylvania. Perhaps you'd like to show me around the island sometime?"

He'd really caught me off guard. Dr. Danger—Will—was definitely attractive in a clean-cut, semi-older way. With his dark hair and large brown eyes, he was handsome enough. I couldn't say my body had anywhere near the reaction to him that it did for Justin, but maybe it would be good to accept his offer.

"Sure. That would be nice."

"Great." He fished inside the pocket of his white jacket for his phone. "Give me your number?"

Justin looked miffed as I recited my digits.

"The nurse will be back in to check on him soon. I'll call you." He winked.

"Okay." I smiled, offering a small wave.

After Will left the room, Justin looked over at me from the bed and huffed, "What a fucking loser."

"Loser? Why? Because only a loser would be attracted to me?"

"What kind of a doctor picks up a patient's friend like that on the job?"

"Oh, now we're friends?"

Ignoring my question, he said, "Seriously, that was lame. He's a cheeseball."

"I happen to like cheeseballs, especially if they come in the form of good-looking doctors. Cheeseballs are better than downright mean people."

"Whatever."

A nurse came in to tell us that the other room was ready. She walked us into an elevator to the second floor, where Justin was placed in an overnight suite. Still hooked up to the IV, he finally fell asleep. Soon after, I followed suit, conking out on the cot next to his bed.

About an hour later, it was sometime early in the morning. I woke up before he did and marveled at how even though he was so sick, he was still handsome as ever with his matted hair and especially with his overgrown stubble. Then, Justin unexpectedly opened his eyes. When he saw me lying on the makeshift bed next to him, he looked surprised.

"I thought you would have gone home."

"No. I couldn't leave you."

"You really didn't have to stay."

"It was fine. I would have been worried."

He didn't respond, but the look on his face softened.

The nurse walked in and checked his vitals and temperature. "Your fever is still high…one hundred and two point five…but at least it's responding to the medicine and going in the right direction. I'm going to check with the doctor on call about you being discharged."

"Thank God," Justin muttered.

———

When we arrived back at the beach house, Justin settled into his bed once again. Thankfully, the vomiting part of the illness seemed to have passed, even though the fever hadn't. Jade texted from time to time, and I continued to give her updates.

The nurse had said it was important for him to eat something and stay hydrated, so I boiled him some chicken broth and brought it upstairs. He was sleeping, and I didn't want to wake him, so I opted to take it back downstairs until he woke up. He must have heard the mug moving against the saucer, though, because as I was heading back out the door, his voice stopped me.

"What are you doing?"

"I made you some broth. The nurse said you need to eat."

Returning to his bedside, I handed it to him as he scooted up against the headboard and began to sip it. I turned around when I felt his hand grab my arm.

"You don't have to leave."

"I'll just come back for the mug."

As I walked out, his voice stopped me again. "Patch."

My body froze. Him calling me by the old nickname had totally stunned me. I never thought I'd hear it again.

"Turn around," he said.

When I did, his face reflected a sincerity that I hadn't seen in years.

He placed the mug and saucer on the table and said, "Thank you…for everything. Thank you for taking care of me."

So caught off guard and overcome with emotion, I simply nodded once and continued out the door, unable to stop thinking about his words for the rest of the night.

Two days later, Justin's fever finally broke, but he still wasn't feeling up to performing. I was watching television downstairs when he sat down on the couch next to me. He put his legs up on the ottoman and crossed his arms. It was the first time he'd ever chosen to hang out in the living room when I was lounging.

He'd just showered and smelled like aftershave. My body immediately reacted to the closeness of his legs to mine even though we weren't touching.

I wish he were mine.

Where had that thought come from?

"What's this crap you're watching?" Justin asked.

"Some reality show. I can change it if you want."

"No. I invaded your space."

"I'm just glad you're feeling better."

"Me too."

Throwing the controller at him, I said, "Seriously, take the remote."

He handed it back to me. "Nah. I owe you. You put up with my shit when I was sick and whiny. The least I can do is sit through listening to these whiny bitches."

"Well, if you really want to thank me for nursing you back to health, there is something else you can do."

He lifted his brow curiously. "All right…"

God, I just realized how that sounded.

"You can talk to me," I said.

"Talk?"

"Yes."

He let out a deep sigh. "I really don't want to open up an old can of worms. We both know what happened. It's not gonna change anything."

Not beyond begging, I looked into his eyes. "Please?"

He suddenly got up.

"Where are you going?"

"I need a drink for this," he said, walking toward the kitchen.

"Can you get me one too?" I hollered after him. My heartbeat began to accelerate in preparation. Was this really happening? Was he going to talk about what happened or just listen to me ramble?

He returned with a bottle of beer for himself and a glass of white wine for me. It surprised me that he knew exactly what I wanted, even though I hadn't specified. It proved that he'd been observant even while pretending to ignore me.

He took a long sip, then placed his beer on the coffee table. "We have to set some rules."

"All right."

"Rule number one: if I say we're done talking, we're done talking."

"Okay."

"Rule number two…after tonight, we don't talk about shit that happened in the past. This is it. One night only."

"Okay. I can handle that."

Grabbing the bottle again, he downed half of the beer before slamming it down on the table. "All right. Go."

Where should I begin?

I just needed to throw it all out there.

"There is no excuse for leaving the way I did. I was young and stupid and scared. My biggest fear had always been getting hurt by you, because you were the one person I could count on besides Nana. When I found out you knew what was happening behind my back…I took it as betrayal. At the time, I didn't realize that you were just trying to protect me."

65

Nine Years Earlier

Mom was out as per usual, so I would be sneaking out with Justin to go to the little red theater. This week, they were playing an Italian film called *Si Vive Una Volta Sola* that I had been wanting to see.

As he always did, Justin met me at the corner.

"We'd better hurry up," he said. "We don't want to miss the nine o'clock show."

"We're good on time. Relax."

We started the walk to the bus stop when I realized I didn't have my bus pass.

"Shoot. We need to go inside your house. My bus pass is in the pocket of my jacket that I left in your dining room when we were doing homework the other day."

He waved his hand dismissively. "I'll just pay for you."

"No, Justin. That's stupid. We still have plenty of time."

I started walking back toward his house.

He grabbed my arm. "Stop. I have it covered."

"I'm going inside."

An uncharacteristically panicked look flashed across his face. "We can't."

"Why?"

As was usual every other week, his mother Carol was on an out-of-town business trip. I couldn't understand why he was so insistent that we not go inside his house.

He looked like he was struggling to come up with an excuse. His eyes moved from side to side, and my instinct just told me something was off.

"What are you keeping from me?"

"Nothing. We just can't go in there right now."

"I don't understand. Your father's car is outside. He's home. Why can't I just run in and get my jacket?"

"My father would get mad if he knew I was going out with you. I told him I was going out with Rob."

"I don't believe that. Your father knows we hang out. He's cool with it."

"Not at night."

"You're lying."

"Patch, will you just trust me?"

I suddenly ran toward the front door and knocked frantically. There was no answer for almost a full minute before Elton Banks finally came to the door.

"Hi. Justin and I were heading to the movies, but I need my bus pass. It's in my jacket that I left in your dining room. I just need to come in and get it."

Justin's dad looked over at him worriedly. Meanwhile, Justin's face was practically white.

When Mr. Banks hesitated to let me in, I pushed my way past him. "I just need my jacket." After entering the dining room, I spotted my sweatshirt hanging on the chair. Something else caught my eye: my mother's faux fur coat.

What was she doing here?

It didn't take me long to figure it out. Storming upstairs, I knew exactly where I was going to find her. I burst through Justin's parents' bedroom to find my mother frantically trying to put on her clothes.

Covering my mouth with my hand, I shook my head in disbelief before running back down the stairs and out the front door.

Justin ran after me. "Patch, wait. Please!"

I turned around and spewed, "You knew about this? You

knew that my mother was here messing around with your father? How long has this been going on?"

"I didn't know how to tell you."

"I can't believe this!"

"I'm sorry, Patch. I'm so sorry."

I ran back into my house and slammed the door, unsure of what hurt more: my mother's actions or Justin keeping it all from me.

CHAPTER 6

The hurt in his eyes was palpable. Justin leaned his head back against the couch as I struggled to find the words.

"My mother was basically an irresponsible child, a selfish person. She'd had so many different boyfriends and affairs with married men. It never really surprised me that she would stoop to that level with your father. At the time, though, I just felt betrayed by everyone, including you. But I was wrong to punish you in any way for their actions."

He rubbed his eyes warily and turned to me. "What do you want to know, Amelia?"

"How did it start? How long did you know about them?"

He turned his body toward me and wrapped his arm around the back of the couch. "I'm pretty sure my father was the one who pursued her. He used to always ask me questions about Patricia before they got together."

"Really?"

"What I know now that I didn't know then was that my parents had an open marriage. My mother went on way too many *business trips*, if you know what I mean. At the time, though, I hadn't figured it out yet. I came home from school unexpectedly early one day and walked in on your mother and him having sex."

I shuddered. "Oh my God."

Justin grabbed his beer and took a long swig. "My father sat me down later that night and explained to me that he believed my mother was having an affair too, and that he and Patricia had just started seeing each other. Your mother made me swear not to tell you. She said you wouldn't be able to handle it, that your relationship with her was already tarnished enough and that you were under a lot of stress that I didn't know about. She somehow convinced me that telling you would ruin your life. She told me if I really cared about you, I wouldn't say anything. I believed her."

"There was nothing I ever kept from you, Justin. There was nothing going on with me. She was manipulating you to keep her antics a secret from me."

"I wanted to tell you, but the more time that passed, the harder it was to admit that I'd been keeping something from you for so long. So, I chose not to say anything. I was only trying to protect you."

"Justin, I—"

"Let me finish," he interrupted.

"Okay."

"We both came from broken homes, but from the moment I met you, my world seemed a little less broken. I always felt like my job was to protect you. And keeping what they were doing from you was only an extension of that. It wasn't meant to be deceptive."

I get it now.

There was so much I was embarrassed to admit about my

feelings all those years ago, but I couldn't hold anything back. He was giving me this one chance to explain myself. Taking a long gulp of my wine, I prepared to lay it all out on the line.

"I ran away because I couldn't handle my emotions. It was more than just you keeping that secret from me. It was what it represented to me: that there would be other things in the future that you would keep from me too." I paused. *Just say it.* "I was developing really strong feelings for you that went beyond our friendship, and I found myself unable to handle them. I didn't know how to tell you. I was afraid to scare you away. It felt like I was destined to get hurt somehow, so I chose to move away before that happened. It was my own way of controlling it. It was rash and foolish."

That was the first time I had ever admitted those feelings.

He just looked at me for a bit, then said, "Why didn't you tell me how you felt, even before everything went down with our parents?"

"I didn't think you felt the same way about me, and I didn't want to lose you."

"So, you ran away and lost me anyway. How did that make sense?"

"It somehow felt like if I left before the worst happened, it wouldn't hurt as badly. The bottom line, though, is that I was a dumb, hormonal, fifteen-year-old girl. Running away to live with my father was the wrong decision. And you never gave me the time of day to tell you how sorry I was once I came to my senses that following year. So, I need to say it now. I am so sorry if my leaving like that hurt you in any way."

"Hurt me?" He let out a slight angry laugh, then shocked me with what he said next. "It *changed* me. I loved you, Amelia. I was *in love* with you." Justin ran his fingers through his hair in frustration. "How the fuck did you not know that?"

His words felt like they'd sliced through my heart, leaving me unable to respond. I had never in a million years expected him to say that.

He had loved me?

He continued, "I would have died for you back then. When you left, it felt like my world ended. Besides your grandmother, you were the only one I could count on. You were always there…until you weren't anymore. Losing you taught me not to count on anyone but myself. It shaped who am I today, and that's not necessarily a good thing."

It hurt so badly to hear him say that. "I'm sorry."

"You don't need to apologize again; you already did."

"If you don't forgive me, then I do need to keep repeating it."

He let out a long, deep breath. "Like I've said to you before, I've moved on from it."

I didn't want him to move on. I wanted to go backward, back in time, and hug him. Never let him go.

Still reeling from his admission, I dug my nails into the back of the couch and said, "I don't want us to be virtual strangers. You still mean so much to me. The fact that you're angry at me won't change that."

"What do you want from me?"

"I want us to try to be friends again. I want us to be able to sit in the same room and talk to each other, maybe have a few laughs. We're gonna always own this house together, in any case. Someday, we'll be bringing children here. We need to get along."

"I am not gonna have children," he said emphatically.

The fact had slipped my mind.

"Jade told me."

"She did, did she? What else did you talk about? My dick size? You tell her you got a good look at it?"

I chose not to entertain the quip and stayed with the subject at hand. "I know why you don't you want children, Justin."

"You of all people should understand that it's asinine to bring a child into this world if you're not one hundred percent sure of your capabilities. My parents are a prime example of people who should have never procreated."

"You're not your parents."

"No, but I'm a fucked-up product of their mistakes, and I'm not gonna repeat history."

It made me immensely sad that he felt that way. Thinking back to how protective he had always been of me, I knew Justin would make an amazing father. He just couldn't see that. Knowing that I had promised we wouldn't rehash the past beyond tonight, an urgent need to get more off my chest overtook me.

"I beg to differ. I think that you are so much stronger as a person because you had to grow up a lot quicker than kids who were coddled and handed everything. You've given to others what your parents neglected to give you. I'll never forget how you always managed to make me laugh even when it seemed impossible, how you always knew exactly what I needed, how you always protected me. Those are the qualities that would make someone a good parent. And whether you have children or not, you are an amazing human being. Not only that, but your musical talent completely blows me away. It makes me so sad to think of everything that I missed because of my stupidity and fear. I know we've both changed, but I still see all the good in you even when you are trying so hard to hide behind a mask." My eyes started to water, and a teardrop fell. "I miss you, Justin." It felt like everything had just come pouring out of me before I could think about the consequences.

He startled me when he reached over and swiped a teardrop from my cheek with his thumb, prompting me to close my eyes. His touch felt so good.

"I think we've talked enough for tonight," he said.

Nodding, I said, "Okay."

He lifted himself off the couch and turned off the television. "Come on. Let's get some air."

I followed his lead out the front door and down to the beach. We walked in silence for what seemed like an eternity. The night was still except for the sound of the waves crashing. The ocean breeze was calming, and as strange as it was, the silence between us seemed like a therapeutic exercise of some kind. It felt as though a huge weight had been lifted, because I'd gotten to say what I wanted to. Even though there hadn't really been a clear conclusion to our conflict, it was more closure than I'd ever had with him.

The sound of Justin's phone interrupted the quiet of our walk. He picked it up.

"Hey, babe. …Everything is good. …That's great. Wow. It's really happening. …Just taking a walk."

I found it interesting that he didn't mention he was with me.

"Me too. Can't wait. I love you too. All right. Bye."

After he hung up, I looked at him. "How's Jade?"

"She's good. She's going to get to perform tomorrow night because the lead's grandfather died."

"Wow. That's amazing. Well, not that the grandfather died…"

"Yeah. I got that."

Not another word was spoken until we started to approach the house.

Justin pointed to something in the distance. "Do you see that?"

"Where?"

The next thing I knew, I felt weightless. Justin had lifted me off my feet and was running toward the shore. Judging from his laughter, there was nothing to point out; he'd just been trying to distract me long enough to snatch me up.

Jerk.

He dumped my fully clothed body into the ocean. Salty water ran down my throat and up my nose. Justin immediately ran back to the sand, leaving me to wade through the water after him. He was still laughing. He'd taken off his shirt, which had gotten wet, and his pants were soaked.

"Do you feel better now?" I huffed.

"A little." He chuckled. "Actually…a lot."

"Well, good. I'm glad for you," I said, wringing out my dress.

He stood up. "Let me." Justin surprised me when he stood behind me and twisted my long hair to help get the water out. His hands lingered for a few seconds, causing my nipples to tingle. I turned around to distract myself from it and was met by his blue eyes staring into mine. They were glowing in the reflection of the light coming from our house. He looked heartbreakingly handsome.

Fumbling my words a bit, I said, "Um…thank you. Well, I suppose I shouldn't be thanking you, because you caused it."

"It was a long time coming. I've wanted to throw you in the water since the first day I got here."

"Oh, really?"

"Yeah. Really." He smiled mischievously.

"By the way, why are you still here?"

He squinted. "What do you mean?"

"You could have easily gone back to New York with Jade. You know that."

"Are you implying something?"

"I'm not implying anything. I just know that you've been using the Sandy's gig as the reason, and I find that hard to believe."

"What do you want to hear, Amelia, that I'm here because of you?"

"No…I don't know. I—"

"I don't know why I'm here. All right? That's the truth. It just didn't feel like it was time to leave."

"Fair enough."

"Are you done interrogating me for one night…pain in my ass?"

"Yes." I smiled. That was another name he'd used to call me. It was a play on my last name—Payne.

"Good."

"For the record, I'm really glad you stayed."

He shook his head and rubbed his eyes, then said, "Trying to hate you is exhausting."

"So, stop trying."

My teeth started to chatter; it was getting chilly out.

"We'd better go inside," he said.

Following him to the house, I couldn't help thinking that the cold air outside had nothing on the warm feeling inside of me from having reconnected with him tonight.

"You hungry?" he asked.

"Starving, actually."

"Go change. I'll make dinner."

"Really?"

"Well, we gotta eat, don't we?"

"Yeah. I guess we do. I'll be back." I smiled all the way to my room, giddy from the idea of him cooking for me.

When I returned with a dry outfit, my heart fluttered at the sight of Justin standing at the stove. He was still shirtless and wearing his gray beanie while frying some vegetables in a pan.

I cleared my throat. "Smells good. What are you making?"

"Just a teriyaki stir fry with rice, seeing as though you have a limited palate. When the hell did you stop eating red meat, anyway? You used to be a carnivore."

He must have remembered how much we'd enjoyed Burger Barn together in the old days.

"One day, I just woke up and thought about how bizarre it was to be eating a cow. It made no sense. And I stopped cold turkey."

"Seriously? That's kind of ridiculous."

"Yes."

"You've always been a little bizarre, Amelia. I can't say that surprises me."

I winked. "That's why you love me." I'd meant it to come out facetiously, but immediately regretted using the word *love* given his prior admission. When he didn't respond, I panicked, and diarrhea of the mouth developed. "I didn't mean that you still love me. I was just joking. I—"

He held out his palm. "Stop while you're ahead. I knew what you meant."

I pursed my lips, trying to think of a quick change of subject. "Do you think you'll go back to playing at Sandy's tomorrow night?"

"Probably."

"Good. I'm really looking forward to hearing you perform again."

He grabbed two plates and emptied the contents of the pan onto each of them, then slid mine across the counter. "Here."

"Thank you. This smells delicious."

The dish he'd made was actually very tasty. He'd added

sesame seeds and water chestnuts. "Where did you learn to cook like this?"

"Self-taught. I've been cooking for myself for years."

"Where are your parents now?"

"I thought we were done talking about this stuff."

"Sorry. You're right."

Despite having said that, he looked up from his plate and answered my question anyway. "My mother moved back to Cincinnati when I was in college. They sold the house. My father lives in a condo in Providence now."

"How long after I left did things continue between my mother and him?"

"About a year. My mother found out about what they were doing under our roof and kicked him out. He'd violated their rule about messing around with other people in our family home. He lived with Patricia for a while before things went sour between them."

"He moved in with her?"

"Yeah."

I couldn't believe it.

"My mother kept that from me, then. That explains why Nana stopped speaking to her around that time."

"I spent a lot of time over there with your grandmother before I moved away. She was the only person who kept me sane."

"Did you ever talk about me to her?"

"She tried to get me to, but I wouldn't."

"Do you think she left us both this house because she knew it would force us to face each other?"

"I honestly don't know, Amelia."

"I think she did."

"I had no intention of coming here and trying to make amends with you."

"No, really? I didn't catch on." When he cracked a slight smile, I asked, "Do you still feel the same about not making amends?"

"Things don't change overnight. We talked. That's not gonna erase years of shit that happened. We're not going to just magically be best friends again."

"I never expected that." Playing with the remnants of my food, I thought long and hard before speaking again. "I'm gonna say one last thing. And then I promise I won't harp on it anymore."

"I wouldn't put money on that." When his mouth curved into another smile, it was enough to give me the confidence to spill my guts one last time.

"I will probably spend the rest of my life wondering what would have happened if I hadn't run away, if I'd just put my fear aside and told you everything I was feeling. You told me tonight that you were in love with me back then. I truly didn't know that, Justin, but I wish I had. I need you to know that I loved you too. I just had a really shitty way of showing it. And to think that you spent all of these years hating me. I just want you to be happy. If being around me makes you angry or stressed, then I don't want to force anything, and if that's the case, maybe it is best that we keep our distance. But if there's a chance that we can truly be friends again, I would want nothing more. And I'm not stupid. Of course, I know it won't happen overnight. That's it. I won't say anything else about it." I got up from the table and put my plate in the dishwasher. "Thank you for dinner and for talking to me. I'm gonna turn in early."

Just as my foot hit the first step to go upstairs, his voice stopped me. "I never hated you. I couldn't hate you if I tried. Believe me, I *have* tried."

Turning around and smiling, I said, "Good to know."

"Good night, Payne in my ass."

"Good night, Justin."

CHAPTER 7

Two days later, I was having my morning coffee when a text notification lit up my phone. It was from Dr. Will Danger.

How about dinner tomorrow night?

I pondered my reply. It would probably do me some good to take advantage of a distraction from Justin. Since our talk the other night, things had been more cordial between us. At least he was no longer avoiding me. After he'd performed last night, we'd actually driven home from Sandy's together. It had been a quiet ride, but it was a step in the right direction. So, things were as good as they could have been.

The problem was me. I still couldn't curb my attraction to him and didn't know where to draw the line on my emotions. I thought about him every second of the day. We'd be going our separate ways soon, not to mention the not-so-insignificant detail of his committed relationship with Jade. I would never do anything intentionally to jeopardize that. But I still couldn't control my feelings.

My fingers forced out a response to Will.

Tomorrow night sounds great. Just let me know what time.

Justin's deep morning voice startled me. "I see you made coffee fusion."

I jumped, quickly putting down the phone.

He snickered. "Oh. Did I interrupt something? You texting a boy?"

"No."

He glared at me suspiciously. "Liar."

A nervous laugh escaped me. "Want some coffee?"

"Trying to change the subject?"

"Maybe."

"So, who was it?"

"Will."

"Dr. Danger?"

"Yes."

"Ever heard of stranger danger?"

"Yes."

"They created that term about him."

"Oh yeah?"

"I'm pretty sure. Yeah." He poured himself a mug of coffee and turned to me again. "Seriously? Dr. Cheeseball? You're gonna go out with him?"

Nodding, I said, "Tomorrow night. What's your problem with him, anyway?"

"He's disrespectful."

"In what way?"

"That guy was eye-fucking you before he even confirmed we weren't together."

"Maybe he's just perceptive."

"How?"

"He sensed your disdain toward me. It was quite obvious."

"Where's he taking you?"

"I don't know yet."

"You should find out."

"What does it matter?"

"In case you go missing, I'll know where to tell the police to start looking."

Evening rolled around, and I had absolutely no clue what to wear. Will said he was taking me to this restaurant on the water in nearby Tiverton. It was going to be a humid night, so I opted for a lightweight floral tube dress that I'd bought one afternoon while out shopping with Jade earlier this summer.

I could hear Justin panting from down the hall.

Not again.

I didn't dare go over there to assess the situation after what had happened the last time I'd found myself witness to that jerk-off jamboree. But after several minutes, what sounded like punching was added into the mix. I broke my vow to stay out of it and marched out of my room to check things out.

It turned out that Justin was in the exercise room beating the shit out of an Everlast punching bag.

Beads of sweat were dripping down his sculpted back. The room smelled of sweat mixed with his cologne. His hair was drenched. He had earbuds in, and I could hear the music blasting through them. Gritting his teeth, he hit the black rubber contraption harder and harder. My heart beat faster with every punch.

When I inched cautiously closer, he growled, "Get out of the way." I flinched as his arm swung dangerously close to me.

I backed up but stayed watching him from the corner of the room. I'd seen him working out before but never like this. He was like a beast, so strong and virile. It occurred to me that with Jade gone so long, he must have been sexually frustrated. Maybe that was why he was taking it out on the punching bag. Whatever the reason, I was transfixed by the energy he was expending and found myself unable to take my eyes off him.

He suddenly stopped, took out his earbuds, and moved over to the doorway where he'd set up a metal bar for pull-ups. My eyes followed the movement of his body as he lifted his own weight, his rock-hard abs tightening and curling with each lift.

He jumped down from the bar and wiped the sweat off his forehead with the back of his hand. "Nothing better to do than to watch me work out? Aren't you supposed to be getting dressed for a date?"

"I *am* dressed."

"That's Jade's dress, isn't it?"

"No. It's the same one she has, but this one is mine. We bought these from the same shop on clearance the same day."

"It looks normal on her. On you…it looks ridiculous."

My stomach sank. "Are you saying I'm fat?"

"No, but your body is different than hers. That dress looks obscene on you."

Looking down at myself, I suddenly felt naked. "What are you talking about?"

"You want me to spell it out?"

"Yes."

He came up behind me, grabbing my shoulders and

positioning me in front of the full-length mirror on the wall. Shivers ran down my spine from the feel of his rough hands on me.

"Look. Your tits are busting out of it. Your nipples are poking out of the middle of those daisy flowers."

My mind was in a fog because all I could see was me in the mirror with Justin's hot, sweaty body behind me. Then, he flipped me around fast, his stare burning into mine. He was too close for comfort, and my legs felt like they were going to collapse under me from the surge of sexual awareness. "Look at your ass in the mirror. The material can barely wrap around it. You think Dr. Doolittle is going to be able to look you in the eyes when you're dressed like that?"

"You really think this looks that bad?"

He suddenly walked away from me and returned to the pull-up bar. My nipples were tingling. I just wanted his hands on me again.

"You really are that oblivious, aren't you?" he said before doing a few more reps in silence. He hopped down, the weight of his body causing a large thump against the wood floor.

"What do you mean?"

"You never did have any clue what kind of effect you have on people."

"Be specific, please."

"When we were younger, you would sit on my lap, put your hands on me, run your fingers through my hair, hug me all the time with your massive tits pressed against me. I spent half of my teenage years walking around with a fucking hard-on that I couldn't do anything about. The entire time, you apparently had no clue."

"I didn't."

"I know that now. And you have no idea how many times I had to defend you behind your back. Guys talking about your body, saying sexual things about you right in front of my fucking face. Do you have any clue how many fights I got into because of you?"

"You never told me."

"No. I didn't. Because I was trying to protect your feelings. I tried so hard to fucking protect you from shit, and that was the one thing that bit me in the ass in the end."

"I'm sorry."

He held his hands up. "You know what? Never mind. My bad. Let's not do this again. I told you we were done talking. And we are."

"Okay."

"I'd like to continue my workout in peace if you don't mind."

"All right."

Back in my room, I could hear that he'd returned to the punching bag in full force. Still reeling from his words, I couldn't help but wonder if he was right. Maybe I *was* really just a clueless person. But he'd never exactly expressed his feelings to me back then, either. Was I supposed to be a mind reader? I felt like I needed to make that point. It was bugging me. I returned down the hall and spoke through his violent hooks to the bag.

"The other night you asked me why I never told you how I felt. Well, clearly you didn't have the balls to tell me how you felt, either."

Justin stopped punching but kept his arms on the bag, leaning against it. He took a few seconds to catch his breath. "I thought it was understood. How much more obvious could I have been? All the fucking songs I wrote you? Did you ever see me with any other girls?"

"No. But you did admit to kissing someone before that night at Brian's."

"I did kiss one girl before that night. Wanna know why? Because I didn't want to be clueless as to what the fuck I was doing when I finally got the courage to kiss you. I never considered it a real kiss. I wanted my first real one to be with you. I wanted everything with you. But I was afraid we were too young, so I was waiting. I didn't want to rush things and ruin it. But you're right. A part of me also didn't have the balls to tell you how I felt."

"I wish you had. You were being careful, and I was just clueless. Together, we were...careless."

"Careful plus clueless equals careless? Did you just make that up right now?"

"Yes."

"That's pretty fucking cheesy."

"Thanks a lot."

"You'd better get ready for your date with Trapper John, M.D. Or should I say Trapper *Con*."

I laughed, relieved that he was smiling about things now. "Will you help me?"

"Help you? What the fuck do you need help with?"

"Help me pick out what to wear."

"You can't figure this shit out on your own?"

"Yeah. But I still want to look good. You know I have a tendency to pick weird stuff. Potato sack couture and all. I feel like I go from one extreme to the other, and I don't know how to dress in between."

"Fine." Justin let out an exhausted breath and followed me to my room.

I started to take dresses out of my closet, throwing them on the bed one by one. "How about this?"

"Ugly."

"This one?"

"Uglier."

"Okay. This?"

"You got Birkenstocks to go with it?"

"All right...this one?"

"Well, that would be one way to get rid of him."

I covered my face. "Aargggh! This is so frustrating."

"I know a solution."

"What?"

"Don't go on the date."

"Because I can't figure out what to wear?"

"Yeah. I think you should stay home."

"You just don't like him."

"You're damn right."

"Again...why?"

"He just wants in your pants, Amelia."

"Well, he's not getting in my pants."

"You sure about that?"

"I don't sleep with guys on the first date."

He lifted his brow skeptically. "You've never slept with a guy on the first date?"

"Well..."

"Exactly."

"Even if I wanted to sleep with him—which I don't—it wouldn't be tonight."

"Why is that?"

"I stabbed myself again."

He shook his head and chuckled when he figured out I was referring to my period. "I see."

"Why do you think that he's only interested in me for my body, anyway?"

"It was his eyes. I don't trust them. You can tell a lot about someone by the look in their eyes. His gave me a bad vibe."

"Well, I have more going for me than my tits and ass. So, hopefully you're wrong."

"You're right. You have nice deep-set dimples when you smile too."

My body felt flush from the compliment that had come out of the blue. I didn't know how to respond, so I simply said, "Shut up."

"Just be careful," he said seriously, reaching into his back pocket. "Speaking of which…bring this with you." It was his old red Swiss Army knife from when we were younger.

"You still have that?"

"I'll never stop needing it."

"You really want me to have this with me?"

"Yes."

Taking it from him, I said, "Okay."

"Are we done here?"

"We still haven't picked out what I'm wearing."

Justin walked over to my closet and ran his hand slowly along the lineup of outfits, eventually stopping at a simple black sleeveless dress that was far from revealing. It looked more like something you could wear to a funeral. Actually, it was the dress I had bought to wear to Nana's funeral before I'd realized she had explicitly written that she didn't want one. She'd wanted to be cremated, with her ashes thrown in the ocean without any fanfare.

"This one? Really?"

He held the dress in his hand. "Don't ask for my help if you're not gonna listen."

"Okay. This one it is." I took it from him and watched as he made his way out the door. My eyes focused on the rectangular tattoo on his back. Even though I'd always thought it was sexy as hell, I had never been able to get a good enough look at it until now.

"Justin."

He turned around. "Yeah."

"What is that tattoo on your back?"

His body stiffened. "It's a barcode."

"That's what I thought. I always wondered. Does it mean anything?"

Refusing to answer my question, he simply said, "Get dressed. You don't want to be late for Dr. Dick."

———

Will was supposed to be picking me up in about twenty minutes. I sat on the kitchen counter sipping a glass of white wine to relax. The black dress that Justin had chosen actually looked pretty nice. There was no unnecessary skin showing, and that was probably the way it should have been. I'd ended up putting my long, dark brown hair up into a twist.

A waft of Justin's cologne prompted me to look to the side. My heart clenched at the sight of him standing in the entryway. I hadn't noticed him until I smelled him. He seemed to be observing me without my knowing.

He'd just showered after his workout and looked so incredibly hot in a simple black shirt that hugged his muscles. The jeans he was wearing were the ones that always displayed his ass in the best way. Even though I had the night off, Justin was supposed to be playing at Sandy's. The women were going to go apeshit over him tonight.

He walked over and pulled up a stool next to me. My nipples perked up at the closeness of his body.

He examined my face and said, "You don't look too excited."

"I'm not sure how I feel, to be honest."

"You're not nervous about going out with that jackass, are you?"

"A little."

"Why? He's not worth your nerves."

"It's the first date I've been on since Adam."

He sucked in his jaw almost angrily. "That's the guy that cheated on you…"

"Yeah. How did you know?"

"Jade told me."

It surprised me that they'd been talking about me. I wasn't sure how I felt about Justin knowing about Adam.

"Oh."

"Don't let what happened with that asshole make you think you should settle for the first Tom, Dick, or Harry that comes along."

"Have you ever cheated on anyone?"

He hesitated before he answered. "Yes. I'm not proud of it. I was younger then, though. It's not something I would ever do today. The way I see it, if you want to cheat on someone, you should just break up with them. Cheating is for cowards."

"I agree. I wish that Adam had just broken up with me."

"I'm glad you're not with him anymore."

"Me too."

"He was trying to have the best of both worlds. He'll end up doing it to the other girl too. Watch."

"Jade is lucky to have you, to be with someone who is loyal."

His expression darkened before he said, "Temptation is natural. That doesn't mean you should act on it."

"Right. Of course."

Justin swiftly changed the subject. "You got your pocket-knife?"

"Yes. I'm not going to need it, but it's in my purse."

"Good. You have my cell phone number?"

"Yes."

"You should be taking your own car."

"Well, I already agreed to have him pick me up."

"If he tries anything funny, call me. I'll come get you."

"But you'll be in the middle of performing."

"Doesn't matter. Call me if you need a ride."

"Okay. I will."

His protectiveness reminded me of the old days. Having someone looking out for me was a really good feeling. In fact, I hadn't felt it since running away from home all those years ago.

I took another sip of my drink. Before I could place it down on the counter, I felt Justin's hand on mine as he intercepted, taking the glass and gulping down the rest of the wine.

My voice was practically a whisper. "I didn't know you liked white wine."

"I'm in a different kind of a mood tonight, I guess." He took the glass over to the small bar area and refilled it before sitting back down and placing it in front of me.

We quietly drank out of the same goblet, passing it back and forth, making silent eye contact. Whenever he licked the Chardonnay off his lips, it was utterly arousing. I felt so guilty for feeling that way, but it was beyond my control. Like he said, temptation was natural, right? Knowing that I couldn't and wouldn't act on it made the feelings that much more powerful, though. The fact that he was unattainable made it all-consuming.

If I were being honest, no part of me wanted to go out with Will tonight. Every part of me, on the other hand, wanted to go watch Justin perform, especially since we were coming up on the final days before he would return to New York.

The knock on the door was loud and confident. Justin rubbed the back of his neck to massage the tension there. If I didn't know better, I would think he was the one nervous about this date.

When I hopped down from the stool to answer the door, he said, "Wait."

"Yeah?"

"You look really nice. I think that dress was the right choice."

My heart fluttered. "Thank you."

My heels clicked on the tile as I walked over to the front door.

Will was holding a small bouquet of flowers. "Evening, Amelia. God, you look stunning."

"Hi, Will. Thank you. Come in."

Justin's arms were crossed. His body language was more like an armed guard at a bank rather than a man standing casually in his own kitchen.

"You remember my roommate, Justin."

"Of course," said Will. "How are you feeling?"

"Very energized at the moment, Dr. Danger."

Will seemed annoyed at Justin's mispronunciation. "Danger," he corrected.

"Sorry. Didn't mean to anger, Dr. Dang-er."

Will wasn't amused. "No problem."

"Where are you kids going tonight?"

"The Boathouse. You been there?"

"Right on the water. Smooth. Pulling out all the stops."

Grabbing my purse, I said, "Well, we should get going."

Justin held his hand out. "I'll take care of the flowers."

Somehow, I wondered if they would end up in the trash the second the door closed behind us.

"Thanks," I said.

"No problem."

When we got outside, Will turned to me. "Your roommate likes to butcher my name. He's a bit of a wiseass."

"Yes. He can be."

Will opened the door to his Mercedes and let me in the passenger side. The conversation was easy on the way to Tiverton. He asked me about my teaching career, and we spoke about his time at the University of North Carolina School of Medicine at Chapel Hill.

My phone vibrated.

> **Justin:** Those flowers were from the supermarket.
> **Amelia:** How do you know?
> **Justin:** He left the orange sticker on. What a tool.
> **Amelia:** It's the thought that counts.
> **Justin:** Look in the back seat. I bet you'll see milk and eggs.
> **Amelia:** Don't you have to be at Sandy's?
> **Justin:** Heading out now.
> **Amelia:** Break a leg tonight.
> **Justin:** Stay out of Danger. Better yet, keep Danger out of you.
> **Amelia:** You're a goof.
> **Justin:** Order the lobster. At least you'll get something out of tonight.
> **Amelia:** Goodbye, Justin!

"What's so funny?" Will asked.

"Oh, it's nothing. Sorry."

He looked over at me. "So, what were we saying? Oh, you were about to tell me when you're planning to head back to Providence."

"The last week of August. I have to get my classroom set up for the beginning of September."

"I bet your students really dig you."

"Why do you say that?"

"I wish I had a teacher that looked like you when I was in middle school."

"Well, I like to think they appreciate me for other reasons."

"Oh. I'm sure they do."

When we arrived at the restaurant, it was already dark out, so the waterfront view wasn't as great as it would have been during the daylight hours. It was starting to get chilly, so we opted for a window seat inside but overlooking the water. Lights from some of the sailboats illuminated the dark ocean. White fairy lights hanging inside the restaurant made for a cozy ambience. The smell of fresh seafood filled the air. I laughed to myself, thinking of how Justin would probably say the place smelled like dirty snatch.

I ended up ordering swordfish with mango salsa while Will opted for chicken marsala. The conversation while we were waiting for our food was pretty mundane. We spoke a little bit about the upcoming presidential election. Will was a republican while I was a democrat. I also told him the story of how I had inherited Nana's house.

My phone vibrated.

Justin: How's it going?

I didn't want to be rude and answer him. So I ignored the text until Will excused himself to use the restroom.

> **Amelia:** Aren't you supposed to be singing?
> **Justin:** It's my ten-minute break.
> **Amelia:** Everything is fine.
> **Justin:** Just checking to make sure you're still alive.
> **Amelia:** I have not had to use the knife, no.
> **Justin:** Did you order the lobster like I told you to?
> **Amelia:** No. Swordfish.

He didn't respond, so I assumed that he was done texting me, which was good, since Will was headed back to the table.

Our food arrived, and the waitress brought me a second glass of wine. We ate in comfortable silence until I felt my phone buzz on my lap. After I was halfway through my meal, I decided to excuse myself to go to the bathroom so that I could check my phone.

In the restroom, I leaned against the sink as I took my phone out.

> **Justin:** You were right.

What did that mean?

> **Amelia:** Right about what?

After waiting for five full minutes, I decided to head back to the table.

"Everything all right?"

"Yes. Everything is fine."

"I was thinking we could drive back to Newport, maybe take an evening walk down Main Street and stop for coffee or ice cream, whichever you prefer."

Truthfully, I wanted to go home, take off my heels, and soak in a nice hot bath.

"That sounds great," I lied.

My phone vibrated again. This time, I looked down to my lap to sneak a peek at Justin's response.

> **Justin:** I didn't stay because of the gig at Sandy's.
> **Justin:** I could have gone back to New York.
> **Justin:** I wanted to stay.

Those words ensured that I was a complete goner for the remainder of our time at the Boathouse. I didn't respond to the text, but that was mostly because I didn't know what to say. My heart just felt inexplicably heavy. He may not have necessarily expected a response, anyway.

Back in the car, we'd just gotten back to Newport when Will said he needed to run into a convenience store for a minute. Out of nowhere, my nose started running. I badly needed a tissue, so I opened the center console in the hopes of finding something to wipe my nose with. While I didn't find a tissue, my hand did stumble upon something: a men's gold wedding band.

What the fuck?

My heart started to pound furiously.

Are you kidding me right now?

The asshole was probably buying condoms for a tryst with me. Without thinking it through, I got out of the car and slammed the door. I wasn't in any mood for a confrontation and honestly didn't care enough to ream him out. All I cared about was going to see Justin.

Looking down at my phone, I realized he would still be playing the last set at Sandy's, which was about a half-mile walk from my current location. Running in my heels, I panted as I made my way across downtown Newport.

I stopped to catch my breath before entering the restaurant. Because it was cooler tonight, Justin was performing on the inside stage. I snuck inside and hid in a corner where he couldn't see me but I could still watch him. This had to be close to the end.

His voice suddenly vibrated through the mic. "This last song goes out to all the people who've ever had a certain kind of friend that drives you crazy—the kind that gets under your skin and stays there even when they're not physically present. The kind with dimples you've been dreaming about since you were a kid. The kind with seafoam-green eyes you get lost in. The kind that's confusing as all hell. That kind. If you can relate, this song is for you."

Oh my God.

Justin began to play a cover of a song I recognized. It was "Realize" by Colbie Caillat. Attempting to listen to the words, I couldn't decipher them all because I was too transfixed on the way he was singing them. The lyrics were mostly about realizing true feelings and how sometimes they could be one-sided. During most of the song, his eyes were closed, even though he was playing the guitar. He didn't know I was here, and I was pretty sure he was thinking of me. I didn't know whether I should leave. It felt like I was invading his privacy. I doubted he would have chosen to sing this song to my face.

When Justin finished the song, he thanked the audience and immediately got up. Ignoring the bevy of women trying to approach him for an autographed CD, he took off to the back of the restaurant. I needed to decide whether I was going to make my presence known.

Still in the corner of the room, I felt my phone vibrate.

> **Justin:** Done for the night. Heading home. Everything kosher?
> **Amelia:** Not exactly.
> **Justin:**???

I opted to pretend that I hadn't heard the song or what had come before it. None of it had been meant for my ears. Making my way back outside, I typed.

> **Amelia:** I'm fine. I just got to Sandy's. I'm outside.

Within ten seconds, the door opened, and Justin was outside carrying his guitar.

The anger was written all over his face. "What the fuck?"

"Hi to you too."

"What happened?"

"Your suspicions about his character were correct."

"Did he try to touch you?"

"No. He didn't lay a hand on me."

"What did he do then?"

"He neglected to mention that he's married."

"What? How did you figure that out?"

"I found a men's wedding ring in the center console of his car."

"Fucker."

"Thank you for looking out for me."

"I guess old habits die hard." He stared up at the starry sky. "Anyway, I'm sorry you wasted your night."

"The only thing I'm sorry about is missing your performance. I left him at the Cumberland Farms convenience store and ran here as fast as I could, but I didn't make it in time."

"You didn't miss much."

"Why is that?"

"I felt a little off tonight."

"I bet that's just your perception."

"No. I was distracted."

A group of girls came outside and lingered around him. One of them approached him with a CD. "Would you mind signing this, Justin?"

"Not at all." He was very gracious about it.

She squealed before scurrying away with her friends.

I chuckled. "So you think I could bum a ride off a local celebrity?"

"I don't know. Your house might be too far out of my way." He nudged his head. "Come on. I'm parked in the lot across the street."

I loved riding in Justin's Range Rover because his intoxicating smell was tenfold inside of it. Leaning my head against the seat, I closed my eyes, so incredibly happy to be with him. It hit me that it was really only a matter of days before he'd be gone back to New York. I'd be closing up the house, and I wouldn't see him every day anymore.

When I opened my eyes, I realized that we were going over the Mount Hope Bridge. He was driving off the island.

"Where are we going?"

"We're taking a little detour. That okay with you?"

Excitement filled me. "Yeah."

Forty minutes later, we arrived in Providence, the city where I lived and where we had grown up.

"I haven't been back here in ages," he said.

"You're not missing much."

"It's more like I try not to think about what I'm missing."

We drove through our old neighborhood and eventually made our way down the packed streets of the city's East Side. When he turned onto a particular side street, it finally hit me where he was taking me. As if it were reserved for us, there was an open parking spot right in front of the little red theater. Justin parallel parked and turned off the ignition.

He sat there for a few seconds, then turned to me. "It looks open. You think they still have a midnight show?"

"I haven't been here in years. We could check it out."

I never expected this trip down memory lane.

Justin walked up to the scruffy old man behind the counter. "You still showing indie films?"

"Whatever you want to call them."

"When's the next movie?"

"Ten minutes."

"We'll take two tickets."

"Number one to your left."

"Thanks," Justin said before leading me into the dark theater.

Looking around, I said, "I'm so glad you thought of this."

"Do you remember this actual room?" he asked.

"I do." I pointed to the middle. "We used to sit right about there. It smells worse than I remember."

"It does smell pretty raunchy."

There was only one other person in the theater, a man sitting diagonally across from us.

The lights dimmed, and the feature presentation started.

Within a few seconds, it became abundantly clear that while the little red theater looked physically the same, everything else had changed.

The opening sequence featured a musical montage of women sucking different men off. It seemed our little red movie house had completely lost its innocence in the years we'd abandoned it. It was now a porno theater.

When I looked over at Justin, he was laughing so hard he was practically crying.

I whispered, "Swear to me you didn't know."

He wiped his eyes. "I swear to God, Amelia. I had no clue. Did you even see a sign...anything?"

"No. But there never really were signs indicating what was playing, so I just assumed..."

"You know what they say about assuming things..."

"You make an ass out of you and me?"

"Close. Sometimes when you assume things, you accidentally end up in an adult movie theater watching anal." He pointed to the screen, which displayed nothing but a gigantic ass getting screwed.

To make matters worse, the only other patron in the place seemed to be jerking his hand up and down under a blanket. We both stared over at the guy, then erupted in laughter.

"Do you think that's our cue to leave?" I asked.

"It might be."

A new scene suddenly popped up on the screen. It wasn't as hardcore as the other and seemed more cinematic, like an actual film as opposed to a cheap triple-X video. The music was softer. The snippet featured two guys going to town on a girl slowly and sensually. She was giving oral sex to one while the other guy was going down on her. We were supposed to be leaving, but I felt frozen in my seat, unable to take my eyes off it. I knew Justin was watching it too, because he was quiet. The entire thing lasted about ten minutes.

When it was over, I looked over at Justin, who was staring at me. Had he been watching the movie, or had he been watching *me* watching the movie? Did he know I was aroused by it? In any case, he didn't make any snide remarks, and he certainly wasn't laughing at me.

When he finally spoke up, his voice sounded strained as he whispered in my ear, "You want to stay?"

"No. We should go."

"Okay."

When I started to get up, he put his hand on my arm to stop me. "I need a minute."

"Why?"

He just looked at me like I should have known why.

I figured it out. "Oh."

I didn't know what turned me on more, watching that scene or knowing that Justin was hard from it. It was all too much for me. He closed his eyes for about a minute, then looked over at me. "It's not going down."

"Staying in here isn't going to help."

"Probably not."

"Let's just go." I didn't mean to laugh, but it was pretty funny.

We both got up and exited the theater. I tried really hard not to look down, but my eyes betrayed me as they wandered to the bulge straining through his jeans. Dirty thoughts flooded my mind. I wished things were different, because I could think of a million ways I could help him take care of it.

The ride back to Newport was quiet. The sexual tension in the air was thick. My nipples had turned to steel, and my panties were soaked knowing that he was probably still hard. It occurred to me that certain situations could be even more arousing than sex itself, when you wanted something so badly but couldn't have it. My body was experiencing an impossible state of arousal.

We pulled up to the house. When he shut off the ignition, he leaned his head back against the seat and turned to me, looking as if he wanted to say something but couldn't find the words.

Breaking the ice, I said, "Thank you for attempting to make my night better."

"*Attempt* is the operative word. It was an epic fail."

"No, it wasn't."

"It wasn't? I accidentally took you to see a porno and got a boner in the process. What the fuck…am I fifteen?"

"I was turned on too. It's just not as obvious."

"I know. I could tell. That was what…" He hesitated and shook his head. "Never mind."

"Well, anyway. It was still better than the date with Dr. Danger."

"I can't believe that asshole. I should go to the hospital and beat the fuck out of him tomorrow."

"He's not worth it." I glanced out the window. "We should go inside."

"Yeah."

Back in the house, we lingered in the kitchen. I wasn't ready to go to sleep, even though it was well past one in the morning. Neither of us budged.

"Jesus, it's so late, but I'm not tired at all," I said.

"If I make some coffee fusion, will you have some?"

"Yeah. I'd love some." I smiled.

I watched his every move as he prepared the coffee.

I love you.

God, the thought had just come out of the blue from my subconscious mind. Did I love him, just as much as I always had? I needed to control these feelings; otherwise, I would be setting myself up for major disappointment.

His back was to me when he said, "Jade is coming back in a few days."

My heart sank. "Really? Are you going back to New York with her?"

"No. After she leaves, I'll stay an extra few days to fulfill my promise to Salvatore."

"Oh."

He placed a steaming-hot mug in front of me. "Here you go."

"Thank you."

Over the past forty-eight hours, it seemed that something between us had shifted. Maybe his change in attitude was a result of the impending end of summer.

Sipping the coffee, I said, "I don't think either one of us will be going to sleep anytime soon after this."

"Might as well just stay up."

Over the next two hours, Justin and I talked, opening up about the things that we'd missed in each other's lives. I found out that before he moved to New York, he'd actually completed a semester at Berklee College of Music in Boston but couldn't afford to continue. His parents had refused to fund his education if he chose to major in music. Instead, he'd moved to New York and taken odd jobs and gigs until he'd eventually gone back to school, majoring in business with a minor in music. He told me he'd met his ex-girlfriend, Olivia, a few years after he'd moved there. They'd lived together for a couple of years and stayed friends even after he'd broken up with her. She'd been his only serious girlfriend before Jade. He said Jade believed that the ex wanted to get back with him, even though Olivia was with someone else now. In between those two relationships, he'd slept around with his fair share of women. I appreciated him being candid with me, but it still hurt to hear that.

I told him stories about my time at UNH and how I had chosen to major in education because it had felt like a solid choice, not because it was something I was passionate about. I admitted that even though I enjoyed teaching, it felt like there was something missing, something else I was supposed to be doing with my life that I hadn't figured out yet.

Amped up on the coffee, we literally talked through the night. I was still wearing the black dress from my date. At one point, I went upstairs to use the bathroom. When I came back down to the kitchen, he was sitting on a stool by the window, tooling around with his guitar.

The sun was starting to rise over the ocean. His back was facing me as he started playing "Here Comes the Sun" by the Beatles. I leaned against the doorway, listening to his soothing voice. The more I paid attention to the lyrics, the more they seemed metaphorical. The past decade had been like a long season of darkness and regret when it came to Justin and me. This reconnection was like the sun coming up again after a long time. Of course, he'd probably just chosen to sing it because the sun was literally rising. Still, I couldn't help where my mind traveled, especially on no sleep.

Stop falling in love with him again, Amelia.

How exactly was I supposed to change how I felt? I couldn't. I just needed to accept that Justin was with Jade. He was happy. I needed to somehow figure out how to be his friend again without getting hurt in the process.

When the song finished, he turned around and saw that I'd been watching him.

I walked over to where he was sitting and gazed out the window. "The sunrise is beautiful today, isn't it?"

"Really beautiful," he agreed, except he wasn't looking at the sun at all.

CHAPTER 8

Jade was arriving tomorrow, and that was making me feel very much on edge.

I needed to talk to someone, so I coerced my friend and co-worker, Tracy, to come for a visit to the island. She met me for lunch at the Brick Alley Pub in town. I hadn't seen Tracy since right after the school year had ended. With her kids' busy summer schedules, she hadn't been able to break away until now.

The first half of our lunch date was spent over nachos, with me giving her the full backstory of my history with Justin and rehashing what had happened at the beach house up until now.

"God, I wouldn't want to be in your shoes," she said. "What are you going to do?"

"What *can* I do?"

"You could tell him how you feel about him."

"He's with Jade, and she's a really good person. I can't try to make a play for him right under her nose if that's what you mean. I won't do that."

"But he obviously wants you."

"I wouldn't say that."

"Come on…the song he dedicated to you? Sure, he didn't know you heard it, but clearly he's got lingering feelings."

"Lingering feelings are one thing. Acting on them is totally another. He's not going to leave his gorgeous, talented, Broadway-star girlfriend who was there for him when I wasn't just because some old feelings were rekindled. Jade's a great girl."

"But she's not you. He's always wanted you. You're the one that got away."

"I'm the one that *ran* away. He won't forget that. He might learn to forgive me, but I don't know that he'll ever fully trust me. It's not fair of me to expect him to."

"You're being too hard on yourself. You were a kid." Tracy took a bite of her corn chip and spoke with her mouth full. "You said you're not selling the house, right?"

"No. We agreed to keep it. That's what Nana would want."

"Then whether he stays with Jade or not, this house is going to bind the two of you forever. Do you really want to spend every summer for the rest of your life watching the man you love moving on with other women?"

My heart felt like it was breaking in two. Flashes of many summers turning into winters ran through my mind on fast-forward. The idea of that sounded daunting. Year after year of unrequited love for someone I couldn't have was not something I wanted to endure.

"You're not helping my dilemma. I was hoping you'd talk some sense into me, help me realize that I need to accept things the way they are and move on."

"But that's not really what you want, is it?"

No. No, it isn't.

Tonight was my night off. I didn't know whether to be disappointed or relieved that I'd be missing Justin play. We'd kept our distance since the all-nighter. It was for the best, since things had teetered on inappropriate that night—at least, in my head they had.

Tracy had decided to stick around and spend the night at the beach house. With Justin out of the house, she'd had the bright idea that we should buy some liquor and have a girls' night in.

We arrived at the house with a paper bag full of tequila, limes, and coarse salt. My stomach dropped when I spotted Justin's car in the driveway.

"Shit. Justin's home."

"I thought he was working," she said.

"Me too."

Justin was nowhere to be found when we walked in the door. I dropped the bag on the kitchen counter and went to show Tracy the upper deck. That was where we found Justin sitting, smoking a cigar with his legs up on the balcony as he looked out toward the water. His hair was wet, like he'd just taken a dip in the ocean, and he was shirtless. The top of his boxer briefs was sticking out of his jeans. He looked like a freaking Calvin Klein ad. Tracy's mouth practically hit the floor when she got a look at him.

"What are you doing here? I thought you were playing at the restaurant."

Smoke billowed out of his mouth. "I was supposed to be. But the place almost burned down."

"What?"

"There was a kitchen fire this afternoon. When I showed up, they told me they had to close to air out the entire restaurant.

They won't be reopening for another week, at least. It doesn't look like I'll get to play there again before I leave."

"Holy shit. Did anyone get hurt?"

"No, but Salvatore was a fucking wreck." He glanced over at Tracy. "Who's this?"

"This is Tracy, a good friend from Providence and a teacher at my school. She came down to spend the day with me. She's gonna sleep over tonight."

Justin placed his baseball cap over his head backward and stood up. "Nice to meet you," he said, offering her his hand.

"Likewise," she said, taking it.

I shook my head, not only about the blaze but about the fact that Justin was probably leaving with Jade sooner than I thought. "Wow. I can't believe that about the fire."

"I wasn't really in the mood to perform tonight, but I would have never wished that shit on Sal."

"Gosh. I wonder if I'll even be working there again myself before the end of summer."

He took another puff of the cigar and flicked away the ashes. There was something so sexy about that. "What are you ladies up to tonight?"

"We were gonna have some drinks and have a girls' night in."

"That sounds like a hot mess."

Tracy laughed. "It's not every night that I get away from my kids. So, this is about as wild as it gets for me."

Justin winked. "Well, I'll stay out of your way then."

"You don't have to," Tracy said. "You should join us for a drink."

"That's all right. I'll pass."

When we returned downstairs, Tracy went to use the bathroom. I was cutting up limes when Justin came down and spotted the gigantic bottle on the counter.

"Jesus Christ. Enough tequila?"

"It was her idea. I've never done tequila shots before."

He squinted his eyes. "You've never done a tequila shot?"

"Nope."

"Damn, Patch. What? Did they not know how to live it up in New Hampshire?"

"I never really drank at all until about a year ago. Actually, I've never drank more than I have this summer."

He flashed an impish grin. "Can I take responsibility for that?"

"Maybe." I laughed.

Our attention turned to Tracy as she came back down the stairs.

"I'm so sorry, Amelia, but Todd just called and said that Ava is sick and throwing up. He really needs me to head back home to Warwick."

"Are you serious? I'm so sorry to hear that."

"I guess you two will have to enjoy the tequila without me. I'm just glad Todd called before I started drinking and couldn't drive myself home."

"Do you need anything for the road?" I asked. "A bottle of water or something?"

"No. I'm good." Tracy pulled me into a hug and said, "I'll see you back at school in a few weeks anyway."

"Thanks for coming down, Trace. I had a great time."

"It was nice meeting you, Justin."

Justin offered a silent wave before I walked her to the door.

With Tracy gone, the mood shifted from light to extremely tense. When I turned around, Justin was leaning against the kitchen counter with his arms crossed.

This was exactly what I had been trying to avoid. Part of why I'd encouraged Tracy to spend the night was to avoid being alone with him. Tonight was likely the very last time we would be alone before he returned to New York.

I slowly walked toward where he was standing.

Justin smirked. "What are we gonna do with all this tequila?"

Shrugging, I said, "I don't know."

"I think we should drink it."

"I don't know how to do tequila shots. Tracy was gonna show me."

"Simple. Lick, slam, suck."

"Excuse me?"

"It's a four-step process. You wet your hand to salt it, lick the salt off, slam the glass down after drinking it, and then you suck the lime. Lick, slam, suck. I'll show you how to do it."

Hearing him say the words *lick, slam,* and *suck* made my body prickle.

Just then, my phone vibrated against the counter. It was right next to Justin. His expression darkened after he glanced down at the screen.

He lifted the phone and muttered, "Real fucking nice," before handing it to me.

All of the blood in my body seemed to rush to my head when I read the text from Tracy.

> Justin totally wants you. You should fuck him hard tonight.

His stare was piercing when I looked up.

Racking my brain for a response, I let out a fake laugh. "She's a jokester. She likes to bust balls. I'm sorry."

He didn't say anything, just stared at me with an uncomfortable intensity.

Shit. Thanks a lot, Tracy!

My heart was beating frantically.

Justin was quiet for the longest time, then simply said, "I really need that fucking drink."

Breathing out a sigh of relief, I said, "Me too."

He examined the bottle. "Did you pick out this tequila?"

Good. He's letting it go.

"Yes."

"This brand sucks. It's cheap."

"I told you. I don't know anything about tequila."

"Actually, it's not the worst thing in the world, because we'll chug it down so fast, you won't even taste it. If it were the expensive stuff, then that would be a waste."

Justin opened the small container of salt, grabbed two shot glasses from the cabinet, and placed them down on the granite before sliding one of them over to me.

Lifting his hand, he spread his thumb and his index finger open and pointed to the space between them. "Put your hand like this, and do what I do." He then licked the space between his fingers. God, that one swipe of his tongue was so erotic. He made it easy to see what that mouth could do in other ways.

Jade is a lucky woman.

Justin watched every movement of my tongue as I did the same. He then sprinkled some salt between his fingers and mine.

"You're gonna lick the salt off real fast before drinking the tequila down in one shot. Don't stop. Drink it all down. Then, grab a lime and suck."

Holy hell, hearing that demanding tone come out of his mouth…it was almost too much.

"Ready? We'll do it together. On the count of three. One… Two… Three."

Following his lead, I licked my hand and slammed the liquid down, the tequila burning my throat.

I'd forgotten to grab a lime. Justin took one and placed it in my mouth. "Quick. Suck on this. It will diffuse the taste." I sucked the juice out, savoring the acidic flavor. My lips were touching his fingers as he held it. He was watching intently as I sucked on it. I wished I could have swallowed his fingers whole.

When he took the lime away, I licked my lips. "God, that was strong. What do we do now? Another one?"

"Easy, drunk-ass. We should wait a bit. You're a lightweight."

We spaced out our shots, each one packing a bigger punch than the last. When I lost my balance a little, Justin said, "All right. That's it. I'm cutting you off."

I watched as he did two more shots. After several minutes, his eyes were starting to look glazed over. We were both pretty drunk.

The room swayed as I made my way over to the couch and closed my eyes. I felt a heavy weight as Justin plopped down on the cushion next to me. He lay his head back and closed his eyes too. He'd taken off his hat, and his hair was disheveled. The recessed lighting in the living room was shining atop his head, bringing out the natural blond streaks. After staring at him for a while, the need to run my fingers through that silky hair became unbearable. I reached my hand over and started to rake my fingers slowly through it. I knew it was wrong, but I'd somehow convinced myself that it was an innocent gesture between friends. Like we'd used to do.

He let out a long, shaky breath but kept his eyes closed as my fingers continued to massage through his hair. At first, he looked like he was in ecstasy, so I didn't stop. After about a minute, though, his breathing became heavier, and he started to fidget.

He shocked me when he suddenly opened his eyes and turned to me. "What the fuck are you doing, Amelia?"

I retracted my hand. My heart started to pound as I attempted to come up with an excuse. "I'm sorry. I...I got carried away."

"I see. Blame it on the alcohol?" he scoffed.

He got up and walked to the other side of the room, pulling on his hair in frustration as he paced. Then, he did the most bizarre thing. He dropped to the floor and started doing push-ups in speedy succession.

Trying to fight the tears of humiliation that were stinging my eyes, I watched as he continued the exercise for several minutes. He was panting and exhausted by the time he collapsed onto his back. He finally sat up, bowing his head toward the floor as he looked deep in thought. Sweat was pouring off his back.

Deciding that I'd already done enough damage for one night, I got up and started to go upstairs.

His voice stopped me. "Don't go."

Turning around at the foot of the stairs, I said, "I think I really need to just go to sleep."

"Come here," he said quietly.

When I returned to my seat on the couch, his voice was more demanding. "I said come...here." He pointed to the floor next to him. As Justin sat with his arms wrapped around his shins, I planted myself on the ground beside him, still too ashamed to look him in the eyes.

He turned his back toward me. "You asked me what this tattoo on my back meant. Look at the numbers in three sets of four under the barcode."

They just seemed like random numerals in no particular order. *Three sets of four*. What did they mean?

The first set finally came to me: 1221. "That's December twenty-first, your birthday."

He nodded. "Yeah."

The next set was 0323. "What's that one?"

"March twenty-third, 2001," he said.

"What's the significance of that date?"

"You don't know?"

"No."

"That was the day we met."

"How on earth did you remember the exact date?"

"I just never forgot."

I looked at the next set of digits: 0726.

Now, that was a date I could never forget.

"July twenty-sixth was the date I left Providence in 2006." I stared off for a bit before saying, "The barcode represents your birth and the beginning and end of our relationship."

"Yeah. Defining moments of my life."

"When did you get this tattoo?"

"The night I got it, I was in Boston finishing my first and last semester at Berklee. I knew I wasn't going to be returning, because I couldn't afford it. I was depressed and missing you like hell that night. But I'd refused to speak to you when you'd tried to contact me the year before, and I wasn't going to budge. I was young and stubborn. I wanted to make you pay for running away. The only way I knew how to achieve that was to do to you what you did to me—disappear. I found a tattoo place near school and had this inked on me. It represented letting you go once and for all."

"Did it do the trick?"

"You know…after that day, I really followed through with my vow to move on. And every year, it did get easier to forget everything, especially after I moved to New York. Days and weeks would go by without thinking about you. I thought I'd put you in the past where you belonged."

"Until you couldn't avoid me anymore."

He nodded. "Coming here, I had no idea what to expect. When I laid eyes on you that first day in the kitchen, I quickly realized the feelings hadn't gone away at all. I'd just been suppressing them. Seeing you again as a grown woman…it was jarring. I didn't know how to handle it."

"Besides being mean."

"At first, I was still so fucking angry at you. I wanted you to be a bitch to me, so that at least the anger would be justified. But instead, you were sweet and full of regret. The object of my anger has slowly been shifting from you to myself…for wasting all those years in bitterness. So you know what this tattoo represents to me now?" He paused. "Fucking stupidity."

"I was the stupid one for ever leaving you. I—"

"Let me finish. I've got to get this out tonight."

"All right."

The next thing that came out of his mouth was totally unexpected.

"We need to talk about our attraction to each other, Amelia."

I swallowed. "Okay."

"That text from your friend…she was right. I want to fuck you so badly right now that I'm practically shaking. My conscience is the only thing stopping me. It's wrong and so messed up."

My body was in flux upon his admission, unsure of whether to feel turned on or sick to my stomach.

He continued, "Ever since that day I caught you watching me in my room…I haven't been able to get you out of my head."

"I shouldn't have done that."

"No, you shouldn't have. But the thing is…I couldn't even

be mad at you because you watching me jerk off was just about the hottest fucking thing I've ever experienced in my life."

Wow. I hadn't thought he'd felt that way about it.

"I figured you thought I was perverted."

"I would've done the same thing if I walked by your room and saw you touching yourself."

"You have a beautiful body, Justin. It was hard to look away."

"What were you thinking about?"

"What do you mean?"

"When you were watching me. What were you thinking about?"

Since he was being so honest with me, I decided to tell him the absolute truth. "I was imagining that I was with you."

His breath hitched, and he turned away for a moment before making eye contact. "Have you always been as attracted to me as you are now?"

"Yes. But even more so now. I know it's wrong, Justin."

"Right or wrong, we can't help who we're attracted to. I don't want to want you like this. Just sitting next to you right now is hard for me. But wanting someone and acting on it are two different things. That's why when you were touching my hair, I had to stop it."

"I really wasn't trying to sleep with you. I just missed touching your hair. That's all. It was selfish."

"Believe me, I understand. I'm not innocent in all of this. I've looked for excuses to touch you too. But I have a girlfriend. We have a good life in New York. There's no excuse. I'm starting to feel like my father, totally out of control with no concern for anyone else."

"You're not your father."

"My mother was just as bad."

"Well, you're not your parents."

"I don't want to hurt you either, Patch. I'm so fucking confused. This situation with sharing the house makes things very awkward." He closed his eyes for a long moment before continuing, "Maybe we should work out an arrangement next year."

"Arrangement?"

"Yeah, like maybe we alternate months, so that we don't have to be here at the same time."

It felt like he'd punched me in the heart.

I couldn't believe what I was hearing.

"Let me get this straight. You can't trust yourself around me, so you don't want to physically see me ever again?"

"That's not it."

"Then why else would you not want to be around me?"

He raised his voice, his tone bordering on angry. "Do you really enjoy hearing me and Jade fucking?"

"No. But—"

"Well, I don't want to hear you fucking anyone, either. I'm trying to protect both of us here."

My blood was boiling. "So, you'd rather just not see me at all?"

"I didn't say that. But coming up with a schedule is something we should at least consider. I think that would be a smart option."

The words were flying out of my mouth. "As hard as this has been for me, I've never once considered that. That's the difference between us. I would deal with any amount of discomfort that it took in order to have you in my life again. I would never choose any option that involved pretending you didn't exist anymore. I would take any fragment of you over nothing at all. Clearly, you don't feel the same about me. So

120

you know what? Now that I know that…I'm perfectly good with a schedule." Hot tears streamed down my cheeks.

"Fuck, Patch. Don't cry."

I held out my hand as I stood up. "Please. Don't call me that name ever again."

He buried his face in his hands and yelled into them, "Fuck!"

I stormed into the kitchen and opened the bottle of tequila, pouring myself another shot. I didn't bother with the salt or lime and instead just drank it straight.

Justin grabbed the bottle before I could pour another. "You're gonna make yourself sick."

"That would be none of your concern."

The door clicked open at that very moment. Both of our heads turned toward it simultaneously.

His face turned practically white before he flashed the fakest smile and said, "Jade!"

She ran toward him and wrapped her arms around him. "I couldn't wait till tomorrow. I missed you so much."

She planted her lips on his, and his body stiffened. You could tell he was uncomfortable kissing her in front of me after what had gone down tonight.

She pulled away from him. "You smell like tequila."

"Yeah. Her friend was here and brought it."

"Glad to see you two are speaking to each other." She looked over at me, then approached to give me a hug and said, "I missed you too, Amelia." Guilt was building within me with each second that her skinny frame pressed into mine.

"I'm so glad you're back," I lied.

She took a look at my face. "Your eyes look red. Are you okay?"

"Yes. I just drank too much. I'm not used to it."

"Tequila is rough." She laughed, looking over at the bottle. "Especially cheap crap like that."

Jade spent the next several minutes filling me in on all of the theater gossip from Broadway while Justin and I stole awkward glances at each other. When she finished rambling, I decided I needed to excuse myself.

"Well, I'm exhausted. I'm gonna head upstairs."

"Hope we don't disturb you too much tonight." She winked and looked over at Justin. "It's been a while."

He looked stoic and extremely uncomfortable.

"Don't worry about me. Go to town," I bit out.

Upstairs in my room, I covered my ears with my pillow to mask the sound of his bed shaking. Listening to them having sex was painful beyond belief, but it didn't compare to the emptiness I was feeling over the conversation Justin and I had had.

My stomach was aching. I suddenly felt violently ill. Running to the bathroom, I swore that I would never drink tequila again for as long as I lived, not only because it made me sick to my stomach but because it would always remind me of this miserable night.

CHAPTER 9

Two days later, and I was still sick. Did hangovers even last this long? I had barely come out of my room. Justin and Jade were preparing to leave the summer house and head back to the city for good. I could hear them slowly packing up their stuff. It was still unclear exactly when they were taking off. Still so furious at his suggestion that we schedule our stays at the house next summer, I had no desire to face him or even say goodbye.

He hadn't bothered to come check on me, either. When Jade had peeked her head in, I had thanked her but told her to stay away from me so that she didn't get sick for her return to Broadway. I preferred the idea of not having to talk to them at all before they left, but I was starting to realize that I needed to leave my room long enough to pay a visit to the doctor.

Today must have been my lucky day because they left the house together just long enough for me to wash up and sneak out without having to face them.

When I arrived at the clinic, they made me wait about

half an hour before being seen. I couldn't risk going to the emergency room at Newport Hospital because the last thing I needed was to end up getting seen by Will Danger. So I had driven out of the way to find this small walk-in facility.

A nurse finally called me. "Amelia?"

I followed her down the winding hallways into a cold, small examination room, where she had me wait for another twenty minutes. When the doctor finally showed, I explained all of my symptoms: nausea, vomiting, fatigue. I told her I'd been feeling sick on and off all summer and admitted to drinking a lot a couple of days prior, but they ruled out alcohol poisoning. I also mentioned Justin's illness in case it was somehow related to that.

When I admitted to not having seen a doctor in over two years, she insisted on running some tests just to be sure that everything was okay with me. She sent me down to the lab, where a phlebotomist drew blood from my arm. I also peed in a cup. This was turning out to be too complicated.

The blood test results would be back in a few days. I was just about to leave the office when the doctor caught me out in the reception area. "Ms. Payne?"

"Yes?"

"Can you come back into my office for a moment, please?"

My heart was racing as I followed her into a room. Something didn't seem right about this scenario. They had told me they would call me. What did she need to see me about all of a sudden?

"As you know, the lab downstairs took your blood..." the doctor said. "Those results won't be in for a bit, but testing the urine sample is a much quicker process. You indicated that you aren't sexually active, but it turns out you're pregnant."

"That's not possible."

"I'm afraid it is."

"I've even had my period."

"That could have been spotting or some intermittent bleeding that wasn't menstruation. You mentioned that you've been drinking a lot lately. Is it possible that you had sexual relations you were unaware of?"

"Absolutely not."

Racking my brain, I thought back to the last time I'd had sex. It had been with Adam a few months ago—the night we had broken up. But we'd always used condoms, so it seemed impossible.

"Are you sure?"

"These tests are quite accurate, yes."

"Can you run it again?"

"I'll tell you what. There's an ob-gyn office in this building. If they can squeeze you in, I'll see if they would be willing to do a quick sonogram. I can't guarantee they will have the availability, but I'll call them. Why don't you wait in the reception area?"

It seemed like they made me wait forever. I was certain that this was all a mistake and thus a huge waste of time.

The doctor peeked her head into the waiting area. "Ms. Payne? Good news. They'll take you right now. Just take the elevator back down to the first floor and look for Reid Obstetrics. Ask for Doris. She's the ultrasound technician. Our office already passed along all of your insurance information."

"Thank you."

When I got to the office downstairs, a girl about my age wearing scrubs with Mickey Mouse heads all over the shirt was waiting for me, smiling. "Amelia?"

"Yes."

"Hi. Come right this way."

Doris took me into a dark room. It was much warmer than the cold examination office upstairs, and there was soft music playing on the radio.

"First off, congratulations." She had a slight Spanish accent.

"Oh, I'm not pregnant. I have a virus. This is just to confirm that they made a mistake with the urine test."

She looked amused. "Those tests are very accurate."

"They usually are but not in this case," I said matter-of-factly.

Ignoring my comment, she pointed to my shirt. "Can you lift this for me? I'm just gonna put some warm gel on your belly."

The tube made a weird squirting sound when she squeezed the clear gel onto my stomach. She touched the nozzle to my abdomen and pressed down a bit. A fuzzy white image appeared on the screen, and within seconds, I saw it. Not just a blob, but a huge head and arms. It was moving and looked gigantic.

"Amelia, I present to you…your virus. As you can see, it has a heart that's beating right here, and it looks like all the parts are where they should be. You are most definitely carrying a child."

It felt like the room was spinning.

"How can this be?"

"I'm sure you can figure it out if you think hard enough. You look to be several weeks along, which would put your due date sometime in March."

Several weeks ago. The last time I had been with Adam. Adam who had cheated on me. Adam who was living in Boston with Ashlyn. Adam who I hated. That Adam.

I'm carrying Adam's baby.

The technician went on, "Unfortunately, it's a little too early to tell the sex, but we can make you another appointment for your eighteen-week visit if you want, and we should be able to determine the gender then. You'll see the doctor next time first, though."

"I'll probably see a doctor out in Providence where I live most of the year, but thank you."

Dazed and confused, I watched as she printed out three pictures of my baby and handed them to me. I stared down at the images of the alien creature and then down at my stomach, which barely looked any different to me. I just looked a little bloated and had attributed that to stress and drinking.

Oh my God. Drinking!

I'd been drinking alcohol and coffee fusion. Was the baby even okay?

Feeling numb, I exited the medical building and sat in my car for several minutes before conjuring up enough energy to drive home. The outside looked different. Grayer. Scarier. The future seemed completely uncertain. For the first time in months, something other than Justin was consuming my mind.

———

Back home, Justin and Jade were cooking dinner in the kitchen while I lay in my bed clutching my stomach in disbelief. I'd managed to sneak back into my room before they returned to the house with their groceries, so I still hadn't made contact with them. The sound of Jade laughing from downstairs was driving me nuts under the circumstances.

I was still in shock. It seemed like I was in the middle of a horrible dream.

How was I possibly going to raise a child? I could barely take care of myself. My salary wasn't enough to cover the cost of day care. There were so many things that were up in the air.

The sound of the front door slamming interrupted my frantic thought process. Before I could wonder if they'd left,

I heard footsteps coming up the stairs and approaching my room.

There was a knock at the door.

"Who is it?"

"It's me." The unexpected sound of Justin's low voice made me shiver.

"What do you need?"

"Can I come in?"

I got up and answered the door. "What?"

He looked tired, like he'd been run ragged.

"You look exhausted. Too much sex?" I scoffed.

Ignoring the question, he said, "Jade is making guacamole. We're out of limes, so she ran back to the store. It's the first opportunity I've had to talk to you alone. We don't have much time."

"What do you need to say?"

"Why haven't you come out of your room?"

"Isn't that what you wanted? For me to disappear?"

Looking filled with regret, Justin shook his head slowly and whispered, "No."

"No?"

"No. The schedule idea was asinine. I'm sorry I ever suggested it."

"Well, guess what?"

"What?"

"It's no longer going to be hard for you to resist me. There won't be a dilemma. Because when I tell you what I found out today, you'll never have a single inappropriate thought about me again. You won't want *anything* to do with me. Your biggest nightmare just became my reality, Justin."

His eyelids were fluttering in an attempt to decipher my words. "What the fuck are you talking about?"

Bursting into tears, I sat back down on my bed and buried my face in my hands. I was suddenly all too aware of my pregnancy hormones. Justin, who had never seen me cry to this extent, sat down next to me and pulled me into his arms. That only prompted me to sob harder.

"Amelia…talk to me. Please."

"I went to see a doctor. It was just supposed to be a routine checkup. I'd been sick, just like you were…"

"Did someone hurt you over there?"

Wiping my nose with my sleeve, I cried, "No. It's nothing like that."

"What then?"

"The doctor ran some tests. One of them was a pregnancy test." So ashamed, I pulled back to look at his face.

"You're…pregnant?"

My voice was practically inaudible. "Yes."

"How can that be?"

"I'm several weeks along. It's Adam's."

"That asshole didn't use a condom with you?"

"That's the thing. We *did* use one. I don't know how this happened. Clearly, they're not foolproof."

"Is it too late to terminate it?"

"I could never go through with an abortion."

Justin got up from the bed and started to pace. "All right… all right, I'm sorry. I was just thinking out loud, making sure you know what your options are."

"I'm so scared."

Jade's voice called from downstairs, "Justin? I'm back!"

He stopped pacing. "Shit."

"Please don't tell Jade," I begged. "I don't want anyone to know yet."

"Okay. Of course."

"You'd better go."

He wouldn't move from his spot. "Amelia…"

"Go! Just go. I don't want her to see me crying."

Still looking shocked and confused, Justin quietly slipped out of the room.

I spent the rest of that night surfing the Internet for information on what to expect in the next six months. I had to figure out how I was going to tell Adam. He might not want anything to do with it, but he still needed to know.

———

Justin and Jade were packing up the car. I'd already said my goodbyes to Jade over an early breakfast, but I hadn't had a chance to speak to Justin. They would be taking off back to the city any minute. I couldn't believe this day was finally here. It was both dreaded and a relief all at once. Seeing him every day would have been even harder, knowing that without a shadow of a doubt, there was no longer the chance of a future for us. Justin didn't want kids of his own, let alone to raise someone else's. This pregnancy was the final nail in the coffin. Maybe I would take him up on that schedule for next summer. Better yet, maybe I would need to sell him my half of the house. As much as that thought was heartbreaking, I didn't know what kind of financial situation I would be in after the baby came.

Standing out my bedroom window, I looked down as they placed suitcases and boxes into the back of the Range Rover. At one point, Justin happened to look up at me. He held up his index finger as if to tell me to wait for something. Soon after, he whispered in Jade's ear. A few seconds later, she took off in the car.

The sound of his footsteps followed. Then, he appeared at my door.

Looking morose, he said, "Hi."

"Hi."

"How are you holding up?"

"Not too good."

"I asked Jade to go get gas so that I could say goodbye, find out if there is anything you need before we leave."

"No. I'm fine. You need to get back to your life."

"I feel bad leaving you like this."

"I'll be heading home in a couple of days anyway. The sooner I get back to Providence and prepare for this new reality, the better I will be."

"Patch…"

"Don't call me that name anymore." Tears sprung to my eyes. "Not because I'm mad at you…it just makes me sad." My lips trembled.

"Okay," he said softly.

"What were you going to say?"

"If you need anything…anything at all…please call me. Promise me you'll keep me updated on what's happening."

"I will."

"Let me know when I'm allowed to tell Jade."

"Okay. It's not like I can hide it much longer."

His eyes wandered to the bed. Earlier, I'd been looking at the snapshots from the ultrasound and had left them lying out in the open. He walked over and picked them up. He stared at the images and looked mesmerized. "That thing is inside of you? You're hardly showing."

"I know."

He shook his head while examining the photos. "God, this is so strange. I think I'm still in shock."

"You wouldn't be the only one."

He placed the pictures back on the bed and stared into

space, deep in thought. Then he reached into his pocket and took out the red pocketknife. "I want you to keep it. You need it more than I do. Keep it by your bed at night. It'll make me feel better because I feel fucking helpless right now."

I wasn't going to argue with him. "Okay."

His gaze moved to the window. We could both see that Jade was pulling in.

I wiped my eyes. "You'd better go."

He didn't move.

We stared long and hard into each other's eyes until we heard Jade entering the house.

Then, he slipped away.

PART TWO

TEN MONTHS LATER

CHAPTER 10

I felt like I was breaking into someone's property, even though it was half my own.

Everything looked the same as we'd left it. The beach house was freezing. The heat needed to be turned on. It was the middle of May and still fairly cool on the island. I wasn't supposed to return until the end of June, but the place where I'd rented an apartment had gotten sold, forcing me to leave. That had given me no choice but to head to Newport early; otherwise we would have been homeless. I was already on maternity leave through the end of the school year, so it made sense.

We'd been unable to find temporary tenants in the off-season here, so the beach house had stayed empty. An unexpected feeling of longing overwhelmed me. This place used to remind me of Nana; now it reminded me of Justin. I could practically smell his cologne in the kitchen. It was my imagination, but it felt real. I also imagined him standing near the coffeepot, smirking while stirring his coffee fusion…his bare, muscled back as he looked out the window toward the ocean...the *lick, slam, suck* as he drank tequila. Gazing toward the living room, I remembered our awkward final night before Jade had returned.

Closing my eyes for a moment, I imagined it was last summer, when life had been so simple. Then, the little cry coming from the baby carrier strapped to my chest snapped me back to reality.

Bea's head wiggled back and forth in search of my breast. "Wait...wait. I have to take you out of this thing first." Removing her from the BabyBjörn, I babbled, "You were so good during the ride. You must be starving, huh?"

Shit. Most of my stuff was still in the car. I carried my two-month-old daughter outside to retrieve the breastfeeding pillow from my back seat. Tracy had bought it for me, insisting it was the one item I'd need the most, and she had been right. It was bright pink with white daisies, and an absolute necessity in order to feed this constantly hungry baby without breaking my back. I stopped for a moment to admire the ocean before returning inside.

Bea was short for Beatrice. She was named after my grandmother. My baby girl had been born in March, one week before her due date. Adam had chosen not to be there. He'd said he wanted proof that the baby was his, and until then, he wasn't going to acknowledge her as his daughter. He was the only person I'd slept with before getting pregnant, but there was simply no way to prove that to him if he didn't take my word for it. I didn't want the stress of having to get Bea's blood drawn right now, and he was in no hurry to be there for us, so I had chosen to put off dealing with him. Ashlyn was surely working this situation behind the scenes, and I was sure she was telling him that I was a liar. With much bigger fish to fry, I didn't need that shit right now. Life was too stressful as it was.

When Bea finished feeding, she fell asleep again. I slowly pulled her off my breast and placed her in the infant seat. I used the rare break to head back outside and retrieve the rest of our items. Most of my stuff was in storage back in Providence. But I had brought all of our clothes and Bea's bassinet. I would have to purchase a crib and figure out how to assemble it.

A man with dark curls who looked to be in his early thirties approached me. His big brown eyes beamed. "Hey, neighbor. I saw your car. I was wondering when I'd get to meet the occupants of this gorgeous home."

I pointed to the house just to the right of mine. "You live in that one right there?"

"Yes. Moved in back in the fall. I'm one of the rare year-round folks, apparently."

"Well, you've met Cheri, right? She's also year-round."

"Yup, but I think that's about it."

Laughing, I said, "You're probably right."

He held out his hand. "Roger Manning."

"Nice to meet you. Amelia Payne."

"I see you have baby stuff in here. Do you have kids?"

"Oh…just one. My daughter was born in March. She's inside sleeping."

"I have a daughter too. She's seven and lives with her mother in California."

"You must miss her."

"You have no idea. I work for the navy, so I've been stationed out here for a while. After her mom and I got divorced, my ex wanted to move back west to be closer to her family."

"I see."

"Will I get to meet your husband?"

"Oh, I'm not married. It's sort of a long story. I'm not with the father of my child. It was an accidental pregnancy."

"I'm sorry to hear that."

"Don't be. It's a blessing."

Roger peeked inside my trunk. "Can I help you carry the rest of this stuff in?"

My fear of trusting this virtual stranger was overridden by my fatigue. Bea hadn't been letting me sleep, and I welcomed any help I could get.

"That would be great."

Roger unloaded all of the items from the car into the house, even bringing the bassinet upstairs for me and setting it up next to my bed.

After we walked back down the stairs together, he knelt down to get a look at Bea while she slept in her car seat on the living room floor.

He whispered, "She's precious."

"Thank you. She likes to sleep during the day and keep me up at night. They say to sleep when the baby sleeps, but I can't. I have too much to get done when she's sleeping."

He stood up and lingered a bit, then said, "Well, if there's anything you need, I'm right next door. Seriously... if something breaks, or you need help lifting something... don't hesitate."

"I really appreciate that, more than you know. Thank you."

When the door shut, a smile spread across my face. Poor Roger had no clue he'd be assembling a crib soon.

With Bea still sleeping, I decided to head upstairs and put some of our clothes away. On the way to my bedroom, I couldn't help stopping in Justin's room. I lay down and sniffed the pillow on his side of the bed. This time it wasn't my imagination; it still smelled like his cologne. There was the feeling of longing again. I hugged the pillow, and a teardrop fell down my cheek. I'd done a decent job of harboring these feelings for almost a year. This was the moment it all unraveled.

I miss you.

Justin had called and texted me many times over the past several months. I would let him know I was okay but insisted that I didn't need his help. He wasn't very active on social media aside from posting a few pictures from gigs—mostly of his audiences—here and there on Instagram. I would stalk Jade's Facebook page for small glimpses into their life in the city, so envious of their freedom. I missed him terribly, but I knew that distancing myself was for the best.

Right after Bea's birth, I'd texted him a picture of her. He had once again offered help, both monetarily and otherwise. I'd refused. He and Jade had ended up sending me a generous gift card to Babies "R" Us, which I'd used to buy Bea's bassinet and bouncy seat.

I hadn't told him I had gotten kicked out of my apartment. I had been ashamed and didn't want the offer of charity again. So he didn't know I was living here yet. I really hoped that by some miracle, they would stay away for as long as possible this summer. I doubted they would appreciate getting woken up by Bea several times in the middle of the night anyway. Truthfully, though, the real reason I didn't want to see him was simply that it would be too painful.

———

Almost a month passed with no sign of Justin and Jade. I was finally getting acclimated to life on the island again.

Roger had ended up assembling that crib for me. It was white, and I'd bought a bedding set online with the remainder of my gift card. Roger and I were becoming friendly. Knowing that it wasn't easy for me to leave the house, he'd occasionally bring me coffee or fresh seafood from the dock. Even though I sensed he might be attracted to me, he wasn't making any moves, which was a good thing, because I was certainly in no position to be dating anyone.

Bea was going through a rough patch. She was colicky and still not sleeping much. It didn't matter how much I fed her, she always wanted more. When I did manage to leave the house, I took her with me, to the market and to doctor's appointments. I hadn't been out alone since the day she was born. It was just the two of us. I was fine with that. The only times sadness would creep in tended to be late at night when I was most tired and worn out from the day.

One such evening, rain was pelting my bedroom window. Bea was screaming and crying. She'd drained my breasts of milk, yet she wouldn't take a bottle. Wanting to sleep so badly, I was starting to see stars from fatigue. I broke out in tears. It felt like this type of torture would be suitable for prison inmates. How was I going to continue to live on no sleep? How would I ever go back to work, and who could possibly take care of her the way I did? A feeling of helplessness consumed me as thunder rolled in the distance. What if we lost power? How would I change her diaper in the dark? It dawned on me that we didn't even have any candles. A minor panic attack started to brew within me. Deciding to head downstairs, I slowly descended the steps as I held onto Bea carefully.

Half an hour later, my emotions had only gotten worse. My nipples were sore and cracked. Bea was still colicky in my arms. The front door rattled, and full-on panic ensued. A rush of adrenaline hit as I frantically reached into my pocket for Justin's pocketknife. I made sure I wore pajamas with pockets for that very reason.

Someone was breaking into the house.

It occurred to me that my cell phone was upstairs. Bea was screaming, so we couldn't even hide. The door was shaking again.

"Damn key," I heard a man say as the door opened.

His eyes bugged out of his head as he caught sight of me. Bea was hanging off my boob. My hair was disheveled, and I was stiffly pointing his own knife at him.

"Justin."

CHAPTER 11

Justin turned his head away from me. "What the fuck, Amelia? Put down the knife and cover your tit."

His surprise arrival had startled me so much that I hadn't even realized that one of my breasts was sticking out of my nursing bra. I rarely slept with a shirt since it was easier to nurse in just the bra. With Bea in one arm, I walked over to the kitchen and grabbed my cardigan off of one of the stools before covering myself up.

The scene was chaotic as I fumbled with my sweater and spoke through Bea's excruciating cries, "What are you doing here?"

"Do you always hang around the house in just a bra now? If so, we're gonna have a problem."

"I didn't think you'd show. It's earlier in the season than you arrived last year. Why didn't you call me first?"

"For one, I didn't think you'd be here. I needed to escape the city for a while. I was gonna spend a couple of weeks opening up the house, getting it ready before you arrived."

Bea's cries hadn't waned. I bounced her up and down in an attempt to calm her.

"What's wrong with her?" Justin asked.

"She's colicky. I can't produce enough milk to satisfy her, and she won't take formula."

He slowly approached where I was standing and took a peek at Bea's face. His mouth curved into a slight smile. "She looks like you."

"I know."

Now that he was close to me, he took a good look at me as well. "Jesus Christ, Amelia."

"What?"

"You look like you've been through a war."

"That's another way of saying I look like shit?"

"Your eyes are bloodshot...hair is knotted. Fuck. You're a mess."

"You don't think I'm aware of that?"

"Have you been sleeping?"

"No. I get very little sleep. She's going through a rough patch, keeps me up at night and sleeps sporadically during the day."

"You've got the rough *patch* part right."

"Very funny."

"You can't live like this."

"What exactly do you suggest I do?"

"You can start by taking a shower."

"I can't just leave her crying like this."

"Did it ever occur to you that maybe she's crying because you stink?" He chuckled.

I was speechless for a moment before breaking out into laughter at my own expense. My God. "You might have a point."

"I'll hold her while you bathe."

"Really? You'd do that?"

"I said I would."

"Have you ever held an infant?"

"No."

"Are you sure you're okay with this?"

"I can handle it."

There was no way I could pass up this opportunity. The thought of a hot shower right now was absolutely heavenly.

Handing her carefully to Justin, I warned, "Watch her head. Make sure it doesn't bend too far back. Support her neck with your arm."

"I've got it."

Bea looked so tiny in his big arms. She seemed to like being there too.

"You've got to be kidding me," I said.

"What?" he asked.

"Haven't you noticed that she stopped crying?"

"I told you. Maybe you smell."

"Maybe." I laughed. "Or it could just be that you're a chick magnet, and that title extends to infants as well."

He rocked his body back and forth to soothe her and waved me off. "Shh. Go, Amelia. Before she loses it again."

"Okay." I turned around at the foot of the stairs. "Thank you...so much."

Upstairs, as the hot water poured down on me, I thanked God for Justin showing up when he had. I had really been on my last leg of sanity. Much like he'd always done when we were kids, Justin had come through exactly when I'd needed it. Even if it hadn't been intentional, he was my hero tonight.

Feeling somewhat human again, I stepped out of the shower and got dressed as fast as I could. The fact that it was quiet downstairs didn't escape me. Still, I felt like I needed to get dressed fast in case Justin was losing patience—or worse, if Bea had pooped.

The reality when I got downstairs was far from what I imagined. Bea's back was rising and falling as she lay stomach-down on Justin's chest. She was out like a light. He was just sitting on the couch, and things were as peaceful as could be. When he saw me approaching, he held his index finger to his mouth to signify that I should be quiet.

Sitting down on the couch next to him, I just stared in amazement. He didn't have to do anything except exist, and he was somehow able to get her to sleep. Who knew that Justin "I Don't Ever Want Children" Banks was the Baby Whisperer.

He turned to me. "Why don't you go sleep?"

"What if she wakes up?"

"I'll deal with it."

"She'll wake up wanting to eat."

"Then I'll bring her upstairs if that happens. For now, she's fine."

"Are you sure?"

"Amelia…"

"Yeah?"

"Does it look like we're going anywhere anytime soon?" He shooed me away. "Go!"

"Thank you," I mouthed before heading upstairs.

I barely remembered my head hitting the pillow. It was the longest I'd slept straight since the day before my daughter was born.

Six hours later, the sound of Bea crying woke me. Rubbing my eyes, I could see Justin standing in the doorway with her.

"I tried to put off coming up here as long as I could…" He

walked over to me and placed her in my arms. "I'll leave so you can feed her. I'm gonna hit the sack for a bit."

"Thank you again so much. I needed that sleep so badly."

"It was no problem."

After he left, I took out my breast, and Bea latched on immediately. She smelled like him. I breathed in the masculine scent, and a sexual desire that had been long suppressed came alive in me. It felt so good not to be the only adult in this house anymore, but I needed to keep my feelings in check. Whatever it took, I was not going to let myself become obsessive over Justin again. Being responsible for another human being meant I could no longer afford to become an emotional wreck.

———

It was midafternoon when Justin came downstairs. Bea was strapped to my chest in the carrier as I cleaned the kitchen.

"Good morning." I smiled.

"Hey," he said groggily.

Just like that, my body awakened with an intense need. He was the very definition of scruffy. His hair was disheveled, and in the daylight, it became apparent that he'd been growing out his stubble. A gray fitted T-shirt looked like it had been painted onto his muscles. And don't get me started on how good his ass looked in those gym pants.

"How is she?" he asked. My body reacted even more as he stepped closer to peek in on Bea.

"She's asleep."

"That figures. The sun is shining. I should've known." He searched my eyes. "How are *you*?"

"I'm feeling good. You were amazing last night."

"That's what they always say." He winked.

Rolling my eyes, I said, "Thank you again."

"Stop thanking me." His face turned serious. "You know... all those times I asked how you were doing, you told me you were okay. You didn't look fucking okay to me last night. You were lying."

"Justin, this whole thing is my responsibility. What is anyone else gonna do for me?"

"Has your mother even come to visit?"

"She came to the hospital when Bea was born, but she didn't offer to stay. She's more concerned with things like traveling to Cancún with her boyfriend and hawking those multicolored leggings all over the Internet, apparently. You know, priorities."

"Un-fucking-believable." He looked around the house, then said, "Nana would have helped."

"Yes, she would have." I closed my eyes for a moment, thinking of my grandmother before my thoughts shifted to my mother again. "As for Patricia, I don't want her with me anyway. Having to deal with her would be like taking care of two babies."

"She should still have the decency to offer help, even if you refused."

"I agree."

He scratched his head. "I forgot to bring my coffee with me. Do you have any lying around?"

"Actually, I stopped drinking coffee fusion when I found out I was pregnant. The withdrawal was killer. I do have some half-caf in the cupboard."

"I guess that'll have to do for now." He glanced over at Bea. "You don't think all that fusion did anything to her, do you?"

"Do you think it could be why her sleep is erratic?"

"I feel guilty getting you hooked on that shit. Neither of us knew what was going on."

"Don't even. It wasn't your fault. Look at her. She's fine."

He rubbed his chin and grinned. "Yeah. She seems all right."

"I'm gonna try to put her upstairs in the crib. Then, I'll come down and make some coffee."

"I've got it," Justin said.

"You sure?"

"Yep."

After I put Bea down, Justin was preparing two mugs when I returned to the kitchen.

"Still take cream and sugar?" he asked.

"Yeah. Thanks."

"How is she?"

"Sleeping like a baby."

"Good." He slid my mug toward me.

I took a sip and asked the question I'd been dying to. "Why didn't Jade come with you?"

"She's got a regular role in a new musical called *The Alley Cats*. She can't leave the city."

"She's not coming at all?"

"I'm not sure."

"How long are you staying?"

He stirred his coffee and shook his head. "I don't know."

Dread filled me. Justin had only been here one day, and I was already sad for the day he'd be leaving me alone again. "Well, I'm glad you're here."

We drank coffee in silence until I noticed Justin staring down at my breasts.

Coughing, he asked, "Did you spill coffee on yourself?"

I looked down and sure enough, breast milk from my

nipples had formed two giant wet spots on my shirt. "Shit. No. I'm leaking milk. I'd go change, but it's just gonna happen again until she wakes up."

"Jesus. I'm so glad I'm not a woman."

God. I'm glad you're not a woman too.

"Welcome to my life." When he continued to look down, I joked, "You don't have to look. My eyes are up here."

"Your tits are massive. You have to know that."

"Oh, I'm quite aware. It's a supply and demand issue. The more she drinks—which is all the time—the more I make. It's all she wants to do when she's awake."

"I can't say I blame her."

I knew my face was turning red. What was happening to me? I couldn't be a walking zombie on no sleep and deal with this infatuation again. I didn't even feel sexy anymore. Nevertheless, I was falling right back into the pattern of lusting after this man.

"Well, even though my breasts are bigger, I've lost weight," I said.

"Oh, I noticed. You haven't been eating?"

"Not as well as I should. I force myself to eat cheese sticks and raw vegetables, but I'm generally too drained for anything substantial."

"When was the last time you had a home-cooked meal?"

"Can't even remember. The only times I've bothered to cook are when the neighbor brings me seafood from the dock."

"What neighbor?"

"Roger."

"Roger."

"Yes. He moved into the house that was vacant last summer. You know, the blue one?"

"Really…" He glared at me. "What else does he bring you?"

"Coffee, sometimes."

"Let me guess. He's single."

"Yes…divorced, but he's just a friend. He's been helpful. He actually assembled the crib for me."

"Right. Of course he did. No guy does that shit without an ulterior motive, Amelia."

"Not every guy's the same."

"And not every fucking girl looks like you. Trust me, that guy is waiting in the wings. Just be aware of that and be cautious."

Feeling hot from the compliment, I cleared my throat. "Well, it wouldn't matter if he had ulterior motives or not. Clearly, I'm in no condition to be with a man. I can't even bathe half the time."

"You shouldn't be letting strange men into this house so easily. You're in a very vulnerable position right now. This guy knows that."

"Well, I was desperate for help, so…"

"You should have called *me*."

"You're in New York. He's right next door. That wouldn't have made sense."

"I would have come for the day if you needed me."

"I don't want to be a burden on you, Justin. I need to find my own way." Even though a part of me loved that he'd said that, another part was equally confused. "Just last summer you were suggesting that we avoid each other altogether." My tone was bitter. "Forgive me if you weren't the first person I thought to call when I needed help."

His expression darkened. "Fuck, Amelia. Really? You're gonna bring that up again? Do you think that was what I truly wanted? I was drunk as shit that night and saying and doing anything I could to keep my fucking dick in my pants. I thought I already explained suggesting that was a mistake."

"Okay. I'm sorry." I held out my hands. "I don't want to fight."

"Good." He exhaled and changed the subject. "So, I told Salvatore I could play a few nights here and there if he wanted. But I didn't commit to anything long-term."

"Because you're not sure how long you're staying?"

"Right."

"Well, he must be so happy to have you back, even if it's just for a few nights."

"Yeah. He was."

"I wish I could go watch you play."

"Why can't you?"

"I can't take Bea to Sandy's. She'd start crying in the middle of your songs. And if I had to feed her there, it would be awkward."

"So what if she cried? People will just have to deal with it. And you could go to the back room to feed her. You need to get the fuck out of the house."

"Maybe I'll consider it."

He suddenly got up and put his mug in the sink. "I've got to get some work done. I'll make dinner tonight, so don't fill up on too many raw veggies."

"That'll be awesome."

———

Bea slept for a few hours that afternoon, allowing me to get laundry and other chores done. Justin spent most of the day holed up in his room working.

When he finally came downstairs, he had just showered and was buttoning his black button-down shirt.

151

He looked too good to be staying home tonight. "Are you playing at Sandy's?"

"No. Not tonight."

"I didn't think so. It's just that you're all dressed up."

"You remember Tom from Sandy's?"

"The old night manager?"

"Yeah. I told him I might meet him for a drink later at the Barking Crab. He wants to pick my brain about some music stuff."

"I see."

"Why don't you go upstairs and change before dinner?"

"We're just eating here, right?"

"Yes, but you have boob milk stains on your shirt. I just thought maybe you'd want to shower and change."

"I would love to."

Justin looked after Bea while I showered. I decided to go all out and put on a tube dress. I brushed my hair and made up my eyes. It kind of felt like I was getting ready for a date, and I needed to stop that train of thought.

I thought I would find Justin cooking when I returned downstairs. I'd told him to put Bea in the bouncy seat. Instead, he was holding her and rocking back and forth, looking out the window. He didn't see me watching him.

"I'm back."

"Oh, hey. She didn't want to go in the seat, started crying, so we've just been watching the sunset."

My heart clenched. "You need to cook, right?"

"Yeah, but it won't take very long."

I reached out my arms, and to my surprise, Bea started to cry in protest when I took her from him. Patting her back, I said, "I don't think she wanted to leave you."

"No. It's just your imagination."

"Really? Want to test it?" I held her out toward him again.

Justin cradled her in his arms, and sure enough, Bea stopped crying. She was looking up at him. It seemed the apple didn't fall far from the tree.

"My imagination, huh?" I said.

He smiled down at her. "I don't know why she likes me. I don't even do anything but hold her."

"To a baby, that's everything."

Suddenly looking a little uncomfortable, he handed her back to me. "You'd better take her."

Back in my grasp, Bea started to fuss again, so I took her to the living room and fed her while Justin got dinner started.

There was a knock at the door.

"Are you expecting someone?" Justin hollered from the kitchen.

"No. Do you mind getting it? She's still eating." I readjusted the blanket over my shoulder for privacy.

I couldn't see the front door from where I was sitting, but I could hear everything.

"Who are you?" Justin asked.

"I'm Roger. I live next door. You are?"

Shit.

"Justin. This is my house."

"Oh, that's right. She mentioned a seasonal roommate."

"Can I help you?"

"Is Amelia here?"

"Yes, but she's feeding the baby."

"I was just down at the dock. I bought her some shellfish."

"Amelia! Roger is here. He brought you some snatch," Justin yelled.

Great.

Covering myself as fast as I could, I shouted, "Coming!"

Trying to seem nonchalant as I approached the door, I said, "Hey!"

"Hi, Amelia," Roger said. "Sorry if I'm disturbing something."

"No, no, not at—"

"Actually, we were just about to eat," Justin interrupted.

Roger looked annoyed. "How long are you staying, Justin?"

"As long as I need to."

"Amelia told me your girlfriend is a Broadway star, right?"

"Yes."

"That's really gnarly."

"Gnarly? What the fuck, are you a surfer or something?" Justin lifted his hands in a shaka sign. "Whoa!"

"Roger, don't mind Justin," I cut in. "That was really sweet of you to bring the crabs. I so appreciate it."

"Crabs...interesting choice," Justin scoffed.

"I'd better let you guys eat," Roger said.

"We'll talk soon." I smiled.

"Take care, Amelia. Nice meeting you, Justin."

Justin did a little salute. "Roger that!"

When Justin slammed the door behind Roger, I turned to him. "You're being a total prick."

"Come on. I was just messing with him."

"You think it's funny, but he's the only friend I have here, and you're going to scare him away. After you take off to New York again, I'm going to need someone to talk to. It's very lonely out here."

"Why would you need *him*? You live in Providence, anyway."

Biting my lip, I said, "Actually...I was gonna talk to you about something."

"About what?"

154

"I might take a year off from my teaching job. I got kicked out of my apartment because the owner sold the building. I don't have a place to live in the city anymore, and I'm not sure I'm ready to put Bea in day care at the end of the summer. I was going to ask you if it's okay if I stay in here in the off-season."

"This house is yours. Of course, it's okay. I would never tell you otherwise. You shouldn't even have to ask."

"All right. Well, now that I got that out of the way, I feel better. Thank you."

"Dinner's ready. Put her down so you can eat."

Justin had poured wine for each of us.

"Oh…I can't drink, Justin."

"Shit. I wasn't thinking."

"Well, they say I can have one drink, but I've still been hesitant."

"That's fine. It won't go to waste."

Justin had made rice casserole. We were halfway through our meal when Bea started crying from her bouncy seat. But when I stood, Justin stopped me.

"Finish your food. I've got her."

He lifted her and brought her over to the table. As always, she quieted in his arms as she stretched her neck to look up at his face. This time, she reached out her little hand and started to play with his scruff.

"Hey, you trying to say I need to shave?" he teased.

Watching him with her gave me goose bumps.

Don't go there, Amelia.

Bea started to babble. It almost looked like she was trying to talk to him.

Justin pretended to understand her. "Oh yeah?" When she passed gas, he didn't even flinch. He just said, "Well, excuse you!"

The whole thing was making me crack up.

After I finished, I took her back from him and fed her on the couch while Justin cleaned up the kitchen. Bea fell back asleep after her meal.

When Justin joined us in the living room, it occurred to me that he'd had plans to go out.

"Aren't you supposed to be meeting Tom for a drink?" I asked.

"Nah. I think I'm gonna skip it. I'm playing tomorrow night. I'll probably meet up with him after that instead." His phone suddenly vibrated and he answered, "Hey."

I wasn't completely sure who he was talking to until he looked over at me and said, "Jade says hi."

"Hi, Jade." I smiled, even though I was starting to feel that old familiar jealousy creep in again. Maybe it was a good thing that she'd called when she had, because a reality check was desperately needed.

Justin walked away to finish the call in the other room. When he returned, he said, "I have to go back to New York this weekend."

My heart felt like it dropped to my stomach. "Oh. Just for the weekend?"

"Maybe a little longer."

CHAPTER 12

It was Friday night, and Justin had already left for his gig at Sandy's. He was supposed to be leaving early the next morning to head back to New York. While I'd originally told him I wouldn't be going to see him perform, I was seriously second-guessing my decision. Who knew if and when he'd be back? After all, he'd come for some alone time only to find Bea and I wreaking havoc on his life. I wasn't sure I would choose to return if I were him.

I suddenly turned to Bea. "Do you want to go see Uncle Justin play? Will you promise to be good?"

I placed her in the crib before impulsively tearing my clothes off, worried that if I didn't hurry up, I'd wuss out and decide to stay home. I put on a red dress that I hadn't worn since before I was pregnant and slipped breast pads inside my bra to avoid wet spots. I styled my hair into loose curls and applied my makeup. Within minutes, Bea and I were dressed and in the car.

Returning to Sandy's gave me the jitters. I hadn't been

back since last summer. I was also inexplicably nervous for Justin to see me in the audience when I'd already told him I wouldn't be there.

He was in the middle of a song I didn't recognize. As usual, the crowd was transfixed on him, with women creeping closer and closer to the front just to get a better look at his beautiful face while he sang.

It was always so emotional for me to watch him perform. Thankfully, Bea was behaving in her carrier, allowing me to soak in every moment of being here.

I made my way to the mahogany bar to say hello to Rick the bartender, who gave me a glass of seltzer on the house. Relaxing in my seat, I closed my eyes and cherished the sound of Justin singing as he began a cover of "Wild Horses" by the Rolling Stones. That haunting song seemed made for his voice.

When I felt my eyes getting watery, I cursed at myself. Why did I get so sentimental whenever he sang? It always felt like every word of every song had meaning and could somehow be applied to my experiences with him.

Halfway through the song, Bea started to cry. This was not the kind of song that masked the frenzied cries of an infant very well. A lot of heads were turning toward me. There were whispers, probably people wondering why I'd brought a baby to this kind of establishment in the first place.

Hot flashes permeated my body. Even though he continued through the song flawlessly, Justin's gaze traveled over to my corner of the room. Our eyes locked. I was mortified for having interrupted this beautiful song.

When it finished, I started to head toward the back room. Justin gestured with his hand to tell me to stay. I continued down the hall anyway until his voice through the mic stopped me in my tracks.

"So that baby you hear crying is actually special to me. Her name is Bea. Her mom is Amelia, who's also special to me—one of my oldest friends. Anyway, would you believe that this is Amelia's very first night out since Bea was born more than three months ago? Amelia didn't want to come tonight. She was afraid that people would stare at her if the baby started crying. I told her not to worry, that the people here were kinder and more understanding than that. She didn't take my word for it, but she took a chance and came anyway. Believe me when I say, she hasn't had it easy. She's doing a hell of a job raising that little baby all by herself. I think she deserves a night out, don't you?"

Raucous applause followed, and Justin motioned for me to come to him. Bea was still screaming.

"Give her to me...the carrier too," he said away from the mic.

Justin placed the BabyBjörn across his chest and slipped Bea inside before securing her. My baby girl was exactly where she wanted to be and finally calmed down. Of course.

He repositioned his guitar to accommodate her and started to sing a song that at first sounded like a lullaby. Then I recognized it as "Dream a Little Dream." I couldn't contain the smile on my face as I watched Bea up there with him.

The women in the crowd were gushing. If they thought they loved him before, now their ovaries were absolutely combusting. The applause from the crowd was the loudest on record after he finished.

When Justin took Bea out of the carrier, her butt was facing the microphone. Magnified by the mic, a sound that mimicked an explosion rang out through the restaurant.

It quickly occurred to me that all of these people just witnessed my daughter's explosive diarrhea.

Justin completely lost it. As he handed her back to me, he was laughing along with everyone else. He whispered, "Bea just busted serious ass."

"I'd better go change her."

As I was walking away, he stopped me. "Amelia."

"Yes?"

"You look beautiful."

I shrugged. "I tried." Even though I brushed his compliment off, I hadn't felt beautiful until that moment. Now my heart was beating a mile a minute.

———

The next morning, when we woke up, Justin was gone. There was a note on the kitchen counter.

It was the first night you both slept. I didn't have the heart to wake you before I left. Take care of Bea. I'll see you soon.

An entire week went by with no word from him.

I tried not to overreact. After all, we weren't his responsibility. The loneliness just seemed so much worse now that I knew what it felt like to have someone around. Bea's insomnia was worse than before too. I honestly thought she missed him. So did I.

In an act of desperation, I'd called my mother and asked if she would be willing to stay with me for a week or so. She'd only been at the beach house for three days, and I already wanted to shoot myself in the head. She spent more time on the phone with her boyfriend or on the upper deck smoking her Benson & Hedges cigarettes than she did with Bea and me. It was stupid of me to hope that becoming a grandmother would change her selfish ways.

While she did manage to watch Bea so that I could get a few hours of sleep each night, inviting her to stay with us turned out to be a mistake. On the last night of her stay, rather than spend quality time with Bea, she chose instead to badger me about taking legal action against Adam.

"When are you going to force that guy to pay up, Amelia?"

Right after Justin had left, I'd taken Bea to have her blood drawn. Adam had also gone to a lab in Boston, and it had been confirmed yesterday that he was definitely her biological father.

"I don't want to put Bea through dealing with him right now. He has to make the first move as far as I'm concerned. He's been so mean that I don't even want him in her life."

"Well, you're not going to be able to support yourself much longer. You need to get a man, even if it's not him."

"I'm not going to bring a man into Bea's life just to use him for financial support. I'll find a way to take care of myself." *I'm not you.*

"Good luck doing that on a teacher's salary."

"At least I have a respectable career to fall back on. I'm sure you think it's better for me to just not work, mooching off strange men like you did. Thank goodness my father was one of the good ones. But I can assure you, I will never put Bea through the kind of childhood I had, with men coming and going."

"You act like you were abused. Your childhood wasn't that bad."

"You wouldn't know. You were absent for most of it."

"Did you really invite me here to fight, Amelia?"

"No, let's stop fighting. You're leaving tomorrow, and I need to sleep. Do you mind staying up with Bea so I can get a few hours in?"

"Sure." My mother flicked her long, blond hair. "Go ahead." She proceeded to grab a mug from the cupboard and help herself to some leftover coffee that had been sitting for hours in the pot.

I figured I might as well take advantage of her last night here. She probably wouldn't come back after this tumultuous experience.

A few hours later, something disrupted my sleep. It was well past midnight. The faint sound of people talking downstairs registered. My mother was supposed to be watching Bea, so who the hell was in my house?

Panic struck, and I crept down the stairs, stopping midway when I realized the other voice was Justin's.

He came back?

The conversation that ensued between him and my mother completely blew me away as I hid in the stairwell listening to them.

"What are you doing here?" my mother demanded.

"This is my house," Justin said.

"Which is a joke, by the way. This house should have been left to me."

"Did you come here on your own, or did your daughter invite you?"

"Amelia asked me to come." She paused, then said, "God, you turned out to be fucking hot."

"Excuse me?"

"You're like a better-looking version of your father. I wish I were fifteen years younger. Unless you like older women…"

"Are you fucking serious right now, Patricia? Haven't you done enough damage to our lives? Amelia invited you here to help with the baby, and I find Bea by herself in the living room while you're smoking on the fucking deck. Now you're trying to pick me up?"

"Calm down. I was just kidding."

"I really wish I believed you were. Do you have any idea what Amelia's been through these past few months? She's doing the best she can. She doesn't deserve this shit. You should have been offering to help from day one, but honestly, she's better off without you."

I'd had enough. I made my way down the stairs and said, "Mom, I think it's best if you leave tonight."

"Tonight? I was planning to leave in the morning anyway."

"Yes. But that was before I knew Justin would be back. This is his house, and you're upsetting both of us. And why were you out on the deck when you were supposed to be watching the baby?"

"She was sleeping. It's no big deal."

"Nothing is ever a big deal to you!"

"You're seriously asking me to leave right now in the middle of the night?"

"No. I'm *telling* you to leave. Please. You're my mother and I love you, but you're fucked-up, and you'll never change."

"I can't believe this," my mother huffed before quietly heading upstairs to pack her things.

When she returned, she lifted Bea out of the carrier she was sleeping in, intentionally waking her up to kiss her. Bea started crying as my mother handed her to me before walking out the door without saying anything further.

When the door shut, I closed my eyes, feeling like I was going to cry right along with the baby. Then, I felt Justin's arms wrap around me.

"I'm sorry," he said.

"I wasn't sure if you were coming back."

He took Bea from my arms. As expected, she immediately calmed down. But something unexpected also happened. Her little mouth spread into a wide toothless smile as she looked up at him.

I gasped. "Oh my God, Justin. She's smiling at you!"

"Has she never smiled before?"

"There have been times I thought maybe she was smiling, but wasn't sure if it was just gas. But there is no doubt about this one. That is most definitely a smile!"

He seemed to be in awe as she continued to grin at him. "Maybe she didn't think I was coming back."

She wouldn't be the only one.

"We're both happy you did."

———

The next morning when I came downstairs carrying Bea, Justin had already made coffee. The smell of the freshly ground beans mixed with his musky scent was a great way to start the day. I noticed that there was also a new Keurig machine set up on the counter.

"Where did that come from?" I asked.

"I brought it back from my apartment in the city. That way, I can make coffee fusion for myself and half-caf in the coffee maker for you."

"That was very thoughtful."

When he handed me my steaming mug, something dawned on me. "What did you use in this? We were out of cream. I haven't had a chance to go to the market."

"I used milk instead."

"We didn't have milk."

He pointed with his thumb to the fridge. "There was a glass bottle of milk in there."

Covering my mouth, I said, "I didn't buy regular milk. Justin...that was my breast milk! I pumped it and poured it into an empty glass bottle. The only good thing my mother did for me while she was here was buy me a breast pump. I've been practicing using it." Cracking up, I pointed into the coffee. "You just put my breast milk in this!"

"Not only that…I already *drank* two cups with your breast milk. I'm on my third."

I covered my mouth again. "Oh my God!"

He took a sip of his coffee. "It's fucking good."

"Seriously?"

"Yeah…it's sweet. I can see why Bea drinks it like crack."

"You're nuts. I'm not drinking this."

"How much of that shit can you make per day? We can sell it."

"You'd better be joking."

"About selling it…yes. About drinking it? No. And I don't want to share with anyone but Bea."

"You're sick."

He winked. "You're just figuring this out?"

It was so good to have him back.

———

A week later, it was a typical evening at home. Justin was playing at Sandy's while Bea and I stayed in. She was being super quiet as she played with her mobile on the floor, so I decided to peruse the Internet while lounging on the couch with my laptop.

I'd been avoiding going on Jade's Facebook page because I didn't want to see pictures from Justin's trip back to New York that would only upset me. But somehow, I'd ended up on her profile anyway, looking through her recent posts. Much of it was the same as always: scenes from backstage, theater friends out on the town after performances, pictures with fans. There was one thing, however, that was far from expected. Jade had recently changed her relationship status from "in a relationship" to "single."

They broke up?

My heart was beating out of control.

When did this happen?

She'd also posted a cryptic status right around the time that Justin came back to Newport: *"To New Beginnings."*

They'd ended it while he was in New York! He'd been back for a week and hadn't told me. Why would he have kept it a secret? My mind was racing. Was he ever planning to tell me?

I stayed in the same spot in the living room, waiting for him to get home. When the doorknob turned, I straightened in my seat.

Justin put down his guitar next to the door and hung up his jacket. "What's wrong? Why are you looking at me like that?"

"Why didn't you tell me you and Jade broke up?"

He let out a slow breath and joined me on the couch. "How did you find out?"

"She changed her relationship status on Facebook."

Letting out another deep breath, he said, "Things had been off for a while. We'd just been growing apart over the past year. The reason I came to Newport early was to have some alone time to think. That was when I found you and Bea here."

"I don't understand. I thought you were in love with her."

"No."

"No? Why did you always tell her you loved her, then? Isn't that misleading?"

"I thought I loved her at one time. So, yes, we told each other we loved one another. Once you start saying that word, it just becomes commonplace to use it. It gets abused and loses its value. We had a good relationship for a while, but it was never gonna work long-term."

"Why?"

"We're too different. She's so caught up in the theater world right now. There was no time for us to work on the problems we had."

"And she wanted kids," I added.

"That too."

I swallowed. Even though I'd known how he felt about kids, a part of me had hoped being around Bea might have shown him that it wasn't so terrible. "You guys didn't sound like you had any problems. Just the opposite, in fact. I had to cover my ears anytime she was home."

"The sex was good. We never had issues in that area. But it takes something deeper than that to last forever with someone. I didn't want to waste her time. Time is precious."

"So it was you who broke up with her?"

"Yes. I was the one who ended it."

I actually felt really badly for Jade. I knew what it felt like to have strong feelings for this man, and she was a good person. She didn't deserve to be dumped. "That was the reason for your trip to New York?"

"My feelings had been weighing on me. I didn't want to go through the whole summer like that. Now she can be free to do whatever she pleases."

"And you?"

He hesitated before saying, "The same."

My body didn't know how to react, whether to feel relief or nausea. Was this a good thing or a bad thing? I honestly didn't know. Justin being single now meant that he could potentially be playing the field, bringing girls home, taking advantage of all of the wanton women gushing over him at Sandy's. I couldn't deal with that. In a strange way, knowing he was committed to Jade had always brought about a bittersweet solace because at least there was only one woman to worry about. Now there could potentially be many.

At the same time, this could be an opportunity for me to finally have a chance to be with him.

I quickly shook that thought from my head, knowing full well that it was a long shot. He didn't want kids; he was emphatic about that. I now came with one, and there was no chance in hell he would go for that kind of package deal.

Then, it occurred to me that maybe he had been intentionally keeping the breakup from me to avoid any expectations on my part. *That was it!*

"Why did you keep this from me, Justin?" I asked.

"I was going to tell you."

"When?"

"I don't know."

"Me knowing doesn't change anything between us, if that's what you think. I don't expect anything from you, especially now."

"What do you mean by 'especially now'?"

"I mean…maybe if I hadn't had Bea…" I shook my head. "Never mind."

"Say what you were gonna say."

"Things might be different if I didn't have a child. Maybe we could have seen where things went."

He looked like he was struggling with what to say next. "You're no less attractive because you have a child. Don't ever think that. But you are right about one thing. Any man you end up with needs to be one hundred percent ready for that responsibility." He pointed over to Bea, who was kicking her legs around as she continued to play on the rug. "It wouldn't be fair to her otherwise."

He's right.

As my head hit the pillow that night, I'd never felt more confused about what tomorrow would hold.

CHAPTER 13

Every evening when the door opened, I cringed, wondering if this would be the night where Justin finally brought a woman home with him. I kept preparing myself for it. He was a very sexual person. Jade had always referenced his insatiable appetite. It had made me want to vomit.

He wasn't going to be celibate forever.

It wasn't a question of *if* he brought someone home; it was *when*. Each time he walked in alone was a bigger relief than the last, though.

The days were passing, and with each one, I wondered how much longer this peaceful camaraderie between us would continue.

Bea was getting bigger every day. She was finally rolling over, which meant being very careful when changing her diaper because she easily could fall off the table. Now that I was pumping milk, it was a lot easier to leave the house from time to time. Justin would watch Bea for little stints while I ran errands. I referred to him as Uncle Justin around her. He seemed to be happy with that. It was a safe title and made it clear that I wasn't expecting him to have a bigger role in her life. He would likely always be Uncle Justin to her. I vowed to learn to accept that.

The best part of my day continued to be the morning, when Justin and I would sit in the kitchen with Bea and have our coffee together. The weirdo was still using my pumped milk as a cream replacement, though. At first, I thought he was continuing the habit just to be funny, but the longer it went on, the more it became clear that he truly liked the taste.

As he poured some out of a bottle into his coffee, I asked, "You think that's completely normal?"

"I'd rather drink from you than some random cow. Think about it. You're the one that stopped eating meat after a similar realization."

"Okay, but despite that, you do realize the average person would find you drinking breast milk very bizarre."

"No. Bizarre would be if I stood in line while you were feeding her and asked to go next."

That actually made me chuckle. "True, but what's gonna happen when you start dating someone? You think she's going to accept you drinking another woman's breast milk? Or even that you had in the past?"

"I'll worry about that when I have to."

It felt like a good opportunity to pry. "So you're not seeing anyone?"

He glanced at me from over his mug with amusement in his eyes. "I'm pretty sure you know the answer to that, Amelia. If I'm not here, then I'm at Sandy's, and then I come home. When would I be seeing said person?"

"I know. I guess I'm just confused."

He slammed the ceramic mug down on the granite. "Okay. Explain why you're confused."

"You're obviously extremely attractive. You're a musician on top of that. You have women literally throwing themselves at you. It's been a month since you broke up with Jade. I keep expecting you to walk in here with someone. That's all."

"You think I'm a man whore when I'm single?"

"I've only experienced you with a girlfriend, so I don't really know."

He placed his hands on the table and leaned in toward me. "I love to fuck. *Love* it. More than anything." Those words gave me the chills. He sat back and crossed his arms. "But the more experience I have, the more I realize that you have to be careful out there. I don't sleep around anymore like I used to."

I decided to mess with him. "That's interesting that you say that because I was thinking that casual sex may be my only option."

He nearly spit out his coffee. "Oh really?"

"Yeah. You actually helped with that realization."

"Did I now? I'd like to hear this."

"Think about it. Like you were saying…any man that's going to end up with me has to be in it for the long haul. It takes time to figure that stuff out, right? I can't be celibate forever while I wait to see if Mr. Right wants to be a father to my daughter. I too, like to fuck."

His eyes widened. "I see."

"Although I haven't slept around in recent years, it might be better for me at this point in my life to just have meaning-less sex with a trusted person who's on the same page. He'd have to be clean, of course, have all the proper tests."

"Are you serious right now?"

"I'm dead serious."

I was starting to become a little convinced of my own argument.

He mocked, "And where exactly are you gonna find a man who is just looking for casual fucking but also happens to be a clean, respectable person that you can bring around your daughter? Oh, and this guy is apparently not sleeping with anyone else at the same time? Yeah. That makes sense."

"I wouldn't be bringing any man around Bea unless it was serious. So he wouldn't be getting to know my daughter."

"Where would you be meeting up with said man, then?"

"Hotels."

"Who's going to be watching Bea when you're fucking this guy in a motel?"

I snorted. "You?"

"Please tell me you're kidding. Because I'm about to fucking lose it."

"Want the honest truth?"

"Yes."

"For the most part I am kidding. But I do think that I may need to find someone to satisfy my needs at some point, someone who I can trust but who understands that it wouldn't be anything more than sex."

He gritted his teeth. "Someone like Roger next door?"

"Maybe."

His face turned red in anger as he got up and put his mug in the sink. "That's just great, Amelia. Just fucking great."

That was the last thing he said before stomping up the stairs to start his workday.

He never came down that afternoon.

Justin was mad...*and jealous as hell*. It hadn't even been subtle.

I'd told him I was giving him the honest truth, but that

wasn't the case. Because the real truth was that there was only one man I'd dreamt of fucking in a hotel—and that was him.

———

Justin still seemed moody that night. He was flipping through the channels at lightning speed without even really paying attention. When my phone vibrated on the coffee table, he picked it up and looked down at the caller ID.

A look of shock washed over his face as he handed me the phone. "It's Adam."

Shit.

I'd left Adam a voice message the other day, asking if he was interested in coming down to Newport to meet Bea. Seeing him was the last thing I wanted, but I felt that I owed it to my daughter to at least attempt to establish a relationship between them.

Justin watched me like a hawk as I answered.

"Hello?"

Adam's voice sounded a bit muffled. "Hey."

"I'm assuming you got my voicemail."

There was some static; he must have been driving. "Yeah. Ashlyn's away. I can come down this weekend. When is a good time?"

He can only come down because Ashlyn is away? Real nice.

"I think it's best if we meet downtown. Maybe at the park. I can text you the location. Would this Saturday work?"

"Yeah. That should be fine."

"Okay. Why don't we plan to meet around three?"

"That'll work."

"I'll text you the info soon."

"All right. Bye."

"Bye."

174

He never even asked how she was.

Justin was still glaring at me after I hung up. "He's coming down here? Since when is he interested in being a part of her life?"

"Since a blood test proved he's the father."

"You never told me you had that done."

"It was just a formality. It happened while you were away, and I didn't even think to mention it because there was never any doubt. Anyway, the only person the test mattered to was Adam because he was accusing me of lying."

Justin's tone was stern. "I still don't want him near her."

"He's her father."

"He's a sperm donor," he said through gritted teeth.

"What am I supposed to do? Keep her from him?"

"He doesn't deserve her." Justin seemed lost in thought for a few moments before he asked, "What exactly are his rights now?"

"I'm not entirely sure. I don't think he's going to want any of the responsibility of caring for her, so I haven't even really looked into that stuff. By the same token, I'm not pressuring him into anything, either. Anyway, it'll just be a quick meeting."

"I'm coming with you."

"No. You don't have to."

"There is no way I'm letting you go see that asshole by yourself."

"That's really not necessary. We'll be—"

"Amelia...it's not a choice. I'm coming with you," he repeated.

The look in his eyes told me this was one argument I wasn't going to win.

———

The weather was perfect: dry with low humidity. We would be meeting at Colt State Park, which was just over the bridge and off the island. Justin and I had visited this park once or twice when we were kids, so it felt a little bit nostalgic.

We packed a picnic lunch and made an afternoon out of it, getting there an hour before Adam was set to arrive. Might as well balance a stressful event with some fun.

I'd dressed Bea in the frilliest pink dress she had and placed one of those thin little ruffled headbands over her head. Her tiny feet were covered in the cutest white patent leather shoes.

Justin gently brushed the back of his finger along her head. "Bea looks adorable, but you know, it kind of pisses me off you got her all dressed up for him."

"I wanted her to look her best, make him feel like shit."

"She always looks her best, no matter what you put on her. He should feel like shit either way, whether she's wearing a dress or covered in poop. She's his fucking flesh and blood, and he hasn't seen her for the first five months of her life."

"You're right."

Our attention turned to a couple of teenagers flying a multicolored kite. We sat in silence, enjoying the scenery. It was a great day to be out on the water, so lots of sailboats could be seen in the distance since the park abutted the ocean.

Justin looked up at the clear blue sky. "Do you remember the last time we were here?"

"Yes," I said quietly. "It was shortly before I moved to New Hampshire. You were starting to get into photography." Justin had brought his camera to Colt State Park during our last trip here and snapped some pictures of me with the water as a backdrop.

"Yeah. That hobby was short-lived, took a back seat to

music." He took out his wallet, which was quite old, the brown leather cracked and weathered. He opened it. "If I show you something, don't laugh."

"Okay..."

He took out a small black-and-white photo that had been tucked inside the back. The edges of the paper were frayed. It was a snapshot of me. "This was one of the images I shot that day. It was the only one I had developed."

I took it from him. "Wow. I never had a chance to see any of them."

"This one was my favorite because I snapped it when you weren't posing. You were laughing at one of my jokes when I took it."

My gaze traveled from the photo to his beautiful blue eyes that were staring into mine and reflected the ocean behind me. "You've always carried this around?"

"Even when I was mad at you, I couldn't get myself to get rid of it. I'd hide it so I didn't have to see you, but I couldn't throw you away."

"Throw it away or throw me away?"

"Both."

We continued to lock eyes as I willed away the pangs of longing that were always there and needed to be constantly suppressed.

Looking down at my watch, I noticed that it was ten minutes past three. "Adam is late."

"What a jackass."

Justin took Bea from me and lay back, placing her on his chest. She reached out her little hand to his mouth while he blew raspberries against her fingers.

The minutes passed, and still no sign of Adam. After an hour of waiting, Justin was irate. "We need to leave."

"I can't believe he would just not show up. Maybe he's stuck in traffic."

"Why wouldn't he text you, then? That's fucking beyond disrespectful. He doesn't deserve a minute more of our time. He's better off not showing up at this point, because he'd get a punch to the face."

I started to pack up, feeling incredibly sad for Bea. Whether Adam was a part of our lives didn't matter to me, but it would surely matter to her someday.

Suddenly, my phone vibrated. It was a text from Adam.

I was on my way but turned around. I'm sorry. I just can't. I can't do this. I'll send you money.

Justin took the phone from me and read the text. He shook his head in utter disbelief, then looked down at Bea, who was still sitting there in her beautiful dress as she watched him. Justin had his knees up, and Bea was resting her back against the slope of his legs. Her tiny hands were enveloped in his large ones.

My daughter was calm as a clam. She had no clue what that text meant for the rest of her life. She had no clue that her father had just abandoned her.

I was pretty sure she thought she was staring into the eyes of her father right now.

After a long moment of silence, Justin whispered, "He doesn't know what he's missing. He's a fool." He moved his face toward hers and said, "Well, we don't need him. Do we, Bea? Fuck him!"

Even though he probably shouldn't have sworn around the baby, the most amazing thing happened. The second Justin said, "Fuck him," Bea started laughing like she understood. It wasn't subtle but rather a contagious belly laugh. When she suddenly stopped, Justin bent his head back, then bobbed it down real fast as he repeated, "Fuck him!" Again, she erupted in laughter. He did it again. "Fuck him!" An even bigger laughing fit ensued. Justin and I were both in hysterics right along with her.

Tears were pouring out of my eyes, and I honestly couldn't have told you whether I was laughing or crying.

That evening, Justin offered to put Bea down for the night. His soothing singing voice carried all the way downstairs. I closed my eyes and meditated to the sound of him rocking her to sleep. The song he'd chosen was no coincidence: "Isn't She Lovely" by Stevie Wonder.

CHAPTER 14

The following week, it was the middle of the day, and Justin was upstairs working. Bea was lying on her belly playing in the living room while I paid some bills. There was a knock at the door. When I opened it, Roger was standing there with two medium lattes from Maggie's Coffeehouse. It had been over a month since he'd last visited.

"Long time no see." I smiled. Taking one of the drinks from him, I said, "You didn't have to do that. But it was time for my afternoon caffeine, so good timing." I waved my arm. "Come on in."

He knelt to greet Bea. "God, she's getting big."

"I know. She's going on six months. Can you believe that?"

"Time is flying."

"Yes…which is why I'm glad you stopped by. I was worried that Justin scared you away."

He sat down and spoke low. "Well, to be honest, I debated coming. Your watchdog is a little intimidating."

"I'm sorry he was rude the last time you were here."

"I'm assuming he's still living here?"

"Yes. Justin's home now. He works remotely and is actually upstairs in his office."

"How long is he staying on the island?"

It was nearing the end of the summer, and Justin had given me no indication of his itinerary. Any time I asked, he said he wasn't sure.

"He can stay as long as he wants because he owns half the house, so we really don't discuss it."

"Can I be a little nosey?"

"Sure. What's up?"

"Is something more going on between the two of you?"

"No. Why do you ask?"

"Well, a man doesn't bark at another man like that about his friend unless he wants her for himself."

"Justin and I have a very long history, but we've never actually been together. We've never even kissed once in over a decade of knowing each other."

"Really…"

"He can be protective, but he doesn't want a serious relationship with me—especially now. He cares for Bea, but he doesn't want kids. He doesn't want to be with me."

Something about having said those words out loud made me incredibly sad—and angry. Why wasn't I enough? Why wasn't Bea enough.

"Sounds like his loss."

"Some things are just better left the way they are."

"Well, now that you've cleared that up…can I ask you another question?"

"Yes."

"Would you want to go out this weekend? The jazz festival

181

is happening downtown. I'd love to take you. We could go during the day."

"I have to be honest because I don't know if you're asking me out on a date. I don't think I'm ready for anything serious. But I do enjoy your company. So if there are no expectations, I would love to."

"I understand. We won't call it a date, then. No expectations...just each other's company. It can get lonely out here on the island, and I feel grateful to have met you, to have found companionship at the very least. Even if it's nothing more than that, I'd love to take you out. You need to get out, Amelia."

"You know what? You're right. Let's do it. Let's go out." I smiled.

Slight wrinkles formed around his eyes when he grinned and said, "Saturday, then?"

"Sure. I'll see if Justin will watch Bea. If not, I'll take her with us." Deep down, I knew Justin was going to go ballistic. But this was necessary. If he didn't want me hanging out with other men, then he damn well needed to explain why. If he wasn't going to give me affection, then I needed to get it somewhere else.

"It's really fine to bring Bea." He winked. "Especially since it's not a date."

"We'll see."

Roger managed to escape the house without Justin coming downstairs.

When my roommate finally emerged later that afternoon, his mood was unreadable. He lifted Bea off the floor and tickled her belly with his hair as he said, "What do you feel like for dinner tonight?"

"Anything is fine."

Carrying Bea over to the cupboard, he scratched the overgrown stubble on his chin. "I have to figure out what we have." He glanced over at the trash bin, taking notice of the Maggie's Coffeehouse cup. "Did you go out for coffee?"

"No. Roger brought it this afternoon."

His jaw tightened as he pondered that. "He was here?"

"Yes." I sighed. "We need to talk."

Justin closed the cupboard. "All right."

Just say it.

"Roger asked if I wanted to go to the jazz festival with him this weekend. I told him yes."

He blinked a few times. "You're going on a date with him?"

"No."

"It's a fucking date, Amelia."

"I explained to him that I'm not ready to date."

"Oh, that's right. You're not looking to date. You're looking for a casual fuck."

"It's just an outing."

He raised his voice. "It's not just an outing. He's a guy. I've seen the way he looks at you. He wants to fuck you."

Justin was really starting to piss me off. My instinct was to scream at him, but I stopped myself. Instead, I looked into his eyes—really looked into them. "What are you doing?"

I hoped he saw the pain and frustration I was feeling. Even though it was a simple question, I knew he couldn't answer me. It was complicated. I didn't even think he understood why he was acting this way. But it had to stop.

Then, something in his eyes shifted. It was as if realization had finally struck as to how unreasonable he was being. He didn't want something more with me, but he didn't want anyone else to have me, either. He couldn't have it both ways.

"I don't know," he whispered, staring vacantly into space. "I don't know why it makes me so mad. I'm confused. Fuck. I'm...I'm sorry." He was still holding Bea and handed her to me before walking over to the window to stare out at the ocean.

I spoke to his back. "I was going to ask you if you could watch Bea, but I think it's better if I take her with me."

"No." He turned around, his hands in his pockets. "I'll watch her. You deserve to get out."

"Are you sure?"

"Yes."

"Okay. Thank you."

That night, we ate in silence.

———

The Friday evening before my Saturday date, I decided to go watch Justin at Sandy's.

Aside from playing with Bea, he'd kept to himself since our altercation about Roger. A part of me was curious as to whether his mood would somehow carry over to his performance.

Bea was asleep in her carrier when we arrived at the restaurant. Tonight, they had Justin playing on the outdoor stage. He didn't notice me sitting in a far corner.

It was a breezy night. A few napkins flew off tables, and Justin's hair was blowing around a little in the wind.

When he started a cover of "Daughters" by John Mayer, it squeezed at my heart because I wondered if he had chosen that song because of the situation with Bea and Adam. I also wondered if he was thinking of her. Most of the songs he'd chosen tonight were slow and melancholy, so much so that Bea slept right through them.

His first intermission finally rolled around. He still hadn't noticed us. He wasn't as observant of the audience tonight in general, seeming very much in his own head. He usually engaged much more with the crowd.

Just as I was about to get up and announce that we were there, an attractive young redhead made her way over to the stage. I watched for several minutes as she flirted shamelessly with him. My stomach was in knots. At one point, she handed him a piece of paper, which he put in his pocket. Whether he'd accepted it to be polite or intended to use it, I had no idea. Even though this type of thing probably happened every night, it still felt like I'd been hit by a brick, and it killed any desire I had to stay for the next set.

Bea and I left, and Justin never even knew we'd been there.

———

The sound of punching came from Justin's exercise room. As I got ready for my sort-of-date with Roger, it occurred to me that the last time Justin had beat the shit out of the Everlast punching bag like that had been the night of my date with Dr. Danger last summer. This felt like déjà vu.

I stood in the doorway and watched him attack the bag until he noticed me and stopped.

Out of breath, he said, "What time are you leaving again?"

"In about forty-five minutes. I just wanted to make sure you were all set to watch Bea."

He wiped the sweat off his forehead. "Yeah. I'll shower and be downstairs in time for you to leave."

"Thank you."

Wanting to make sure she had a full stomach before I left, I nursed Bea while Justin took his shower. She ended up falling asleep, so I put her in her crib before checking myself out one last time in the mirror. The jazz festival was a casual event, so I wore a simple tank top with a denim jacket and flowy floral skirt.

Back downstairs, I waited for Justin so that I could give him some last-minute instructions. I started loading a couple of bottles of pumped milk into the refrigerator when I heard his voice behind me.

"She's asleep?"

"Yup."

"So, what do I need to know?"

When I turned around, Justin was leaning against the counter, looking gorgeous. A few strands of his wet hair fell over his forehead. He hadn't bothered to put on a shirt, and my eyes couldn't help traveling down to his cut abs. His thumbs were hooked into the belt loops at his waistline. While his jeans were zipped, they were unbuttoned at the top. I imagined what it would be like to lick a line straight down that happy trail. On top of that, he was barefoot.

Fuck. Me.

I had some instructions to give him, yet I'd forgotten them all. My mind went completely blank.

"Not to steal your own words from you, Amelia…but my eyes are up here."

Feeling embarrassed, I simply said, "I know."

He wore a smug grin. "So, answer me. What do I need to know while you're gone?"

"Um…I have two bottles of milk that I pumped. They're sitting in the door."

"I won't drink them." He winked.

"She should have a serving of rice cereal when she wakes up. That will help keep her stomach full while I'm out in case the two bottles aren't enough. But I literally just fed her before she went down."

He crossed his arms. "All right...anything else?"

"You should change her diaper as soon as she wakes up too."

"Got it."

I tilted my head. "Any questions for me?"

"How late are you staying out?"

"Probably not more than a few hours. I should be back by eight."

When he didn't say anything further, I asked, "Any more questions?"

He was silent, but his stare was burning into mine. "Yes, in fact," he finally said.

"Okay. What?"

"Why were you looking at me like you wanted to eat me?"

"Are you being serious right now?"

"Are *you* being serious, Amelia?"

"I'm lost."

"Are you being serious about going out with Roger Podger when you'd rather stay home with me?"

"Who said I'd rather stay home with you?"

"Your nipples."

I squinted my eyes incredulously. "My nipples?"

"Yes. While you were looking at me, I was watching them, and they literally hardened before my eyes." He walked slowly toward me, then leaned in. "No part of you—body or mind—really wants to be with him, and you know it. You're doing this to fuck with me because you think I don't want you. You're doing this to make me jealous."

"That's not true. Not everything is about you."

"Not everything. But this...this is definitely about me."

"No."

"Bullshit. You wanted to see how far you could push me before I reached my breaking point."

"If that's what you want to believe, then fine. In the meantime, you egotistical ass, I'm going to a jazz festival." I started to walk away, not even sure where I was going since Roger was supposed to be coming here to pick me up.

Justin gripped my waist to stop me. Flipping me around, he pulled me closer into him, his eyes telling me I wasn't going anywhere until he damn well let me. Justin then slowly pushed me toward the door until my back was against it. His lips hovered over mine as he panted into my mouth. But he withheld.

Needing to taste him, I couldn't take it anymore. Wrapping my hands around his head, I pressed my lips into his. We opened for each other, the feel of his hot tongue swirling inside of my mouth more incredible than the countless times I'd imagined it over the course of a decade. I ran my fingers through his silky hair as we kissed. His mouth was insanely wet, and his taste was addicting. I no longer had a concept of time.

Nudging my legs open with his knee, he wedged himself between them. His hot erection was pressing against my body, and he took my hand and slid it down to his crotch as we kissed. Speaking over my lips, he said, "Fuck, Amelia. You think I don't want you? Feel how much I don't want you."

I moaned against his mouth to confirm that I absolutely felt it; it was practically halfway down his thigh. Experiencing a complete loss of restraint, I was completely at his mercy. His kiss wasn't ordinary or like anything I'd felt before. He kissed with all of the force in his body, as if the very act were necessary for survival. If he kissed like this, I could only imagine what it was like to have sex with him.

The vibration of Roger knocking against the door hit my back. Shamelessly, Justin didn't even flinch. Instead, he kissed me harder, deeper. He made it really hard to want to stop.

Finally prying myself away from Justin, I yelled, "Just a minute!"

His lips were still just inches from mine. He glared at me mischievously, knowing full well that even though I was going out with Roger, I wasn't going to be able to think about anything else but him.

He wiggled his brows and said, "Have fun."

Then, he turned around and walked away, disappearing up the stairs.

———

Roger never suspected that Justin and I had been sucking face just moments before he'd picked me up. I'd checked my reflection in the mirror before opening the door and attributed the delay to breastfeeding.

We stopped at Maggie's for takeout lattes on the way to the jazz festival, which was held on the grounds of Fort Adams at the mouth of Newport Harbor. Three stages were set up, each featuring a different jazz band. It was a gorgeous afternoon with only a slight chill in the air. The location featured panoramic views of the Newport Bridge and the East Passage.

I tried my best to focus on the scenery and music, but my mind was elsewhere. I could still feel Justin's kiss, could still taste him on my tongue. My panties were soaked. I wondered what it all meant, if things were going to be different now.

A text alert sounded.

Justin: Stop thinking about me.
Amelia: You are egotistical. You only kissed me because I was going out with Roger.
Justin: Technically, you kissed me.
Amelia: How is Bea?

Justin: Changing the subject?

But he answered my question by sending me a selfie of Bea and him. They were both lying flat on the living room rug. Bea was smiling. It was freaking adorable.

Amelia: Looks like you guys are having a good time.
Justin: We miss you. You should ditch him and come hang out with us.
Amelia: I'm a little scared to come home, to be honest.
Justin: I won't bite. I promise. Unless you ask me to, in which case I'll do it so gently, you won't feel any pain.
Amelia: I can't text anymore. It's rude.
Justin: We need to talk later.
Amelia: About what?
Justin: I'd like to apply for the position.
Amelia: What position?
Justin: Your casual fuck buddy.
Amelia: What???
Justin: We'll talk later.

I didn't even know what to say, so I put my phone away.

Roger put his hand on my shoulder. "Is everything all right at home?"

Not exactly.

"Oh, yes. I was just checking on Bea. Everything is fine."

"Want to go grab an early dinner?"

Even though Justin's text had managed to squelch my appetite, I said, "Sure. That would be great."

Roger and I left the festival grounds and had dinner at the Brick Alley Pub. We talked nonstop throughout our meal. He spoke about his upcoming trip to Irvine to visit his daughter. He beamed with pride whenever he mentioned Alyssa, and it occurred to me how lucky she was to have a father who cared for her so deeply; Bea wouldn't have that. I could only hope that someone would fill that role for my daughter someday.

Despite the sexual game Justin was playing all of a sudden, he'd still given me no assurance that he wanted to be with us long-term as more than just Bea's "uncle." His assertion that we should be "fuck buddies" certainly didn't count. Justin and I couldn't really be together so long as he didn't want children long-term.

Roger drove me home after dinner. I intentionally didn't invite him in because I wasn't in any mood for Justin's antics.

He lingered. "I hope we can go out again soon."

"I'd really like that," I said.

Despite obsessing over Justin throughout the day, I really did enjoy Roger's company. He was smart, articulate, and a really good listener.

When I opened the door, Justin was sitting on the couch watching television. Bea was cradled in the crook of his arm. "How was it?"

"It was a lot of fun, actually. You would love the jazz festival. You should check it out. Tomorrow is the last day," I said, plopping down on the couch next to him.

"Good." He smiled, but it was more of a chastising grin.

I took Bea from him and kissed her. "I missed you, Bea Bee."

"I'll get up so you can feed her in private. I suppose you're not hungry for dinner."

"No. Roger took me to the Brick Alley Pub."

His expression darkened. "Great."

Pots and pans clanked as Justin not-so-quietly prepared himself something to eat in the kitchen while I fed Bea. She fell asleep on my breast, so I put her upstairs in her crib. It was earlier than her normal bedtime, so I knew she would probably be waking me up in the middle of the night.

When I returned to the kitchen, Justin looked like he'd been waiting for me. He was wearing a gray hoodie that was halfway zipped up over his bare chest, the hood over his head. Looking quite tense, he pulled at his sleeves.

"We need to talk, Amelia."

"All right."

He lifted his face to look me straight in the eyes. "I don't want you going out with him again."

"You can't dictate who I go out with."

"Well, I don't want you going out with anyone."

"I don't understand how you think you have a right to say that."

"Then hear me out."

"I'm listening."

"You said you don't want anything serious right now."

"That's right."

"Neither do I. I just got out of a long-term relationship. I really can't handle serious at the moment."

"So you think I'm the perfect candidate to screw around with? Don't you have enough options? How about that redhead who gave you her number the other night when you didn't even notice Bea and I standing right there?"

His expression turned angry. "What? You came to Sandy's that night?"

"Yes. You played 'Daughters.' It was very touching."

"Why the fuck didn't you tell me you were there?"

"You were busy."

"You were all I could think about that entire night, Amelia. Every fucking song, I was thinking about you or Bea. That's the truth. I don't even remember that woman's name."

"Well, that's irrelevant I suppose. Get back to what you were saying…about wanting me to be your whore."

"It's not like that. *At all*, Amelia." Looking uncharacteristically nervous, he said, "I've been doing a lot of thinking lately. You've made it clear that you need someone to satisfy your needs. I don't want you fucking around with some random guy who doesn't care about you. Contrary to what you might think, I do give a real shit about you. So I want to be the one to take care of it for you."

"Take care of it? You're making it sound like having sex with me is a surgical procedure."

"Far from it. And 'take care of it' isn't the right term, anyway. Technically, I'd be fucking you into oblivion."

"I'm not going to be anyone's mercy fuck, Justin."

"That's not what I'm saying." He slipped his hands under his hood and pulled on his hair in frustration. "Fuck. Do you have any clue how badly I want you? I need this just as much as you."

"I'm sorry, but you're really confusing me. You care about me, but you don't want to be with me. You just want to fuck me. It seems like an oxymoron."

"I want to give you what you need today…not tomorrow or ten years down the line. Today. It just so happens that what you need is also what I need. I need to satisfy this fucking itch that has been eating away at me for over a decade. I need to be with you on a physical level before I fucking explode. But I can't put a label on it right now. I can't make promises for the future because that would be irresponsible. There is too

193

much at stake. I won't make a promise to that little girl only to let her down."

"So you're suggesting that we forget everything else and start a physical relationship with no expectations."

"That was what you said you wanted with some random guy, right? Why not with me? It's a fuck of a lot safer."

"Because I don't think that's possible with you. I don't think I can compartmentalize years of feelings in order to have a casual sexual relationship with you. You matter too much to me. I will always want you in my life. If we have sex, we can never take that back. I would never be able to look at you the same."

"You'd never be able to *walk* the same."

"Can you be serious?"

"I *am* being serious." He smiled. "Okay...in all honesty, I want you to think about my proposition. I'm just asking you to consider living in the moment, having a little fun with me, taking things day by day."

"Taking things day by day and then one day waking up and finding you gone?"

"I'm not going anywhere anytime soon."

A part of me wanted to leap into his arms and take him up on his proposition right there on the kitchen counter, but the logical part just couldn't agree to this. "I don't know."

"If there's anything I can do to help make your decision easier, let me know. Just think about it. You don't have to make a decision right now. Sleep on it. Or sleep *on me.* Whatever you decide."

He started to walk toward the stairs.

"Where are you going?"

"Upstairs. I'll leave the door open in case you decide there's something you'd like to watch later."

CHAPTER 15

I went straight to my own room that night and didn't come out because I couldn't trust myself around him. Was he even serious? A small part of me pondered whether he was just pulling my leg with that proposition. Maybe this was some grand scheme to get back at me for hurting him a decade ago...get me to succumb to his sexual charms, then tell me it was just a joke.

Tossing and turning, I considered the pros and cons and came to the conclusion that while sex with him would be amazing, it would only result in me getting hurt. It would also ruin our second chance at friendship, which was still new and on shaky ground.

At the same time, I was completely turned on, my panties soaking wet from the way he had spoken to me. Just the thought of being with him was getting me off.

At some point in the middle of the night, I must have fallen asleep while ruminating. When I woke up the next morning, it was after 11 a.m. I hadn't slept that late in ages.

The sun was streaming through the sheer white curtains of my bedroom window. Had I dreamt my conversation with Justin last night?

Then it occurred to me that Bea was missing from her crib. I ran downstairs to find Justin sitting in the living room.

"Where's Bea?" I asked.

"She's right here. Check this out." Bea was slowly crawling toward him as he lured her with a new stuffed toy. It was a long, rainbow-colored stuffed caterpillar that squeaked.

"Come on, Bumblebee," he said to her. I loved his nickname for her.

Bea was inching toward him; it was her most impressive attempt at mobility yet.

"She's crawling!" I exclaimed.

"I know. We've been practicing all morning."

"Where did you get that toy?"

"I picked it up for her the other day from the toy shop downtown."

"So you came inside the room this morning and took her out of the crib?"

"No, she walked downstairs herself, Amelia," he quipped. "Of course. I peeked in on you because you never sleep that late. I wanted to make sure you didn't pass out from diddling yourself to thoughts of me last night."

"Not quite. Although you *were* on my mind."

"Anyway...she was just sitting there in her crib, looking at me, quiet as a mouse while you were snoring. So I took her downstairs so you could stay sleeping. You had a pumped bottle in the fridge, so we finished that off." He looked down at Bea. "She's my breakfast buddy now."

"Thanks for doing that."

"It's no problem."

Our eyes locked, and I felt like I needed to break the ice. "Justin, about last night…"

He got up suddenly from the couch. "Don't worry about it. I was out of line. I went a little crazy, got jealous."

I was surprised that he'd changed his tune so fast. "Really?"

"Yeah. I wasn't thinking with the right head."

"Okay…then I'm glad we both agree."

"Well, I have a lot of work to get done. So…" He picked up Bea off the floor, lifting her over his head briefly. "I'll see you later, Bumblebee."

He then retreated to his room and didn't come out for the rest of the afternoon.

More confused than ever, I went about my day, cleaning the house and doing Bea's laundry.

It was the beginning of September, and the weather was starting to get chilly on the island. A few weeks back, I'd officially notified the school department back in Providence that I wouldn't be returning to my job this year. It was a tough decision but one that was best for my daughter. My savings would carry me through about twelve months. In a year's time, I would reassess my situation and either return to teaching or maybe try to find a work-from-home job.

A knock on the door prompted me to place my broom in the corner.

Upon opening the door, my heart nearly skipped a beat at the sight of a familiar leggy blond with a pixie cut. "Jade. Oh my goodness. This is unexpected."

"Surprise!" She leaned in to hug me before stepping back. "Gosh, you look great, Amelia. Did you lose weight? Don't people normally gain weight after having a baby?"

"My daughter didn't let me eat or sleep for the first few

months." Trying to mask my discomfort, I asked, "Is Justin expecting you?"

"No. Not at all. Is he upstairs? I saw his car outside."

"Yeah. He's in his office working."

She took notice of Bea playing in the Exersaucer. "She is so beautiful. She looks just like you. Can I take her out of this thing?"

"Sure."

An uneasy feeling developed as I watched Jade crouch down to see my daughter.

What was she doing here?

Had he invited her?

Was that the reason for his sudden change of tune?

Blinding jealousy bombarded me.

Jade lifted Bea up to hold her. "She smells so good. What is that?"

"It's Dreft, the baby detergent I use on her clothes."

"Maybe I should give you some of my clothes to wash. She smells so fresh and clean."

I was totally over the small talk. "What brings you here, Jade?"

Sitting down on the couch and placing Bea on her lap, she said matter-of-factly, "I screwed up."

"What do you mean?"

"I fucked everything up with Justin. This past year, I gave everything I had to my job and nothing to him. I took him for granted. Did he say anything to you about why we broke up?"

"He just told me that he ended things when he went back to New York earlier this summer. He didn't really go into the details."

"It was a misunderstanding."

"How so?"

"He'd come to surprise me and found me having dinner at the apartment with my costar, Greg Nivens. Justin jumped to conclusions. Nothing was going on with Greg. It was a business meeting. Things had been rough between Justin and me for a while before that, but I would have never cheated on him."

"So you're here to—"

"Get my man back. Yes. I never fought for him. I never pleaded with him. I was in such shock with the way things ended that I never truly reflected on my responsibility in it. It was basically all my fault. I still love him so much."

No.

No.

No.

This unexpected and imminent threat was putting my true feelings to the test. I was terrified to lose Justin, terrified he'd go back to New York with her. My body stiffened in defense, preparing to go to war in a battle it was destined to lose. "Wow. I don't know what to say. I—"

Justin's deep voice startled me. "Jade. What are you doing here?"

She stood up, still carrying Bea. "Hi."

His eyes shifted over to me briefly, then back to her.

"How long have you been here?" he asked.

"Just a few minutes. I came all the way here because we need to talk. Can we go somewhere? Maybe take a walk on the beach?"

My chest felt heavy, and I was sweating from nerves.

Justin gave me another fleeting glance before saying, "Let me get my jacket."

When the door shut behind them, all the fear I'd been holding in released from me in one swift breath only to start building up again in my gut.

I looked over at Bea and spoke to her like she could under-stand. "I don't want him to leave."

She cooed and babbled while she smacked her hand down on one of the squeaky toys attached to her playset.

"I'm afraid to be with him and afraid to be without him."

She blew a couple of raspberries, drool dripping down her chin.

"You really adore him, don't you?"

"Ba...ba," she answered.

My heart hammered against my chest. "I know. Me too."

———

Justin was gone for almost six hours. I was sure he wasn't coming home.

When the key turned in the door around ten thirty that night, I straightened up on the sofa, trying to look casual so that it didn't appear like I'd been anxiously awaiting his return.

Justin rubbed his eyes and threw his coat on a chair. He went to the kitchen to grab a drink before taking a seat next to me.

I swallowed, afraid to ask, "Where is Jade?"

He took a sip of his beer, then stared blankly down at the bottle as he twirled it mindlessly in his hands. "She's on her way back to New York. I drove her to the train."

"I wasn't sure if you'd be coming back tonight."

He was silent for a long time, then looked into my eyes. "Nothing happened, Amelia."

"You don't owe me an explanation."

He spoke louder. "I don't? Are you kidding yourself?"

"What do you mean?"

"You seem to think that I can't see right through you. I saw your face when she showed up. Why can't you admit that you're just as fucking scared of what's been happening between us as I am?"

I don't know.

When I didn't respond, he simply said, "We took a walk on the beach...talked. Then, I drove her to the train."

"You were gone so long. I just assumed..."

"That we were somewhere fucking? No. I drove around for a while alone to think."

"I see. What did you and Jade decide?"

"She thinks the real reason I ended it was because I found her hanging out with that guy, but that's not the truth. I went to New York with the full intention of breaking things off before I even saw her having dinner with him."

"You explained that to her?"

"I couldn't be completely up-front about everything."

"Why not?"

"Because I'd have to admit stuff to her that I haven't even admitted to you...and I didn't want to hurt her even more."

"Things like..."

"Remember what I said about cheating?"

"That if you have the urge to cheat on someone, it's better to just break up with that person?"

"Yeah. Well, I had the urge to cheat...with you...multiple times last summer. I thought that maybe you becoming a mother would make me see you in a different light, make me less attracted somehow, but that hasn't been the case. It's been the opposite. You've never been sexier to me. But even if nothing were to happen between us, my attraction to you is a sign that something was off between Jade and me. You shouldn't covet someone else like that if you're in a healthy relationship. It's an indication that something is missing, even if you don't know exactly what it is. I don't believe in dragging things out if the outcome is already determined in your mind."

"Is Jade okay?"

"Not really."

It pained me to know that she was hurting.

"What do we do now?" I asked.

"I've already told you what I want to do."

"I thought this morning you came to the conclusion it was a bad idea and you didn't want that with me anymore."

"I never said that. What I meant was that I was out of line in the way I presented it to you. I was being overly aggressive because I felt threatened, and I came on to you like a caveman. I never explicitly said I didn't want it, and for the record, neither did you."

"I explained my reservations..."

"And I understand them. I fully get why you're afraid to take things to a sexual level with me. The logical side of me thinks you're right, but the *illogical* side of me doesn't give a fuck and is only thinking about lifting you over my face right now and making you come while you ride my mouth."

Those words hit me straight between the legs.

He went on, "The fact that you just squirmed in your seat is proof that you also have an illogical side. Maybe our illogical sides need to meet sometime." He leaned into me and grinned. "But not tonight. Despite threatening to find a fuck buddy...you're not ready. That would be like jumping over all the letters of the alphabet between A and Z."

"You've been watching too much *Sesame Street* with Bea."

"Fuck. Maybe. Anyway, you're at level A right now. My dick is at level Z. And it doesn't match up. That was one of the things I figured out on my drive tonight. That you're not there yet." He got up. "I'll be right back."

When he returned, he was holding something behind his back. "What's the one thing we did when we were younger whenever we were in a shitty mood or just didn't know what the fuck to do with ourselves?"

"We'd watch *The Big Lebowski.*"

He displayed the DVD from behind him. "Bingo."

"I can't believe you still have that."

"Always have it on hand."

"I'll pop some popcorn," I said, eagerly running to the kitchen, relieved that the tension in the air had lessened. He was right. I wasn't ready. I didn't want to lose him, but as much as I wanted him, I wasn't ready for a sexual relationship with him or anyone.

We sat in comfortable silence watching the cult movie that in retrospect had probably been way too inappropriate for our former thirteen-year-old selves. But neither of us had parents who'd monitored what we'd watched back then. The opening scene where the main character got his head shoved in a toilet brought back so many memories. We'd used to think it was the greatest thing ever.

Midway through the flick, Justin lay on his back, resting his head on my lap. Without thinking it through, I did what felt natural and massaged my hand through the silky strands of his hair.

He let out a slight groan of pleasure as he continued to watch the movie while I played with his hair.

At one point, he turned to me, and I instinctively moved my hand off of him, remembering the time last summer when he'd told me to stop. "Why did you...?" He realized it on his own. "No way I'm telling you to stop this time, Amelia. Please keep doing it. It feels so good."

I kept at it for the better part of a half hour.

My attention was no longer on the movie when I asked, "What else did you figure out on your drive tonight?"

"That I still love your dimples." He looked up at me. "I haven't figured it all out, but I know that for sure."

CHAPTER 16

September turned into October as we welcomed autumn and the changing colors of the leaves on the trees surrounding the island. In the month since the night we'd watched *The Big Lebowski*, things had stayed pretty innocent between us; we hadn't discussed sex again nor attempted to define our relationship. But we were getting closer organically.

Bea was now seven months old and developing more of a personality every day.

Justin had taken one short trip to New York at the end of September to meet with his music agent, who'd set up a studio session to record some of his original songs for a demo.

Overall, we were still taking it day by day, and there was no clear indication of when, or even if, he'd be going back to the city for good.

Halloween fell on a Saturday this year. We decided to take Bea to a local pumpkin patch. Justin snapped lots of photos of me and my daughter amongst the sea of orange and hay. We took a few selfies of the three of us as well. I knew I would always treasure those pictures. Justin and I sipped hot cider as we enjoyed the crisp air with a rosy-cheeked Bea, who was bundled up in a hat and mittens. Despite the fact that there were thousands of days in the course of a life, this was the kind of day you just knew you'd never forget for as long as you lived.

The plan was to spend a few hours out, then return home to give out candy while dressed in our costumes.

Knowing that Halloween had always been my favorite holiday, Justin went all out. After the pumpkin patch, he dropped Bea and me off at the house before heading to the Christmas Tree Shops in nearby Middletown, where they sold lots of seasonal Halloween items.

It was nightfall by the time he returned with a ton of bags. He'd purchased a plethora of orange and black decorations along with packages of candy and a bumblebee costume for Bea.

"They didn't have any suitable costumes for us at the Christmas Tree Shops, so I went to a couple of other places. That's why I'm late. I couldn't decide on yours, so I got more than one."

"Well, let's see." I reached out my arm. "Hand them over." One of the bags was from Island Costumes, and the other was from…Adam and Eve. "Isn't Adam and Eve an adult novelty store?"

"Yeah. It was right next door to the costume place."

He flashed a wicked grin as I squinted suspiciously. Opening the other bag first, I took out a Catwoman costume, which was a one-piece and made out of black spandex. It also came with a mask.

"That's for tonight…for the trick-or-treaters," he said.

"What's the other one for?"

"For…whenever. I just thought you'd look good in it."

I reluctantly opened the Adam and Eve bag and pulled out a sheer white piece of material with red accents. There were little patches in the shapes of crosses at the nipple areas, and you could literally see right through the fabric.

My eyes widened as I read the tag. "Nurse Feel Good?"

"It reminded me of when you took care of me when I was sick." His face was unusually flushed, like he'd actually been embarrassed to give it to me.

"You want me to wear this?"

He bit his bottom lip. "Not now."

I looked down at the tag again. "Panties not included. Something tells me that's because I'm not supposed to wear any?"

"Look…I know I may never actually get to see you in that. Honestly, I just got really turned on in the store thinking about you in it. I had to buy it. A guy can dream, right?"

He had gotten turned on thinking about me, and now I was getting turned on thinking about him getting turned on thinking about me.

I cleared my throat. "What are you going to be?"

Winking, he said, "It's a surprise."

We had about an hour before the trick-or-treaters were set to start arriving. Justin hung the orange lights along the window and put some lit carved pumpkins outside along the steps. He dimmed the main lights in the house and lit candles. It was a cross between spooky, romantic, and cozy.

"Living in the city, I really missed Halloween," he said, ripping open bags and filling the bowl with candy. "You don't get trick-or-treaters at the apartment."

I smiled inwardly, noticing he'd bought extra of my favorite candy bars from when we were kids, Almond Joy.

"I'm gonna go upstairs and get Bea dressed, get into my costume too," I said.

"All right. I'll change after you."

Upstairs, I slipped into the slinky black outfit, which looked like it could have been spray-painted onto my body. Placing the mask on, I looked at myself in the mirror. It was pretty damn sexy, actually. It was no wonder why he'd chosen it. My own knee-high, black leather stiletto boots completed the look. Bea was standing in the crib, looking amused at seeing her mommy in this getup.

After getting her into the furry bumblebee costume, we returned downstairs.

Justin's eyes popped as he looked me up and down. "Wow. Look at you. I definitely picked the right costume."

"Not very scary. More sexy."

"Well, you're scaring me stiff." He wriggled his brows before taking Bea from me and kissing her on the cheek. "You are officially a bumblebee now, Bumblebee." Carrying her over to the window, he said. "Look at the lights, Bea. I put them up for you." He went off with her, his voice no longer audible as he whispered in her ear while showing her the decorations. He took her outside to look at the carved pumpkins.

I stood back and watched them, wondering when we'd become a little family. Had there been an exact moment when we had crossed over? As much as I wanted to deny it as a self-protective mechanism, the past four months with Justin had felt more like a family experience than anything in my life ever had. Scary or not, it had happened naturally, without discussion—both of us unable to admit it to each other. But while Bea was my entire life for at least the next eighteen years, was Justin only temporarily playing house? That remained to be seen.

Justin walked over and handed her to me. "I'm gonna go change. Be right back."

The first group of trick-or-treaters arrived before Justin returned. Carrying Bea in one arm, I grabbed the large bowl and headed to the door to give out the candy.

As I was waving them off, I felt the warmth of his body behind me.

"I'm back."

When I turned around, the sight of him nearly knocked the wind out of me. Justin was dressed in all black. He was supposed to be a SWAT team officer. A short-sleeved black shirt displayed his muscular arms. A black vest with the letters SWAT in white covered the shirt. He was wearing sleek black pants and heavy combat boots. It was one of the hottest things I'd ever seen.

"Oh my..." My body was burning up beneath my tight spandex getup.

"You like it?"

"Yeah...I love it."

"They didn't have a ton of costumes left in my size. It was either this or a clown. I didn't want to scare Bea."

"This was...yeah...a very good call."

"I'm glad you think so," he whispered close to my neck.

We only got a few trick-or-treaters, but it was still exciting anytime anyone knocked on the door. I was grateful that Roger was out in Irvine visiting his daughter so that I didn't have to deal with any potential awkwardness between him and Justin. If Roger were home, he might have stopped in to say hello. We hadn't gone out again since the jazz festival.

It was almost time to call lights out. Cheri from next door had stopped in to see Bea in her costume. As I lingered at the door after saying goodbye to her, I looked over at Justin and

Bea in the kitchen. As I watched him rocking her to sleep, a realization hit me. Whether I avoided a sexual relationship with him or not, my heart was already invested. In my mind, he belonged to me. So avoiding him physically out of fear just meant that I was missing out on something I desperately needed and wanted. Looking over at him in that sexy-as-hell SWAT uniform, I knew I couldn't let fear prevent me from experiencing it any longer.

I walked over to the both of them and kissed Bea's head softly. When I looked up at him, he was already looking down at me with an intensity that almost seemed as if he knew exactly what I'd been thinking seconds earlier. He cupped my entire face in his hand and pulled me firmly into his lips. It was the first time we'd kissed since the moment right before my date with Roger. This kiss was different than that one; it was tender.

My whole body felt limp as he spoke gruffly over my lips, "Why don't you put her to bed?"

I simply nodded. My legs felt wobbly as I walked up the stairs. In my room, I carefully removed Bea from her costume so as not to wake her and placed her in the crib.

As I took off my Catwoman leotard, I stared over at the Adam and Eve bag taunting me on the bureau.

Should I?

I thought about Justin's admission that he'd fantasized about me in it and decided to shock him by putting it on. I placed the sheer material over my head. My swollen breasts were completely exposed with only the red crosses barely covering my nipples. It seriously looked obscenely hot; he was going to freak.

Slipping my own red thong on, I was already wet just thinking about his reaction. Tonight, I was going to be able to touch him, taste him, do all of the things I'd dreamt about. Goose bumps covered my entire body as I tiptoed down the hall.

Justin's door was halfway open, and he stood shirtless looking out the window as the moonlight shined on his gorgeous silhouette. He had been waiting for me.

He'd kept the black trousers on from the SWAT getup. They hugged his round ass so perfectly that my mouth watered from the urge to bite it. I'd admired his beautiful body like this so many times before from afar, yet I knew this time was different.

"Hi," I said, prompting him to turn around.

As he took me in from top to bottom, Justin's breath hitched, his hungry eyes soaking in every inch of me. "Fuck," he growled under his breath. "Holy shit. You're wearing it."

He slowly approached, then took my face in both of his palms. I was shivering with need. He slid his hands down, then traced his index finger down my neck, over my breasts, and stopped at my navel. He looked like he was in a trance as he examined every inch of my body, which was completely exposed through the sheer fabric.

He closed his eyes briefly. When he opened them, the same look of awe remained on his face. It was as if he hadn't expected to still see me standing there. "No one's ever compared to you, Amelia. You have to know that." My heart felt like it was going to combust upon hearing him say that.

Then, he dropped to his knees. He wrapped his hands around my waist as he pulled me into him, kissing my navel and swirling his tongue slowly over my stomach. He lowered his mouth in soft kisses, stopping between my legs.

Slipping his hand into the back of my thong, he roughly gripped the material before sliding it down my legs. As he stood up with my underwear in his hand, he said, "Fuck.

They're drenched." He slowly sniffed them and let out a long breath before shaking his head. "I can't wait to taste you." He pointed down to his crotch. "Look at me." His pants could barely contain him. His cock was so swollen, it seriously looked like it could puncture the material. "I don't think I've ever been this excited about anything. I've dreamt of this moment for what feels like my whole life. I never thought it would happen. I want to savor it."

He took my hand and led me over to his bed. Sitting down on the edge, he lifted me onto him. My knees were wrapped around his thighs, and my bare pussy was straddling his erection over the material of his pants.

His eyes were hazy as he looked up at me. "Tell me what your deepest, darkest fantasy is. I want to make it come true tonight." When I hesitated, he said, "Let's play a little. Tell me what you want. Don't be afraid; nothing is off-limits. Anything you want."

I knew exactly what I wanted, what I'd been fantasizing about almost every single time I'd masturbated since last summer.

"I want you to stroke yourself like you were doing the day I was watching you, except this time I want it to be while you're looking at me. I want to see how much you want me."

His lips curled into a smile. "I have a fucked-up confession."

"What?"

"I was thinking of you that day. When you appeared at my door, for a split second, I thought my mind was playing tricks on me, thought I was imagining you at first."

"Really?"

"I haven't been able to picture much else for a long time." He pushed my body into him. "So your fantasy is to watch me jerk off to you, naughty girl?"

I swallowed. "Yes."

"That can be arranged. Three conditions, though…"

"Okay."

"One…you'll strip down completely naked for me."

"All right."

"Two…you'll help me."

"All right. And three?"

"It ends with me inside of you. I need to fuck you tonight. I can't wait any longer."

No longer able to form coherent words, I simply nodded and waited for direction as he moved his body back against the headboard.

He slid his hand down over his crotch and began to rub his cock slowly and firmly through his pants. "You have the most amazing tits, Amelia. Take that off so I can see them."

My breasts were tingling, so turned on by his demanding tone. There wasn't anything I wouldn't do for him right now. Sitting atop his lower legs, I slipped down my spaghetti straps. The material didn't fall completely off my chest, offering him only a partial view.

"Such a tease." He gritted his teeth and clutched his dick harder. "Take it off."

Lifting the material over my head, I tossed it aside. Suddenly stark-naked in front of him, I instinctually covered my breasts for a moment.

"Don't you dare," he warned with a sly smile. "I need to see all of you."

Justin unzipped his pants, and his fully hard cock sprung out. He wrapped his fist around it and began to slowly pump it up and down as he looked up at me. It was the sexiest thing I'd ever experienced.

"This is what you wanted?" he whispered, jerking himself hard while his eyes traveled over every inch of me.

I nodded as wetness trickled down my thigh.

He spoke between labored breaths. "You're so fucking beautiful, baby. So fucking beautiful."

I grinded against him, turned on beyond belief by the way he was looking at me along with his words.

"I can feel how wet you are against my legs. Keep rubbing yourself on me like that. I want to be covered in you," he said as he stroked himself harder.

I rocked against his legs and licked my fingertips, circling them around my nipples before squeezing my breasts together.

"Shit. Keep doing that."

He was covered in precum from shaft to tip. Knowing it was me who'd caused his arousal was so damn exciting.

He stopped and lay back to catch his breath for a moment, then simply said, "Now, you touch me."

I thought he'd never ask. Reaching over, I wrapped my fingers around his thick girth, which was so hot and wet in my hands. It felt incredible to touch him. I jerked him slowly at first, then moved faster, absolutely loving the feel of his precum all over my hand. Wanting so badly to taste him, I stopped to lick my palm as he watched every movement of my tongue. Then, I swallowed as he watched me intently.

"Fuck, that's hot," he said. When I started to lower my mouth to lick the fresh bead of moisture on his tip, he stopped me. "Don't do that. Not yet. I'll come in two seconds, and I want this to last."

"Okay." I smiled as I continued to stroke his cock, enjoying the moans escaping from him as he tried hard to control himself.

He eventually placed his hand over mine and said, "I can't take it anymore. I need to taste you too." He suddenly slid his body down under me, lifting me effortlessly over his mouth.

I gasped, shocked by the sudden sensation as he voraciously licked and sucked, alternating between penetrating me with his tongue and lapping over my clit. He held on to my hips as he guided me over his mouth, his stifled sounds of pleasure vibrating through my core. He devoured me unapologetically and roughly. It was the most unbelievable thing anyone had ever done to me.

When Justin sensed me losing control, he stopped. "As much as I'm dying for you to come on my face, I want us to come together with me inside of you." He slid back and kneeled above me. His cock was so unbelievably engorged. He continued jerking himself as he looked down into my eyes.

He suddenly took my face and began to kiss me deeply. He pushed his weight down onto me, and I landed on my back. His slick cock rubbed against my stomach as he kissed me with everything he had in him.

"Why the fuck did we wait so long?" he said against my lips.

I shook my head and pulled his hair, egging him on to kiss me harder, unable to get enough of his taste.

It felt like I was going to die if he didn't enter me soon. Intuitively, Justin pulled away from me and reached over to the bedside table. I heard the crinkle of a wrapper as he ripped the condom package open with his teeth. "I'm gonna fuck you so good, Amelia. I can't wait to hear what you sound like when I make you come. You ready?"

Biting my bottom lip, I nodded in affirmation. "God yes."

As Justin slid the condom on effortlessly, I heard Bea's frantic cry coming from down the hall.

We both froze, me with my legs wide-open, ready to receive him, and Justin with his hand on his dick.

No.

No.

215

Please no!

Not. Now.

We continued to stay still, as if not moving would somehow make it stop. When it became evident that we weren't going to get that lucky, Justin got up and slipped his underwear and pants back on. "I'll go check on her. Maybe she just needs to be changed."

"Are you sure?"

"Yeah. Stay right where you are...spread-eagle. Don't move. I'll be back."

Justin stopped in the bathroom to wash his hands before venturing down the hall.

Too worked up to argue in my stark-naked state, I waited impatiently for him to return.

After a couple of minutes, I heard his voice. "Amelia!"

I jumped up. "Is everything okay?"

"She's fine, but I need your help."

I ransacked Justin's drawer for something to throw on, then slipped one of his white T-shirts over my head before running toward Bea's room.

As soon as I entered the room, what smelled like a poop explosion fogged the air. Justin was holding Bea out away from him with both hands as he said, "We have a hazmat situation. She's covered in shit...got it all the way up to the back of her neck."

Bea started to laugh, prompting Justin to say, "You think this is funny? How do you shit all the way up to your head anyway? That's a special talent, Bumblebee."

She giggled again, and we both couldn't help cracking up right along with her despite the mini-disaster.

Once I calmed down, I said, "Okay. Here's what we're gonna do. Just stay holding her. I'm gonna get a plastic bag for her clothes and clean her as best I can with wipes. Then, we'll take her to the tub."

Justin continued to hold Bea while I cleaned her off. He was making me laugh while he spoke to her. "No wonder why you're smiling. I bet you feel real good now, don't you, Bumblebee? I'm gonna call the Guinness World Records tomorrow and report the biggest dump ever."

Even though I knew she couldn't really understand what he was saying, Bea responded to him as if she could. She thought he was the most amusing thing in the world.

I ended up just throwing her clothing in the downstairs trash while Justin stayed upstairs holding her out in the same position.

We took her to the bathroom and plopped her in the tub, using the removable showerhead to hose her down in an extra sudsy bath. She smelled like heaven once we were done. She was wrapped in a warm towel as Justin cradled her while I dried her feet.

He looked at me. "How did we go from what was happening in the other room to this?"

I kissed her toes. "Sort of the story of my life."

"She's wide-awake now, you know."

"Well, that just figures. I think I should go feed her," I said.

"Yeah. I'd be surprised if there was anything left in her stomach after that."

Justin followed me back to my room and lay his head on my shoulder while I nursed Bea. It was the first time I hadn't bothered to cover myself in front of him. The three of us ended up falling asleep together in my bed.

Even though there was no sex that evening, it was still one of the most memorable nights of my life, not just because of all that happened but because the next day, everything would change.

CHAPTER 17

Justin was still sleeping while I made coffee in the kitchen. It was a typical lazy Sunday morning until a simple text turned my entire world upside down. I looked over at Justin's phone, which was charging on the counter.

Olivia: Ok. Call me when you decide.

Olivia?

Immediately remembering that Olivia was his ex-girlfriend, the only long-term relationship he'd had besides Jade, my heart started to palpitate.

What did that mean? They'd been talking?

I didn't even think twice about whether snooping was right or wrong; I had to know. Scrolling up, I read the two other messages above the first.

Olivia: Have you given it any more thought?
Justin: Yes. I need a little more time.

A feeling of dread formed deep within my stomach. Last night had been a turning point in our relationship—or so I'd thought. Justin had made me feel like I could trust him implicitly. Knowing that he'd been communicating with his ex—that he'd been keeping something from me—felt like someone had just poured a bucket of ice water over my head, waking me up from a delusion.

Staring blankly out the large kitchen window, I noticed it was drizzling outside. It was going to be a cold, raw day. I didn't even turn when Justin came downstairs. I heard the smack of his lips as he kissed Bea, who was playing on the mat nearby.

My body stiffened when he came up behind me, pressing his morning wood against my ass as he kissed my neck and said, "Good morning."

When I turned around, he could immediately tell that something was wrong from the look on my face.

His expression dampened. "Amelia...talk to me."

Instead of answering him, I walked over to the counter and handed him his phone. "What do you need more time for?"

Justin stared down at it and blinked a few times. "I was going to talk to you today about something. I didn't want to take away from Bea's first Halloween."

It felt like the walls were closing in on me. "I feel so stupid for trusting in all of this."

"Whoa. Hang on!" His face started to turn red in anger. "Exactly what conclusion are you jumping to right now?"

"It doesn't take a scientist, Justin. You've been texting back and forth with your ex-girlfriend. Trying to decide on something."

"That's right. Something is going on, but it has nothing to do with her. There's a reason she's an ex. You have nothing to worry about. Did you not see what you fucking did to me last night?"

"Why else are you in discussions with her, then?"

He raked his fingers through his hair and took a deep breath to compose himself. "Olivia is the tour manager for Calvin Sprockett."

"Calvin Sprockett the singer?"

"Yes." He laughed slightly at my reaction. "The legendary Grammy-winning artist. That one."

"Okay...so what is she discussing with you?"

"He's going on a North American and European tour for five months. The performer who was supposed to be opening for him just unexpectedly went into rehab. Olivia's tight with my agent, Steve Rollins. They met when we were dating. Olivia was sort of like a manager to me back then too. Anyway, I guess Steve gave her one of my recent demos from the September recording session, and she played it for Calvin. He asked her if I was interested in being the replacement opening act on the tour."

"Are you kidding me? Oh my God. Justin...that's a dream!"

It was strange to feel happiness for him and also like my world was crumbling at the same time. The one thing I knew for sure was that I was not going to let my fear stand in the way of supporting this once-in-a-lifetime opportunity.

Justin went on, "I'm sorry I haven't mentioned it yet. I really just wanted yesterday to be perfect. I swear to God I was going to tell you before the weekend was over."

I racked my brain to think of something to say that wouldn't show my apprehension. "Does he know you've never toured before?"

Justin nodded. "At first, I thought it was strange that he would take a chance on someone like me, but I've since learned that Cal is apparently known for introducing brand-new talent on his tours. That was how Dave Aarons got his start."

"Really? Wow...and he chose you."

He smiled hesitantly. "Yeah."

"Your style totally jives with his too."

"I know. It's a good fit."

Panic aside, my heart also filled with pride. I reached up to hug him. "Holy crap. I'm so proud of you," I said, despite the fact that it felt like everything was falling apart.

"I haven't accepted it yet, Amelia."

I pulled back suddenly to look him in the eyes. "You're going to, right?"

He frowned. "I don't know."

"You can't turn it down."

"I wanted to discuss it with you first."

"What is there to discuss?"

"I'd be leaving you and Bea for five fucking months."

"You never exactly said your stay here was permanent in the first place. Technically, you've been on borrowed time. You realize that, don't you?"

He didn't address my question when he said, "This would be different than simply being in New York. I won't be able to come to the island whenever I want or when you need something. The tour is continuous. They stick to a tight schedule. He likes to do two or three shows in each city."

"You don't have to worry about me." As much as I didn't want him to leave, there was no way I was going to let him give up an opportunity like this out of guilt. He would come to resent Bea and me. That was the last thing I wanted.

"I don't have to worry about you? Do you remember the state I found you in?"

"A lot has changed since then. Bea has grown. She's less dependent on me and sleeping better. Don't use me as an excuse. Five months will fly by." In truth, it seemed like an eternity. So much could happen in five months. In fact, so much *had* happened between us in that same amount of time. We'd grown into our own unique version of a family.

"You say it will fly by now, but when you have no one around to relieve you when you want to leave the house or go grocery shopping, you'll feel it. When you get lonely at night, you'll feel it...unless you call the asshat next door. I'm sure Roger will take full advantage of me being gone."

It seemed like he was trying to make up any excuse in the world as to why going was a bad idea.

"I don't want you to leave, Justin. It scares the hell out of me, but I just know you'll regret it for the rest of your life if you don't go. There isn't even a decision to make with an offer like this."

He looked down at his shoes and stared at the floor for the longest time before he conceded, "You're right. I'll always wonder what could have been. And I don't think I'll get another opportunity like it in my lifetime."

My throat felt like sandpaper when I swallowed. "Well, then you have your answer."

Justin stared into space and said, "Shit. This is really happening." He then turned to me with a nervous expression, as if he wanted me to make one last attempt to talk him out of it.

"Bea and I will still be here."

"I'd be coming back about a month after her first birthday." He looked over at where Bea was playing. "I'll miss it."

Trying to remain calm, I asked, "When do you need to let Olivia know by?"

"No later than the next couple of days."

I hesitated before asking, "Are you sure Jade wasn't right about her?"

"What do you mean?"

"That she's trying to get back together with you. It seems like a very big gesture on her part, to work to get you on this tour."

"She's always been a big supporter of my music. There's nothing else going on there, Amelia."

"Is she actually going to be on the tour the whole time?"

"Yes. She manages it."

"Is she still dating someone?"

He answered reluctantly, "I don't think so."

Adrenaline pumped through me as jealousy took hold. My cheeks felt hot. "I see."

"I told you the story about my breakup with Olivia. She wasn't the one for me. It's over. It doesn't matter that she's on the tour. Please don't focus on that. It's a waste of energy."

"Okay. I'll try, but just imagine how you would feel if I were going on a bus tour with an ex for five months. You can't even deal with Roger next door. You lived with her for two years. You can surely see why it makes me uncomfortable."

"Of course, I get it, but I can't stress enough that Olivia and I are over. Yes, she happens to be going on this tour, but it means nothing to me."

"All right. I'll try not to let it bother me."

My heart felt like it weighed a thousand pounds. I couldn't allow him see that I was devastated by his impending departure. I suddenly said, "Hey, is it okay if I take a quick jog on the beach? Will you keep an eye on Bea?"

"Since when do you run?"

"I'd like to start."

He stared at me suspiciously. "Yeah. Of course I'll watch her."

Without delay, I ran upstairs and changed into my exercise clothes as fast as I could.

Once outside, my legs took off faster than my heart could sustain. I couldn't keep up with my own will to run away from the heartbreak of knowing he was really going away. It wasn't him leaving that was devastating, but rather the fear that he wouldn't want to come back to this mundane life on the island. He would be experiencing something completely new. A music tour would be chock-full of excitement—temptation. No limitations.

But the only thing worse than him leaving would be if he decided *not* to go because of my insecurities. While I couldn't stop him, the one thing I *could* do was attempt to protect myself in the only way I knew how. For the remainder of his time on the island, I couldn't allow myself to get any closer to him physically or emotionally. If we could survive him going away, then I would know that he was serious about us. Until then, it was necessary to live my life under the assumption that he may not be coming back. This tour would be the ultimate test.

The beach air filled my throat as I ran. It was so windy that sand flew into my eyes and mouth as I dodged seagulls.

Finally arriving back at the house, I stopped just inside the door before entering. Justin had the radio on and was dancing around the kitchen with Bea. She laughed every time he spun her around real fast. The music faded into the background, taking a back seat to the loud noise of the anxious thoughts passing through my mind. It hit me that I wasn't going to be the only one devastated by Justin leaving. Bea had no clue he would be gone in a matter of days. She wouldn't even be able to understand *why* he left. My heart hurt for her, and he wasn't even gone yet.

———

It was always when you wanted time to stand still that it flew the fastest.

After Justin accepted the tour gig, he found out he only had a week and a half before he had to report to Minneapolis. He was going to drive the Range Rover back to New York, then catch a flight to meet Calvin and the rest of the crew in Minnesota, where they would kick off the tour.

Because the other musician had dropped out so suddenly, there wasn't a lot of time to prepare. Justin had gotten lucky because when he'd explained the situation to the managers at his day job, they had agreed to grant him an unpaid leave of absence. The president of the software company that Justin worked for was a huge Calvin Sprockett fan, so that had helped.

While on the outside, everything was falling into place, in my mind, everything was falling apart. I wanted so badly to be thrilled for him—and a part of me was. I just couldn't separate that part from my own sadness and fear.

Though we used those final days wisely, spending time together with Bea, things were extremely tense between us. Right after he'd made the decision to go on the tour, I'd explained to Justin during coffee one morning that I didn't think it was a good idea for us to take things any further physically before he left. I'd told him it would only make him leaving more difficult for me. Even though he claimed to understand, I knew deep down he saw it for what it was: a lack of faith in his loyalty to me. I retreated to my own room every night, and he didn't try to stop me.

Two days before his scheduled departure, I had to go to Providence to grab my stuff out of storage. I could no longer afford to keep it there, since I wasn't working. I planned to donate as much of it as I could and have a yard sale in Newport for some of the smaller items. Most of it was stuff I no longer needed, anyway. My friend Tracy's husband met me with his truck and helped me load most of the belongings before he transported the majority to a Salvation Army store.

Justin had stayed behind in Newport with Bea while I made the trek to Providence.

The entire ride back home to the island, I could almost hear the clock ticking in my brain. The past several months played in my head like a movie that was nearing its end. There was no doubt in my mind that this exposure would give Justin unprecedented fame. He was about to be swallowed up whole, and I really didn't think he knew what was coming. Having witnessed it firsthand on a smaller scale, I knew how women reacted to him. That was about to be multiplied by a thousand. His life would never be the same again. Neither would mine.

When I returned to the beach house, things were unusually quiet. Something that smelled like tomato sauce was baking in the oven. With a click of the stove light, I could see it was lasagna.

"Hello?" I yelled.

"We're upstairs!" I heard Justin call out.

It sounded like it was raining inside of Justin's room. The sound was mixed with tranquil music. When I opened the door, my heart nearly stopped.

Justin's bed was gone. In its place was Bea's white crib. A fluffy butter-yellow area rug had been placed on the floor. Illuminated stars were projected onto the ceiling as they slowly moved. The sounds of nature were coming from a machine on the bureau. A framed Anne Geddes picture was mounted onto the wall, depicting a sleeping baby dressed as a bumblebee.

I covered my mouth. "How... When...did you...?"

He was holding Bea. "She needed her own room. Bumblebee's getting big. She can't sleep in there with you forever. It's time. You being in Providence today was the perfect opportunity to surprise you before I left."

Bea's eyes were transfixed upon the floating stars on the ceiling as she moved her little head, stretching her neck to follow their path.

I smiled. "She really loves those, huh?"

"I knew she would. Sometimes when she's up at night with me, I take her out on the deck. We look up at the stars together. Maybe she'll look at these and think of me while I'm away." His words squeezed at my heart.

"I never knew you did that with her." I walked around the room, admiring the transformation. "Where is all your stuff?"

"I broke down my bed, threw it in the corner of my office for now."

Something about him vacating the bedroom and turning it over to Bea suddenly seemed so final and didn't sit right with me. My heart started to pound in panic. "You're not coming back."

"What?"

"You gave up your room because you know you're not coming back here. You'll go away, become a big star. You'll visit, but deep down, you know you won't be living here anymore."

It was like all of my insecurities suddenly had a voice. I really hadn't meant to lay everything out on the line like that. It had all just come out after a long, stressful day.

Justin was speechless at first. When he finally spoke, his tone bordered on angry. "That's what you think?"

"I don't know. I guess I'm just thinking out loud."

"I made this nursery because she shouldn't be sleeping in your fucking room. She deserves a nice space of her own. I was planning this long before I ever knew about the tour. I gradually collected this stuff over the past month, hid everything in my closet." He reached into the bureau drawer for a pile of receipts, took them out, and roughly threw them up in the air. The white slips rained down onto the floor. "Look at the dates on these. They're from weeks ago."

I felt really stupid. "I'm sorry. I've just been stressed over you leaving. I was trying not to let it show, and I guess it finally caught up with me."

"You think I'm trying to separate myself from you? You're the one who put up a gigantic wall the second I told you about the tour. If I had my way, I would want nothing more than to sleep in *your* fucking bed tonight—inside of you—because I'm leaving in less than two days. Two days, Amelia! Instead of enjoying each other, you've been shutting me out. I'm respecting your wishes and not pushing anything because I know this is hard enough for you, but fuck!"

Feeling ashamed, I said, "I'm sorry for overreacting. I made this about more than the nursery. The room is beautiful. Really."

"I'm gonna go check on the food." Justin placed Bea in her crib and abruptly left the room, slamming the door behind him. I looked up at the stars on the ceiling, deeply regretting my loss of composure. The sound machine had switched to a medley of thunder and lightning. It was a fitting representation of the mood.

Dinner was a quiet one that night.

With no permanent bedroom anymore, Justin slept on the couch.

I didn't sleep at all.

———

Justin would be gone tomorrow.

I needed to fix things before he left, or I would regret it. Bea was quietly napping in her new nursery, so I figured I would take the opportunity to talk to him.

Justin's mountain of black luggage was piled in the corner of his office. The sight of that alone gave me anxiety.

As I made my way down the hall, I heard the sound of him beating the punching bag coming from the exercise room.

Standing in the doorway, I watched as he hit the bag with more force than I'd ever seen him exhibit before. Justin was completely in the zone and either hadn't noticed me or pretended not to.

"Justin," I said.

He didn't stop. It was unclear whether he could hear me, since he was wearing earbuds. I could hear the music blasting through them.

"Justin," I repeated, louder.

He continued to ignore me as he hit the bag even harder.

"Justin!" I screamed.

This time he looked over at me briefly, but he didn't stop punching. That confirmed that he was *definitely* ignoring me.

Determined not to run away from this situation no matter how painful, I stayed in the doorway watching him for several minutes until he finally stopped. Leaning against the punching bag and gripping it, he looked down at the floor, gasping for air but saying nothing. After a long moment of silence, he finally spoke.

"I'm losing you, and I haven't even left yet." He turned to me. "This tour is not worth that."

"You have to go. You're not losing me. I just don't know how to handle it."

A stream of sweat trickled down the length of his glistening chest as he walked toward me but stopped short of touching me. The smell of his skin mixed with cologne served as a reminder as to just how much I was kidding myself when it came to my ability to steer away from him sexually.

"It's understandable. Completely understandable," he said.

"What is?"

"All of your worries...I would feel the same if you were the one going on a tour. That scene is no joke. I get why you're scared."

It didn't exactly comfort me to know that he felt my worry was founded.

He continued, "It's not that you don't trust me now, but you think that environment will somehow change me, make me want different things than I want now."

"Yes. That's exactly right. If you understand my fear, then why are you so angry at me for it?"

"It's more like...frustrated. Everything is happening so fast, and I'm running out of time to fix this before I leave. We have to trust that what we've been working toward is worth more than all of the crazy shit that life might throw at us in the next five months. I'm also scared because I don't ever want to let you or Bea down." The look of fear in his eyes was unprecedented, and the uncertainty in them made me uneasy.

"Let me down?"

"Yes. Bea is getting attached to me. While she won't remember these past several months, she's only getting older and will start to understand more as time passes. This isn't a game. I know that. I would rather die than hurt her."

Even though he wasn't saying it in so many words, I took his statement to mean that he still wasn't sure if he wanted a child, which in turn meant he might have been unsure about us. It pained me to know that he still held doubts, given how phenomenal he was with Bea.

And with me.

This tour was forcing Justin to do something he never would have done otherwise; it was forcing him to leave us, to step back and reflect on the responsibility he had unknowingly walked into the day he'd decided to come to Newport one month early last summer, expecting an empty house. He had certainly gotten way more than he'd ever bargained for. He'd been our rock ever since. Even though I didn't want to lose him, he needed this separation to figure out what he truly wanted.

I knew that I truly wanted *him*. I also knew that I loved him enough to let him go. And I certainly didn't want Bea to get any more attached to him if we weren't strong enough to survive this. It was more important now to protect her heart than my own. I vowed not to make him feel guilty any longer.

I reluctantly admitted my realization to him. "Maybe this time away is necessary. It will help you realize what you really want out of life."

He surprised me when he admitted, "I think you're right."

His agreement caused my stomach to drop a bit. At the same time, I vowed to be strong, to let fate take its course. I wouldn't act stupidly and sabotage anything one way or the other, because I loved him. So much. I wanted the best for him, wanted him to be happy even if that didn't involve Bea and me.

The universe had already shown that it had plans for me, ones beyond my control. Bea was proof of that. I had to trust that something bigger than us was at the helm and that this latest challenge had a purpose. The only thing I was sure of was that it would either tear us apart or make us stronger than ever.

At the end of five months, I'd have my answer.

———

It rained that entire day.

As if Bea could sense that something was off, she refused to sleep in her new crib that night. It made me think that it was quite possible babies had a sixth sense. Ever since Justin had redone the nursery, she'd loved sleeping in there and watching the stars. But tonight—Justin's last night—Bea only quieted in the safety of my arms. Intuition, maybe. So, I let her lie next to me in my bed, even though, like me, she couldn't fall asleep.

The closer it got to midnight, the more melancholy I became as insomnia continued to win out.

Justin's knock was light. "Amelia, are you awake?"

"Yeah. Come in."

He entered and lay down on my bed next to us, repositioning the covers. "I can't sleep."

"Are you nervous?" I asked.

"Scared as hell is more like it."

"About what in particular?"

He let out a single sarcastic laugh. "Everything. I'm scared to leave you alone, scared Bea won't remember me…scared she *will* remember me—remember that I left. I'm scared to perform in front of thousands of people, scared to fuck up. You name it—I'm worried about it."

"You shouldn't be worried about performing. You're gonna knock 'em dead."

Ignoring my assurance, he took Bea from next to me and placed her on his chest. Her breathing started to even out.

It broke my heart when he softly kissed her head and whispered in her ear, "I'm sorry, Bumblebee."

My mood had been all over the place throughout the day, alternating between feeling sorry for myself and Bea to feeling proud and excited for Justin. In this particular intimate moment, I felt compelled not as his lover—but as his friend—to help him understand that he deserved this opportunity he'd worked his entire life for. He had nothing to be sorry for. That was how I knew I truly loved him, because in the eleventh hour, all I wanted was to take away his guilt and make him feel good, regardless of how much his leaving hurt.

"Nana would be so proud of you, Justin. She always used to tell me that she believed you were destined for greatness. When you go out there, don't even think about how many people are watching. Just sing for her, sing to Nana...do this for her."

"She'd be pleased with how you turned out too, Patch... all you've undertaken. The mother you've become despite how shitty your own mother was. Nana would be so damn proud. *I'm* so damn proud."

With Bea now fast asleep on his chest, Justin leaned in to kiss me. He began to devour my mouth, firm but tenderly. We kissed for several minutes, careful not to wake Bea.

He said into my mouth, "I want to make love to you so badly right now. But at the same time, I get why you think that would make tomorrow even harder. I don't know if I could ever walk out of here after that."

233

"I don't think Bea would allow it right now, anyway. She looks too comfortable."

He looked down at her and smiled. "You're probably right." He turned to me, his blue eyes luminescent in the darkness. "Promise me a few things."

"Okay."

"Promise me that we'll video chat at least every other day."

"Sure. That'll be easy."

"Promise me that if you get lonely, you'll call me anytime—day or night."

"I will. What else?"

"Promise me that we won't keep anything important from each other and that we'll always be honest with each other."

That one made me feel a little queasy as I started pondering what things he anticipated having to be honest with me about.

"Okay. I promise." I swallowed. "Anything else?"

"No. I just want to sleep next to you and Bea tonight. Is that okay?"

"Of course." I took his hand. "It's going to be okay, Justin. We'll be okay."

He smiled and whispered, "Yeah."

Justin placed Bea between the two of us. As she lay in the middle, Justin and I looked into each other's eyes until sleep finally claimed us.

———

When I woke up the next morning, panic hit me for a brief moment because Justin was gone from the bed. Looking at the clock, I calmed down, realizing it was only 9 a.m. He wasn't scheduled to leave until around noon.

The smell of his signature coffee brewing wafted up the

stairwell and immediately made me sad. It would be the last time I would smell his coffee fusion for a long time.

Feeling my eyes getting watery, I took my sweet time before going downstairs, hoping to regain my composure before then. I did some mindless things: cleaned the bedroom, threw a load of laundry in, anything so he wouldn't have to see me break down. Bea watched me from her Exersaucer as I ran around my room like a maniac.

Justin walked in as I was vacuuming my rug. I wouldn't look up at him as I moved the vacuum back and forth.

"Amelia."

I pushed it faster along the carpet.

"Amelia!" he yelled.

I finally looked at him. He must have seen the sadness in my eyes because his expression slowly darkened. I just stared at him as the vacuum continued to run even though I'd stopped moving it. A teardrop fell down my cheek, and I knew I had officially lost my ability to hide my feelings.

He slowly approached and shut off the vacuum, his hand lingering over mine, which was still gripping the handle.

"I've been waiting to have coffee with you," he said. "I *need* to have breakfast with you and Bea one last time before I leave. It's my favorite thing in the world."

I wiped my eyes. "Okay."

"It's fucking okay to be sad. Stop trying to hide it from me. I won't hide it, either." His voice cracked a little. "I'm so fucking sad right now, Amelia. The last thing I want to do right now is leave you guys. But time is running out. Don't waste it hiding from me."

He was right.

Sniffling, I nodded. "Let's go have coffee."

Justin lifted Bea into his arms as he closed his eyes tightly and breathed in her scent as if he wanted to burn it into his memory. When he pulled back, he lifted her up into the air as she looked down at him. "Are you my Bumblebee?"

She smiled at him, and if that didn't feel like a knife to the heart, I didn't know what did. My emotions were all over the place again. A part of me was still selfishly angry at him.

How could you leave us?

Why haven't you told me you love me?

Why haven't you told Bea you love her?

You don't love us.

A bigger part was angry at myself for even having those kinds of thoughts again. I was coming to realize that it wasn't so much the fact that he was leaving that bothered me as it was the fact that he was leaving me so unsure about where things really stood with us.

He treated me as if he loved me, but even when we were acting like a family, he'd never defined our relationship, never even labeled me his girlfriend.

As Justin prepared the mugs of coffee like he always did, I followed every move he made and couldn't help but wonder what the next time I watched him make coffee would be like.

When he handed me my cup, I put on the best smile I could. I didn't want him to leave thinking of my sad face. But his own expression turned sullen.

"What is it, Justin?"

"I just feel helpless. If you need anything, I told Tom you might call him from time to time. I left his number on the fridge. He said anytime, day or night, don't hesitate. Call him instead of that tool next door, please. I also installed a new alarm system." He waved a hand, leading me to the door. "Come on, I'll show you how to use it."

Everything he was saying was muffled as my eyes followed

his fingers, hands, and lips as he explained how to maneuver the alarm control pad. His voice was fading into the background, losing the battle with my accumulating panic.

Justin took notice and stopped talking. "You know what? I'll email you the instructions." He stared at me for a bit before pulling me into an embrace. He held me for what seemed like several minutes, slowly rubbing my back. There wasn't anything we could do to slow down time.

I watched from the window as Justin loaded his luggage into the back of the Range Rover.

When he came back inside, we took a quick but quiet walk on the beach with Bea. At one point, I stayed behind as Justin took Bea closer to the shore. He whispered something in her ear. That made me curious, but I never asked him what he'd said to her.

Once we returned to the house, it was time for Justin to leave. The morning had flown by way too fast; it almost seemed unfair.

Trying to suppress my tears, I said, "I can't believe this moment is finally here."

Miraculously, I was able to keep the crying at bay because, mostly, I was in shock. The best thing I could do for him right now was to reassure him that I would support him while he experienced this new chapter, let him know that I would be there for him in the very way we'd started—as a friend.

I returned his own sentiments from earlier. "The same goes for you, Justin. If you need me, or you get lonely, or maybe you're feeling doubtful, you call me day or night. I'll be here."

Justin was still holding Bea as he placed his forehead against mine and simply said, "Thank you." We stayed like that for a while with Bea sandwiched in the middle of us.

Still wanting to avoid bursting into tears, I forced myself away. "You'd better go. You'll miss your flight."

He kissed Bea's head gently, then said, "I'll call you when I land in Minneapolis."

Bea and I stood in the doorway, watching as he walked away. He got in the car but didn't move. He looked over at us as we continued to wait. Bea was reaching out her hand to him and babbling; she obviously had no clue what was going on.

Why isn't he moving?

He suddenly got out of the car, slamming the door. My heartbeat accelerated with each step he took toward me. Before I could ask him whether he'd forgotten something, his hand wrapped around the back of my head, pulling me into him. He opened his mouth wide over mine, plunging his tongue inside and twirling it around at an almost desperate pace as he groaned into my mouth. He tasted like coffee and a flavor all his own. This was not the time to be getting aroused, but I couldn't help my body's reaction.

When he forced himself back, his eyes were hazy, filled with just as much confusion as passion. I had to once again remind myself of the old adage of setting someone free, that if they came back, they were yours; if they didn't, they never were.

Please come back to me.

He said nothing else as he walked back to the car, started it, and this time...drove off.

CHAPTER 18

Blind faith.

That was the only thing helping me get through this first month with Justin away. Somehow, I just had to convince myself to trust his actions and judgment, even though I couldn't be there to see what was actually happening.

He called us every night. Sometimes, it would be during what he referred to as his "relaxation time" around 8 p.m., right before their 9 p.m. performances. Other times, it would be during his lunch or dinner break. From what he'd told me, his daily itinerary was jam-packed with sound checks and rehearsals at each new venue. The only downtime was after the show, and by then, he was roped into after-parties or just plain exhausted. If the band stayed more than one night in the same city, they would all check into a hotel. If they had to be in another locale the next day, they would drive through the night and sleep on the bus.

There were two buses, one for Calvin and the main band and one for Justin and the rest of the crew. According to

Justin, each bus slept about twelve people. I never asked him which bus Olivia slept in because I was afraid of the answer.

Blind faith.

Okay, well, even though I chose to have faith in him, I still discovered a little window into their world that satisfied my episodes of paranoia. It came in the form of Olivia's Instagram page.

Back when Jade had lived at the beach house and used to complain about Olivia commenting on all of Justin's posts, I had searched his page to check out Olivia's profile. I'd stalked her online occasionally even before Justin had left. Now, each day, she posted pictures from the tour. Many were just scenic shots, like the sunrise taken from the bus as they entered a new city or whatever the band and crew happened to be eating. Other shots were of Calvin and his band backstage.

One particular night when Bea was sleeping, I opened up Instagram. Olivia had posted a picture of Justin performing. It was just a standard shot of him leaning into the microphone with the spotlight shining down onto his beautiful face, which was framed by that five-o'clock shadow. It made me long to be there, to see him perform on the big stage. When I looked lower, I noticed the hashtags.

#LadyKiller
#JustinBanks
#UsedToTapThat
#ExesOfInstagram

Despite the fact that it bothered me, I refused to bring it up to Justin, refused to play the role of jealous girlfriend, especially when he hadn't labeled me his girlfriend at all.

A knock at the door startled me. I shut my laptop.

Who would be coming by this late?

Thankfully, in addition to the alarm system, Justin had drilled a peephole into my door before he'd left.

A woman with long brown hair like mine was standing there shivering. She looked innocent enough, so I opened the door. "Can I help you?"

"Hi." She grinned. "Amelia, right?"

"Yes."

"I wanted to introduce myself. My name is Susan. I live in the blue house next door."

"Oh. Did Roger move?"

"No. I'm actually his wife."

Wife?

"Oh. I thought he was—"

"Divorced?" She smiled.

"Yeah."

"He is…technically. We reconciled when he came to Irvine to visit our daughter recently. It was supposed to be a one-week visit, but it turned into three weeks. Alyssa and I ended up coming back here with him."

"Wow. I had no idea. That is fantastic." I waved my hand. "My gosh, where are my manners? Come in. Come in."

"Thank you," she said, wiping her feet and entering the house. "Our daughter is sleeping now, but I'd love for you to meet her as well. She just turned eight."

"My daughter, Bea, is also sleeping. She's almost nine months."

"Roger mentioned you had a baby."

"I've heard so much about Alyssa as well."

"Roger also mentioned that you and he were friendly."

"We're just friends, in case you were wondering."

241

She hesitated. "It's okay if it was more than that. We weren't together at the time."

"No. It wouldn't be okay. At least for me, it wouldn't. I would want to know. I get what it's like to wonder about stuff like that when you care about someone."

A look of relief washed over her face. "Well, thank you for clarifying. I'd be lying if I said that I hadn't wondered."

"I'm sort of in love with my roommate, actually. He's currently on tour. A musician. I totally understand jealousy."

She pulled up a chair and sat down. "Oh, man. You want to talk about it?"

"Do you drink tea?"

"I do. I'd love some."

Susan and I became fast friends that night. I opened up to her about my history with Justin, and she offered to help me out with Bea if I ever needed a babysitter. She said Alyssa would get a kick out of watching Bea with her. It made me thankful that nothing ever had happened between Roger and me, because that would have made things awkward.

I had to admit, when she'd first showed, finding out that Roger was back with his wife made me feel even more alone. But that selfish thought was quickly replaced by the happiness brought on by a newfound female friendship, something my life had been seriously lacking.

Susan and I hung out regularly. She encouraged me to try new things and to get out more. I joined a Mommy and Me class with Bea and started utilizing the day care at the gym to be able to work out a few times a week. I was doing the best I could to develop a new routine with Justin gone.

The daylight hours were becoming more bearable; night-time was the tough part. With Bea asleep and Justin busiest in the evenings, I always felt the most alone when darkness fell.

Late one night, around midnight, a text came in.

> **Justin:** We're in Boise. One of the crew members is from here and brought his baby into the bus before the show tonight. It made me miss Bea even more.
>
> **Amelia:** We miss you too.
>
> **Justin:** The tour is stopping in Worcester, Massachusetts, in a couple of weeks. What are the chances you could come see me?

That was only a little over an hour away from me. It would be the closest and only tour stop anywhere near Newport for the remainder of his time away.

> **Amelia:** I don't think the noise and environment would be good for Bea. But maybe I can find a sitter.

It was likely that Susan could watch Bea for me, but I specifically hadn't told Justin about her for selfish reasons. I quite liked his jealousy toward Roger. It was the only upper hand I had at the moment. So, I decided to keep their reconciliation to myself for a while longer.

> **Justin:** I agree. It would be too loud and crazy for her.
>
> **Amelia:** I'll work on it.
>
> **Justin:** It's only one night, unfortunately. The bus leaves for Philly sometime after the show.

Amelia: Fingers crossed I can make it.

Justin: It's not just Bea I miss.

My heart fluttered.

Amelia: I miss you too.

Justin: Sweet dreams.

Amelia: xo

———

It was the day of the concert, and I was getting really antsy. Since it was unclear whether I would be able to secure a babysitter to see Justin in Massachusetts, he'd sent me a laminated backstage pass that would allow me exclusive access in the event something came through at the last minute. He said he wasn't sure he'd be available to greet me if and when I arrived. Having the card would be a safer bet in case he was in the middle of a sound check or even in the middle of performing, depending on how late I got there.

I wasn't going to know until the last minute whether I would be able to make it, since my only babysitter option was Susan. She happened to have an important appointment in Boston today that she couldn't cancel. Depending on traffic, she wasn't sure if she'd make it back in time.

I'd toyed with the idea of driving up there with Bea during the day, but that was no longer an option, since she'd come down with a cold. Taking her out in the freezing weather to a crowded venue like that was not a good idea; she could catch pneumonia.

By the time evening rolled around, Susan called from the road to say that she'd gotten stuck in traffic and hadn't even made it out of Boston's Ted Williams Tunnel yet. At that point, I knew I would miss the start of the show, if I were lucky enough to make it at all. I was honestly heartbroken. This was my one chance to see Justin for the entire tour. It didn't seem fair.

Nevertheless, I got myself dressed up anyway, continuing to hold out hope. Donning a short and tight blue satin dress with black lace accents, I looked more like a lingerie model than a stay-at-home mom. In the event that I got to see him tonight, I wanted to knock his socks off. I was, after all, competing with an entire world of models and groupies vying for his attention. That thought made my stomach turn as I curled my hair into long, loose tendrils and put on my matte plum lipstick. Something told me all of this effort was in vain, but I needed to be prepared to fly out the door if Susan made it back here.

When the clock struck eight, it became clear I was going to miss his performance no matter what happened.

At eight forty-five, Justin called right before he had to report to the stage.

"No luck?" he asked.

"I'm so sorry. I wanted to make it work so badly, but she's not here yet. There's no way I'll get there in time tonight." My voice was shaky, but I refused to cry or else my mascara would run down my face.

"Fuck, Amelia. I'm not gonna lie. I was looking forward to seeing you so much. It was what got me through this week. Of course, I understand though. Bea comes first. Always. Kiss her for me. I hope she feels better."

We stayed on the line, the disappointment audible through our silence and the long sigh of frustration that escaped him.

I heard a man's voice before Justin said, "Shit. They're calling me."

"Okay. Have a good show."

"I'll be thinking of you the whole time."

Before I could respond, the line went dead.

Fifteen minutes later, there was a frantic knock at the door. When I opened it, Susan was panting. "Go. Go, Amelia!"

"It might be too late. The show will be over when I get there."

"Yes. But you'll get to see him before they take off, right?"

"I think so. I'm not sure exactly when the bus leaves for the next city."

"Don't waste time talking to me. Just tell me where Bea is."

"She's sleeping. I left a long note with instructions on the counter."

"I've got it." She waved me off. "Go get your man, Amelia."

Blowing her a kiss, I said, "I owe you big time. Thank you for this."

It had been a while since I'd last driven on the highway at night. The beginnings of a panic attack started to creep in as I sped up I-95. Trying to focus on seeing Justin and not the cars whizzing past me, I was able to keep from escalating into a full-blown attack. The GPS served as my copilot because I had no idea where I was going. This part of Massachusetts was completely foreign to me.

Sweat permeated my body as I got closer. Even though it was cold out, I turned on the air conditioner for circulation to calm myself. What was I doing? The show was over. I hadn't texted him. I told myself it was because I wanted to surprise him, but a part of me wanted to see what things were like when he *wasn't* expecting me.

Parking in the large lot outside of the venue, I wrapped my arms around myself. I'd rushed out of the house so fast, I'd forgotten a coat. Running in my high-heeled boots—the same ones I'd worn with my Catwoman costume—I made my way to a tall chain-link fence that separated the VIP area from the parking lot.

Two black tour buses with tinted windows sat just inside the gate. A guard wearing a headset stood at the entrance. Groups of women gathered nearby, probably hoping for a glimpse of the artists.

My breath was visible in the night air as I flashed my special badge and spoke to the guard. "Is the show over?"

"Almost. Calvin is in the middle of the last set."

"Where can I find Justin Banks? He gave me this access card."

"Justin is in Bus Two. That's the one on the right."

My heart was hammering against my chest as I made my way through the gravelly lot to the bus.

I opened the door. To my surprise, no one seemed to be inside. Or at least, that was what I assumed until noises coming from the back bedroom proved otherwise. There were several coffin-like beds on the sides, but Justin had mentioned that each bus had one master suite in the back. He and the crew alternated who got to sleep in it each night.

A lump formed in my throat as I approached the closed wooden door. The sound of a woman moaning could be heard from behind it.

The guard had said Justin was in here.

I had to know.

I had to open it. I had to see it with my own eyes.

My faith might have been blind, but it was about to get an eyeful.

Slowly turning the knob, I inched the door open a crack. All I saw was a mane of dark hair. A woman was riding him as he lay flat. It looked like Olivia, but I didn't know for sure.

It could have been any woman. It didn't matter who it was. They didn't notice me.

My stomach started to turn, and bile was rising. I couldn't look anymore. I just couldn't.

Exiting the bus, my legs felt wobbly. I walked in a daze as numbness consumed me. My vision was blurry. My heart felt like it was cracking slowly with each step off the bus.

Had I been an idiot for thinking he would wait? That he could withstand the enormous temptation being thrown in his face every day? He had never made any promises, and that was for good reason.

You're a fool, Amelia.

I would have expected to be crying, but for some reason, the shock seemed to have frozen my tear ducts. My eyes felt raw, cold, devoid of any ability to produce moisture.

My phone chimed from an incoming text.

I missed you tonight so fucking much.

CHAPTER 19

What?

How can he be texting me while he's fucking someone else?

Adrenaline rushed through me, taking my nerves on a roller coaster of emotions.

> **Amelia:** Are you on the bus?
>
> **Justin:** No. At Dave and Buster's down the road from the venue, getting a drink. How's Bea feeling?

It wasn't him.

It wasn't him fucking that girl on the bus!

Clutching my chest, I let out the breath that seemed to have been trapped inside it, suffocating me a moment earlier. It felt like I'd been shot with a tranquilizer gun full of euphoria.

> **Amelia:** Still has a cold. She's with my friend Susan because I'm here. Right outside your bus.

Justin: Holy fuck! Don't move. I'm heading
back.

Rubbing my hands over my arms, I stood waiting in the
cold for at least ten minutes. The two people who'd been
screwing inside the bus suddenly exited. The man was good-
looking, but he was no Justin. I also confirmed that the female
participant definitely wasn't Olivia.

A crowd of women suddenly gathered toward the entrance.
The guard could be heard saying, "Back. Back! Let him by!"

It was then that I saw Justin break through the swarm of
people. He passed through the chain-link fence and looked
around frantically before his gaze locked on me.

The commotion around us seemed to dissipate as he
walked toward me and enveloped me in his arms. I practically melted into him. He smelled like a mixture of cologne,
smoke, and beer. It was intoxicating and made me want to
bathe in it. I wanted him all over me.

"You're cold as ice," he whispered into my ear.

"Just hold me. Keep me warm."

"I really need to do more than hold you right now." He
pulled back to take me in, giving my outfit a once-over.
"Fuck," he growled. "Don't take this the wrong way, but why
do you look like a stripper?"

"I was dressing for the occasion. Too much?"

"Hell no. This is exactly what I needed. It just pisses me
off that you were waiting around for me in public dressed like
that. The fucking guys around here are worse than the girls.
Anyone mess with you?"

"No." Looking down at myself, I said, "I'm sorry. I figured
I had to compete with all those groupies."

"Don't apologize. But you don't have to compete with

anyone, Amelia. You never did." He put his forehead on mine, and time seemed to stand still. "When I was performing tonight, all I could think about was how badly I wished you were here. I was at the bar drowning my sorrows when you texted. I still can't believe you made it." He took a deep breath of the skin of my neck. "I'm hard as a rock just smelling you right now. We need to go somewhere to be alone. We don't have a lot of time before the buses leave."

"Where can we go?"

He placed his hands on my cheeks. "Fuck. I want to take you with me on the bus, spend the night with you until the sun rises over the next city."

"I would love that so much. I'm sorry I can't be the kind of girl that can just go on tour with you."

"You have bigger things to be taking care of. By the way, you sure this friend watching Bea is someone you can trust?"

"Yes. I wouldn't be here otherwise."

He rubbed my shoulders. "Stay right here. Let me go check what time we're leaving Massachusetts."

I waited as Justin ran to the other tour bus. When he returned, he looked anxious. "We have exactly two hours before the buses take off for Philly. I would introduce you to the band, but they'll talk your ear off, and I really don't want to waste this time."

"What are we gonna do?"

"They told me there's a small hotel down the road. We can go there to be alone if you want. Or, we can stay here, but then we'd have to socialize."

"Being alone sounds good to me."

Justin brushed his thumb along my cheek. "Good choice."

He took the keys from me and drove us to the hotel in my car. During the ride, he held my hand tightly and didn't let go.

At one point, he flashed me a sexy side glance. "God, you look good."

I joked, "Even though I look like a cheap groupie?"

"*Especially* because you look like a cheap groupie." He winked. His gaze returned to the road for a bit before his voice lowered. "I wasn't prepared for how lonely this tour was going to be. Seeing you makes me realize it even more."

We pulled into the hotel, and Justin checked us in and got us a key card. We had exactly one hour and forty-five minutes before he had to report back to the bus.

The room was dark, but neither of us turned on the light. Unsure of what was supposed to be taking place here, I waited for him to take the lead after the door clicked shut behind us.

He slowly prowled toward me, then pressed his chest against mine. "Jesus. Your heart is pounding. Are you nervous to be alone with me or something?" Nuzzling my neck, he added, "The way I'm feeling right now, maybe you should be."

Scared to admit what was really eating away at me and also not wanting to ruin the mood, I remained silent, just staring at him at the moonlight coming in through the window before my gaze dropped to the floor.

He took my chin in his hand. "Look at me." When our eyes met, he said, "I haven't been with anyone else, Amelia… in case there was any question in your mind. I don't *want* anyone else. I hope you don't, either."

"How did you know what I was thinking just now?"

"I guess I'm in tune to you like that. I had a feeling you needed reassurance. I don't want you wondering about that anymore." He kissed me on the forehead. "But with that out of the way, I do need to be honest with you about something."

I swallowed the lump in my throat. "Okay."

"I somehow thought I could handle five months with no sex, but the reality is…I'm feeling more like an animal in heat than a celibate monk."

I laughed. "Oh, really." My tone turned serious. "Maybe I can help. Tell me what you need."

"Confession," he said over my lips. "I didn't exactly bring you here so we could talk."

I kissed him. "Confession. I didn't exactly dress like a dirty groupie so you could sing to me."

His mouth was against mine as it curved into a wry smile. Within seconds, he took my face in his hands before his lips swallowed mine whole. A stifled moan escaped from me into his starving mouth as our tongues moved frantically to taste one another. I loved the controlled way he always grabbed my face when he kissed me.

But this was different from any other moment we'd been together because it lacked any trace of caution or hesitation. He was unapologetically taking what he wanted, and I was fully letting him. We were both on the exact same page, surrendering to what our bodies needed, and nothing was off-limits. If it weren't for the fact that he was leaving in an hour, this would have been like a dream come true. But we were on borrowed time, and we both knew it.

His hands slid down my back as he grabbed my ass, pulling me against his erection and kissing me hard. He sucked my bottom lip before releasing it slowly. "Last chance to stop me."

"Make every second count," I said in between kisses. "For the next hour, my body is yours, Banks."

"I've only waited a decade to hear you say that."

That was where the conversation ended. Justin pressed his rock-hard chest into me, pushing me into the window. My back was against the glass as he began to kiss me so hard that my lips hurt from the suction. My hands took on a mind of their own, eager to explore him. I threaded my fingers through his hair, rubbed my palms down his chest, gripped his ass. Overwhelmed, I wished I could touch every single part of him at once.

"It's going to be a while before we get to do this again. We need to make it last," he said as he fisted my hair and bent my head back. He kissed down my neck slowly. "Don't ever forget that I respect the hell out of you," he said as he stuck his hand up my dress and grabbed onto my panties.

"Why do you say that?"

"Because I'm about to fuck you full of disrespect." He ripped my underwear off, the elastic burning my thighs from the friction.

My pussy was already wet and ready for whatever he had in mind. Whereas before he had gently kissed down my throat, now he was sucking hard on the skin at the base of my neck.

I felt two of his fingers slip inside of my opening. His mouth stilled on my neck the moment they were fully inside me. He said something unintelligible as he shook his head in ecstasy before suddenly flipping me around so that I was facing the glass.

He pulled his fingers out, and almost immediately, I felt the burn of his cock replacing them as he sunk into me. "Fuck," he muttered.

I hadn't expected him to take me so soon. From the sound he let out when he was all the way inside of me, I didn't think even *he* had expected to lose control so fast.

It felt painfully pleasurable as I stretched to open for him. Justin's cock was thick. I'd always admired its girth, but it was another experience altogether to actually feel how completely he filled me—skin to skin. He hadn't put a condom on, which surprised me. I was too weak to question it, enjoying the raw sensation too much to think about anything else. But I'd come prepared.

"Please tell me you're on the pill," Justin said. "I've never done it like this before, but I don't think I can stop either way. It feels too damn good."

I'd never seem him lose control like this.

"I am. I just started taking it. Don't worry."

"Thank fuck." His muscles seemed to relax.

As he moved in and out of me, he lifted my dress over my head before throwing the frock aside. There was something so sexy about being completely naked while he was still fully clothed. His pants were hanging halfway down his legs, and his belt buckle clanked as he pounded into me.

I could see our reflection in the window. He was looking down at my ass, mesmerized as he watched the place our bodies joined together. He wouldn't take his eyes off it. His palm was firmly planted on my ass cheek to guide the movements of his thrusts, his nails inadvertently digging into my skin.

He began to suck on his finger, and before I could wonder what he was doing, I felt it inside my ass as he continued to penetrate me with his cock at the same time. No one had ever done that to me before, and while his finger there felt foreign, the pleasure derived from the double penetration was incredible.

He pushed it inside slowly until it was all the way in. I let out a long breath.

"You like that, huh? When we have more time, we'll try it the other way around. I want to fuck that ass so badly. But we need time for that."

I simply moaned in agreement, too turned on by what he was doing to form words.

He pulled his finger out. He was now holding onto my ass with both hands, spreading it apart with his thumbs as he fucked me harder and faster.

"I love the way your ass jiggles when I'm pounding into it." He slapped me. "Fucking beautiful."

My muscles tightened every time he opened his mouth. I'd always loved to be talked to during sex, but his dirty, gravelly voice was the sexiest I'd ever heard.

"Tighten against my cock like that again."

I clenched around him.

"Fuck. That feels good," he growled. "I want you to do that when I'm coming inside you."

I wanted him to spank me again. I'd never imagined the pressure of his hand would feel so good, but it did.

What was happening to me?

My voice was throaty when I said, "Slap my ass again."

He obliged, and when he struck me this time, the sting of his hand was perfect.

Everything about this experience was unlike anything I'd ever felt before, from the skin-to-skin contact to the forceful way he fucked me. He'd broken through a barrier of pleasure that I hadn't known I was capable of feeling. I didn't know how I was going to live without this now that I knew what it was like.

I could feel his body trembling at my back. "I need to come. Tell me when you're close," he said into my ear.

I watched his face in the reflection and now, instead of looking down, he was looking straight at my face.

"I'm coming," I said as I tightened my muscles like he'd wanted.

"Fuck. Oh God, Amelia. That feels…oh shit…I'm coming," he groaned out, then muttered low, "Yeah, baby. I'm coming. So good. So fucking good."

Warm cum filled me as I continued to squeeze around his cock. Justin stayed inside of me, fucking me long after he came, kissing my back softly.

"Shit. I don't know what that is that you do when you tense your pussy around me, but I'm going to be jerking off to it for the next four months."

"What *was* that we just did?" I asked facetiously. "That didn't feel like just sex. That was far too incredible."

"That was a decade's worth of frustration barreling out of me, baby."

"You're so good, Justin. It was worth the wait."

He slowly pulled out of me and turned me around, planting a firm kiss on my lips. "We have forty minutes."

"What are we gonna do?"

"I need you again."

My eyes widened. "Can you go again so soon?"

"With you? I could go all night. No one's ever made me lose control like that. That's how it should feel every single damn time, like it's all that matters. I couldn't give a shit if the world is crumbling around me when I'm inside of you."

We smiled at each other, and the streetlights from outside shined into his beautiful blue eyes. Forty minutes wasn't long enough. To squelch the dread creeping in, I took off his shirt and began to kiss his chest softly.

"This time is gonna be different, okay?" he said.

I simply nodded, anxiously awaiting his direction. He stripped out of his underwear, and I could see his dick was still gloriously hard, glistening with arousal.

"Lie down, Amelia."

Admiring his chiseled body, I lay on the bed and backed up against the headboard.

When he turned on the small desk lamp, I asked, "What are you doing?"

"I want to look at you for a while. Is that okay?"

I nodded again. "Yes."

"Spread your legs apart," he demanded.

Justin kneeled at the foot of the bed as he took in the sight of me.

"So sexy…seeing you wide-open like that with my cum dripping out of you. Fuck, Amelia," he breathed out as he started to jerk himself off. He looked down at his engorged shaft. "I'm ready to go again. This is fucking crazy."

"We don't have a lot of time. I need you inside of me again."

"Touch yourself for a little bit."

I positioned my fingertips at my clit and began to circle them around. The room was quiet except for the slick sound of his cock moving against his hand.

"Open wider, Amelia."

Spreading my knees farther apart, I had to curb the need to come.

"You ready?" he asked.

"Yes," I whispered.

This time when he sunk into me, it was slow and controlled. He stopped when he was fully inside and just stayed there without moving for a while.

"How the fuck am I going to be able to leave you after this?" he asked.

When he picked up the pace again, it felt better than ever, not only because of the pressure of his weight on top of me but because we were both fully naked, our skin rubbing together. The room was cold, but the heat of his body warmed me.

I held on to his ass, pushing him deeper into me as he

circled his hips. His breathing matched the rhythm of his movements. When my orgasm suddenly rolled through me, he must have been able to feel it because he also came without warning, grunting loudly in my ear. There was no sweeter sound than the noises he made when he came.

He collapsed over me and said, "Thank you for giving this to me. It's the only thing that's gonna get me through the rest of this time away."

Looking at the time on my phone, I felt sick. We had ten minutes before we had to drive back to the bus. It was odd to feel sated and scared at the same time. He'd left my body completely satisfied, yet my heart was still yearning for more.

It just wanted to hear those three words so desperately.

———

When we arrived at Justin's bus, I gripped his black jacket, unable to let him go. After what we'd just done, my attachment to him was stronger than ever.

"I want you to meet the crew before we leave," he told me.

Although I wasn't feeling very social, I said, "Okay."

Justin brought me inside the bus. A bunch of guys were sitting around eating pieces of a gigantic apple pie that looked like it was from Costco. The air smelled like a mixture of coffee and beer. Justin went down the line, introducing me to each crew member. They were all super nice and down to earth. I didn't have a chance to meet Calvin Sprockett, since he was on the other bus.

A few minutes later, the one person I'd dreaded meeting the most finally made her appearance.

"Is everyone accounted for?" Olivia asked, holding a walkie-talkie.

Justin looked at me and whispered, "That's Olivia."

He didn't realize I already knew what she looked like from my stalking. I was starting to feel nauseous, and it only got worse with each step she took toward us. With luxurious dark hair and a megawatt smile, she was even prettier than her pictures.

I couldn't stand her.

"I see we have an extra passenger," Olivia said.

Seeming to lose my ability to speak, I smiled like a fool without saying anything.

"Olivia, this is my girlfriend, Amelia," Justin said.

Girlfriend.

The fear inside of me began to slowly evaporate. He hadn't said the "L" word, but he'd finally given me the validation I so desperately needed, especially now with him leaving again.

Olivia didn't seem too surprised. "It's nice to finally meet you, Amelia."

"Likewise." I smiled.

"Are you coming with us to Philly?" she asked.

"No. I have a baby girl at home, so I'm not able to travel."

"That's right. Justin showed me her picture."

It further calmed me to know that he'd also spoken to her about Bea.

"Well, it was nice meeting you," Olivia said before giving Justin a slight look of warning. "Buses are leaving in five."

Waiting for her to get out of earshot, I said, "So that's Olivia…"

"Yep."

"She sleeps on the other bus?"

"Yeah. The tour manager goes on the main bus." He smiled, examining my expression and seeming amused at my transparent relief.

He nudged at my dress, and my nipples immediately

perked up. "Let's get you a jacket," Justin said. "Then I'm gonna tell the driver to hold up while I accompany you to the car. I don't want you walking alone."

Justin retrieved one of his black hoodies and held it open for me. I zipped it up, loving the smell of his cologne that saturated it. He led me by the hand across the VIP lot to the regular parking area.

Justin gazed into my eyes as we stopped in front of my car. He held me tightly as he buried his nose in my hair. "You're lucky we don't have any more time. I'd take you right against this car."

"I'd let you."

"Thank you for tonight, Amelia. I'm gonna fucking miss you so much."

I spoke against his chest. "Can I ask you something?"

"Yeah…"

"When did you decide I was your girlfriend?"

He looked up at the sky and hesitated, as if he had to really ponder it. His answer wasn't what I was expecting. "The matinee show of *El Amor Duele* at the little red theater, circa 2005. I wasn't even paying attention to the movie. You were really into it. I was really into *you*. You didn't realize I was staring at you the whole time. You were so enthralled that you didn't even notice that you'd finished your popcorn. Without you knowing, I replaced your empty bucket with my full one. You just kept eating. I decided at that moment that whether you knew it or not, you were my girlfriend. I kept telling myself…that after the show, I was finally gonna make you aware of that fact too."

"What happened?"

He shrugged. "I chickened out." We both laughed, and our breaths collided in the cold air. Justin looked down at his phone. "Shit. They're texting me to hurry up. I have to go."

"All right."

He pulled me into him as tightly as he could and planted one final kiss on my lips. "Thank you again for coming." He wriggled his brows. "And for coming again. And for letting me come." As I giggled against his lips, he said, "You were so amazing."

"Call me tomorrow."

"Be careful driving home."

"Okay."

He lingered, then said, "It's never been that way for me. I've never felt that way with anyone else."

I loved hearing that. "Me neither."

Our hands stayed intertwined until the pull of him walking away naturally ripped our fingers apart. Justin ran across the lot.

I got into my car and turned on the heat. I stayed idling until the two buses pulled out and disappeared from sight.

Later that night, I'd just arrived back at the beach house when my phone chimed with a text from Justin.

All that time I spent mad at you...I could have been fucking you. What a dumbass.

CHAPTER 20

The hardest days with Justin gone were those leading up to the holidays. This was going to be Bea's first Christmas, and we'd be spending it without him.

Justin's tour had made its way out west. He would be performing two shows in Los Angeles, one on Christmas Eve and one on Christmas Day, so there was no way that he could sneak any time away to come home. After those gigs, the band would only remain in the US for another week before flying to Europe, where the tour would continue until they returned to America in the spring. It made me tired just thinking about all of the traveling he was doing.

I had to give Justin credit, though. He'd stuck to his word about Skyping every other day with us. But as much as I looked forward to those chats, it was getting harder and harder to be away from him. As the days went on, so did the fresh memory of our time together in Massachusetts. The reassurance that night had given me was slowly being replaced by fear and insecurity again with each day that passed. While

I trusted him more after we'd made love, he still hadn't *told me* he loved me. In my mind, that meant nothing was set in stone. Couple that with the fact that he would be away for over a dozen more weeks, and that made for one paranoid girlfriend.

It was two days before Christmas. Bea and I had been invited to an ugly sweater party over at Roger and Susan's house. Justin had called earlier to say he'd just arrived in California. I was grateful for the distraction that the party would bring. At least for a couple of hours, it would prevent me from sulking in front of the Christmas tree at the beach house.

I'd gone to a local thrift store and bought a hideous red sweater with little Christmas bulbs sewn onto the front. I'd even managed to find an ugly Christmas sweater onesie online for Bea. So, we were all ready for the festivities.

The temperature was frigid as I bundled Bea up and ran across to the neighbors' house, which was lit up in multi-colored lights. An inflatable snowman blew in the wind out front. Living near the water in the middle of winter was less than ideal.

Carrying some freshly baked sugar cookies, I knocked on their door with my foot, since I had no extra hands.

Roger opened the door. "Amelia, you made it! Susan wasn't sure if you were coming."

"I wouldn't miss it," I said, handing him the plate of cookies. "Is Susan in the kitchen?"

"She is. You're the first one here."

"Figures." I grinned. "I have the shortest commute."

Just as I was about to head to see Susan, Roger's voice stopped me. "Hey, Amelia?"

"Yes?"

"Since Susan's been back, we really haven't had a chance to talk. I've always felt a little strange about not telling you myself about us getting back together."

"You didn't owe me any explanation. I already explained to her that nothing happened between you and me."

"I know you did. I'm really happy that you two have become friends. And I want you to know that I was truly grateful for your friendship too, at a time when I really needed it."

"I'm really happy for you guys."

"Thank you." He paused. "What about you?"

"What *about* me?"

Roger tilted his head. "Are you happy?"

"I am. Just a little lonely with Justin gone."

"You know, you used to tell me that there was nothing going on between the two of you…"

"At the time, there wasn't. I'd always had feelings for him, though."

"He's coming back, right? After the tour?"

"Yes."

"Is that what he wants to do with his life? Be a touring musician? Live on the road?"

"I'm not sure if that's how it's always going to be. He works in software sales, but that's not his dream. Music is his dream. This was a once-in-a-lifetime opportunity, so he had to take it."

"Who's he on tour with again?"

"Calvin Sprockett."

"Wow. Yeah. That's pretty big stuff."

"It is."

After a bit of awkward silence, Roger asked, "Are any of those guys still married?"

"You mean Calvin and his band?"

"Yeah."

I had to think about it. "Now that you mention it...I don't think they are."

Roger hung up my coat as he said, "I suppose marriage doesn't really mesh with sex, drugs, and rock 'n' roll. Not to mention constantly traveling. You know, things had never been harder for me than when I was physically away from Susan and Alyssa. I don't know too much about Justin, but it seems like he's very fond of Bea. If he wants to be a father to her, absenteeism really doesn't work. I figured that out the hard way, and that was without the additional complication of fame."

"I don't think he's figured out whether he wants kids."

"Well, don't you think it's time he did, if he wants to be with you?" Roger must have sensed that he was stressing me out. "I'm sorry, Amelia. I'm just looking out for you."

"I appreciate that. But I'm only looking for eggnog tonight, nothing more complicated than that, all right?"

Closing his eyes briefly in understanding, he chuckled and said, "You got it. Let me grab some for you."

Through the muffled laughter of their guests, who were dressed in a rainbow of ugly sweaters, my thoughts kept me distracted. Even though my conversation with Roger had long ended, I spent the remainder of the party pondering everything he'd said. It was nothing I didn't already worry about, but hearing the concern come from someone else—someone who understood the long-term responsibilities of fatherhood—was eye-opening.

————

Back at the house later that night, I rocked Bea to sleep in front of the tree to the sounds of a children's choir CD of Christmas carols. Earlier in the week, I'd wrapped some

266

presents and placed them under the tree. They were all for Bea and included a small box that Justin had shipped to her to be opened on Christmas morning.

I didn't need anything this year; Bea *was* my Christmas gift. She was the greatest gift from God and had taught me more about unconditional love than anyone or anything else. She'd given me a purpose.

I kissed her head softly, vowing to always be there for her no matter what happened with Justin. I vowed to be the type of mother that I never had.

Still in my Christmas sweater, I placed a sleeping Bea in her crib, taking a moment to look around and admire Justin's handiwork in the nursery.

Back in my room, I couldn't sleep. I'd just nodded off when my phone chimed, waking me up.

Justin: You asleep?

Amelia: Wide awake now.

Justin: Will you call me? I don't know if Bea is near you and don't want to wake her.

He picked up on the first ring after I dialed him. "Hey, beautiful."

"Hi."

His voice sounded sleepy. "I woke you, didn't I?"

"Yes, but it's okay. I'd rather speak to you than sleep. Where are you?"

"I'm at the hotel in Los Angeles. We're off the buses till Christmas night."

"That must be a nice change, getting to sleep in a real bed."

"It only reminds me that you're not here with me."

"I wish I were."

"It's really bugging me that I can't be with you guys for Christmas."

"I don't understand why they don't give you Christmas off."

"Calvin's always done Christmas shows. It's sort of his tradition. It sucks. You'd think none of these people have families. I feel bad for the crew members with kids."

"It doesn't ever end, does it?"

Justin sounded confused by my comment. "What in particular?"

"I mean, this tour will end. But the life of a musician never really does."

"It's not like I won't have a choice in the matter. I don't have to go anywhere or do anything I don't want to."

"Yes, but after this tour, so many more people will know who you are. The opportunities will start coming, and fame will be addicting. That was the point of all this, right? To grow your music career? Are you really going back to your software job like none of this ever happened? What exactly *is* going to happen?"

"I don't know. I haven't thought that far. I just want to come home to you first. I won't be going away again anytime soon after that."

"But you might be going away again at some point. This isn't just a one-time thing, right?"

"Why the worrying all of a sudden, Amelia?"

"I don't know. I guess I have too much time alone to think."

"I'm sorry. But the truth is, I just don't have all the answers tonight. I can only tell you what I'm feeling right now, and that's that I don't want to be here and would give anything to be home for Christmas with you and Bea."

Rubbing my tired eyes, I said, "All right. I'm sorry. It's late, and you must be tired."

"Don't ever be sorry for talking to me about how you feel. Remember, you promised to be honest with me if something is bothering you."

"I know."

Just when my nerves had started to calm down, it sounded like there was a knock at his door.

"Hang on," he said.

My heartbeat started to accelerate when I heard a woman's voice in the background.

I couldn't make out what she was saying but could hear Justin say, "No, thanks. I appreciate it, but no." He paused. "All right. Good night." I heard the door click shut.

He returned to the phone. "Sorry."

"Who was that?"

"Someone wanted to know if I was interested in a massage."

"Massage?"

"Yes. Calvin sometimes hires people to give massages. He must have sent someone up here to ask if I wanted one."

The eggnog from earlier was starting to come up on me. "So it was just a random girl coming into your room to give you a massage?"

"Amelia...I didn't ask for one, nor did I want one. I sent her away. I can't help it if someone knocks on my door."

"Have you ever had one?"

His tone was angry. "No!"

"I can't handle this."

"I get why a strange woman coming to my hotel room door would piss you off, all right? But you either trust me, or you don't. Trust is a black-or-white issue. There is no such thing as trusting someone a little. It's either there, or it isn't. Fuck. I thought you trusted me."

"I do! I never said I didn't trust you. It's just...that lifestyle

269

makes me uncomfortable. And I'm lonely. I don't know if this is the kind of life I want."

"What exactly are you saying?"

"I don't know," I said, my voice barely audible.

There was a long moment of silence as I listened to his breathing. Then, he finally said, "I can't even see the faces of the people in the audience. When I'm singing, I'm singing to you, counting down the days till I come home. Wouldn't that just be a fucking hoot if there was nothing left to come home to?"

Why haven't you told me you loved me?

I'd really pissed him off. I needed to end the call before I said something further that I'd regret.

"You have two big shows coming up," I said. "You can't afford to get all stressed out. I'm sorry for causing a fight."

"I'm sorry too."

"I'm gonna try to get some sleep."

"All right," he said.

"Good night."

"Good night."

After we hung up, I had a hard time falling back to sleep. Ending the call on bad terms made me feel like shit. I thought I couldn't feel any worse.

———

Call it mother's intuition.

Something woke me up, even though it was quiet. The clock showed nearly 4 a.m.

As I tried to fall back to sleep a few minutes later, what sounded like light wheezing came through the baby monitor; I could barely hear it.

Panicking, I hopped out of bed so fast that it made me

lightheaded. Running down the hall to Bea's room, it felt like my heart was in my mouth as I practically tripped over my own feet.

Everything seemed to be happening so fast, yet at the same time, they were the longest, scariest moments of my life. Bea was struggling to breathe, her little eyes looking up at me helplessly. She was choking but unable to cough. My mind raced as I scrambled to remember the steps from the infant CPR class I'd taken back in Providence.

Turning her face over my forearm, I held her jaw with one hand to support her head. I slapped her back five times between her shoulder blades. She still couldn't breathe, and nothing came out.

Turning her face up, I placed two fingers in the middle of her chest and pressed down in quick thrusts. The object still wouldn't dislodge. I ran with her to my room to grab my phone and dialed 911. I couldn't even remember what I said to the operator, because when Bea became unresponsive, I lost my own ability to breathe.

I alternated between back blows and chest compressions as the dispatcher guided me. The object finally flew out of her mouth, and I realized it was one of the small bulbs from my sweater. It must have fallen into her crib.

While the bulb had come out, Bea was unconscious.

The next thing I knew, sirens were blaring. I ran downstairs with her to let them in. Men rushed into the room. They began performing CPR on my baby girl.

My entire life hung in the balance as I watched helplessly, paralyzed by fear. It was no different than being unconscious myself.

When one of the EMTs indicated that she was breathing again, it was as if I'd come back from the dead. The tears pooling in my eyes blinded me from getting a clear view as they put her onto a stretcher and directed me to get into the ambulance. Because she'd been unconscious for so long, she needed to be taken to the hospital for treatment and to ensure that there wasn't any brain damage or internal injuries.

Still in my sleep sweats with no coat, I sat in the ambulance alongside her as one of the men held an oxygen mask over her face.

Too shook up to speak, I typed out a series of choppy texts to Justin.

> Bea is alive.
>
> Choked on a small ornament.
>
> Got it out.
>
> EMTs performed CPR.
>
> In ambulance heading to hospital.
>
> I'm scared.

Within seconds, my phone rang. It had to be one thirty in the morning in LA.

Justin's voice was shaky. "Amelia? I got your message. Oh my God. Is she okay?"

"I don't know. She's conscious and breathing. I just don't know if there was any other damage."

"Can you see her? Is she with you?"

"Yes. She's got an oxygen mask over her face, but her eyes are open. I think she's scared."

I heard rustling, and then he said, "I'm getting on the next flight out there."

Still in shock, I was silent.

His voice seemed to be fading into the distance. "Amelia?

272

Are you there? Hang in there, baby. She's going to be okay. She will."

"Okay," I whispered through my tears.

"Where are they taking her?"

"Hasbro Children's Hospital in Providence."

"Call me as soon as you know anything."

"All right."

"Be strong, Amelia. Please."

CHAPTER 21

Those first few hours waiting with Bea in the intensive care unit were excruciating, truly the scariest of my life.

They had her hooked up to an IV and were giving her oxygen. The doctors ran a series of tests to check for internal injuries and neurological problems. Apparently, after respiratory failure, there could be delayed brain injury that wasn't apparent right away. It would be a while before all of the results came in.

With no clear prognosis, my silent prayers were nonstop. I begged God to spare my baby from any irreversible damage. Bea was sleeping a lot, probably exhausted from the trauma, so it was hard to gauge how she was really doing.

She was able to open her eyes, though, and I had to be grateful for that and for the fact that she was alive and breathing. Thank God I'd randomly woken up when I had. If I had gotten to her room even a minute later, the outcome could have been very different. I couldn't even bear to think about that. Someone had definitely been watching over us last night. Until I had answers, I had to just focus on the positive and continue to pray.

It was midmorning now, and I hadn't moved from my spot at Bea's side, afraid to miss the doctor coming in with information. A nice nurse finally forced me to go get something to drink and to use the bathroom. She promised to watch Bea and assured me that nothing would happen while I was gone.

In the bathroom just off of the nurse's station, tears began to pour out of my eyes. Riddled with guilt, I was finally losing it. If it hadn't been for that stupid sweater and my carelessness, none of this would have ever happened. How could I not have checked her crib before I'd put her down?

I needed to put on a strong front before returning to my daughter. She was intuitive; I couldn't let her sense my fear.

The doctor came in shortly after I returned to my spot at Bea's bedside. "Ms. Payne..."

I stood up, feeling the weight of my heavy, terrified heart. "Yes?"

"We just received the results of the tests on her condition. There are no internal injuries aside from a slight fracturing of the ribs, which will heal on its own. Her neurological assessment seems okay too, but that's what I want to watch over the next day before we can consider releasing her. I no longer think she needs to be in the intensive care unit, so we're going to move her to a regular room on one of the main floors."

A massive sense of relief washed over me. "Doctor, thank you. Thank you. I could hug you. Can I hug you?" When he nodded uncomfortably, I embraced him. "Thank you so much."

"It could have been very serious. We see this very same scenario end differently all too often. Babies or toddlers choking on grapes, hot dogs, small toys. You're very lucky."

After the doctor left, I typed out a text to Justin.

> Thank God! The doctor thinks she's going to be okay. They want to watch her for at least the next twenty-four hours, though. I'm so happy right now!

There was no response.

Soon after, they moved us to a new room on the third floor. Lying in bed, Bea had her eyes open and looked confused as she gazed up at the panels of fluorescent lights on the ceiling. She seemed alert but not her typical happy self. She was probably wondering what the hell she was doing here.

They told me I could hold her again. Even though she'd been getting vitamins and fluids through an IV, they suggested I feed her. I'd been giving her more formula than breast milk lately, but I chose to nurse her because I knew it would comfort her.

I was relieved when she ate with no problem. With every minute that passed, I became more confident that my baby was going to be okay.

She had to be.

After I returned Bea to her bed, Shelly, the nurse, came in to check her vitals. So focused on everything Shelly was doing, I almost didn't notice him standing there.

Justin was in the doorway, his chest rising and falling as he took in the sight of Bea lying in the hospital bed. Even though he'd said he was getting on a plane, I hadn't heard anything from him for the past several hours and wasn't sure if he'd been able to get a flight. His hair was a mess and his eyes were red. Despite looking ragged and almost strung out, he was still stunningly handsome.

My heart leaped. "Justin."

He said nothing and didn't take his eyes off Bea as he walked slowly toward the bed. He looked like he was in shock to see her looking so weak. "She's okay?"

"We think so, yes. You didn't get my texts?"

His eyes still glued to Bea, he shook his head. "No. No, I was on the plane, and my phone died. I took the first flight I could get out of LAX and came straight here."

Shelly looked at him. "Are you her father?"

Justin reached out to Bea's cheek and gently rubbed it as he said, "Yes." His answer was a shock. Chills ran through me when he looked at me and repeated, "Yes, I am."

When he turned his attention back to Bea, his red eyes filled with moisture. In all the years I'd known him, I had never seen Justin shed a single tear. He sat down in the seat on the other side of Bea.

Shelly noticed that Justin had started to cry and said, "I'll give you some privacy."

When the door clicked behind her, Justin lowered his face to the bed and kissed Bea lightly on the cheek. Still equal parts stunned and touched, I waited for him to speak.

It took a while for the words to come. He just stared at her, a look of awe and relief ever so slowly replacing the shock from earlier. I knew he noticed that she wasn't her normal self. It was hard not to see it. Bea would have been smiling or giggling at him by now. Instead, she was merely awake but quiet. I hoped it was just because she hadn't seen him in a while and not a sign of something more serious.

"I love you, Bumblebee. I'm sorry it's taken me this long to tell you." He wiped his eyes, then turned to me. "I've never been more scared in my life, Amelia. I was afraid something would happen to her before I could get here, that I'd never see her smile again, that I'd never have a chance to tell her how much I want to be her father. The whole flight here, I prayed to God, bargained that if she turned out to be okay, I wouldn't let another second go by without telling her I loved her. The thing is…even without me saying it…she already thinks I'm her daddy. I know I'm not her biological father, but she doesn't know that. Blood doesn't make someone a father, anyway. What makes me her father is that she chose me. She owned me from the moment she first smiled at me. And while that used to scare the shit out of me, I couldn't imagine life without her now."

"I thought you didn't want kids."

"So did I. Maybe I didn't want some generic, imagined kids. But I want her." He repeated in a whisper, "I want her."

Now I was crying too. "She loves you too, you know. Very much."

"I'm the only father she's ever known. And she thinks I left without explanation. That kills me every day."

"What's happening with the tour?"

"Well, they're without an opening act now for the Christmas shows in LA, but Calvin understands my situation. They're gonna wing it. They all know how much Bea means to me. They said they would make do for future shows if need be. I'm not going back until I'm sure she's okay and home."

Our attention turned to Bea when she suddenly started to babble.

Justin teased, "Hey, you have something to say for yourself?" He smiled at her for a bit before turning to me. "Is it okay to hold her, or is it better not to?"

"They told me I could take her out. It's okay. Just don't toss her up into the air or anything."

Justin slowly lifted her out of the bed and cradled her in

his arms. "You scared the crap out of me, Miss Bee. You sure this wasn't a ploy to get me home for Christmas? If so, job well done."

It had completely skipped my mind that tonight was Christmas Eve; we'd be spending her first Christmas in the hospital.

Tilting my head, I admired the two of them together. I'd always felt their connection but had worried that Justin would never truly give in to it. I felt so happy for Bea, that this wonderful guy wanted to be her father. I knew no matter what happened between Justin and me, he would always be there for her.

When Bea fell asleep in his arms, I told Justin the full story of what had happened as best I could remember it.

Bea was still asleep when he returned her to the bed and asked, "When was the last time you ate, Amelia?"

"Sometime yesterday."

"I'm gonna go get us some food and coffee while she's sleeping."

"That would be great."

With Justin gone and Bea asleep, my tired mind went into overdrive. It was getting dark outside the hospital windows. Left alone with too much time to think, I started to push guilt on myself for allowing this to happen. I had one job, and that was to take care of my daughter and keep her safe; I couldn't even do that.

When Justin returned, he was carrying a paper bag of food and a small Christmas tree that had probably come from a pharmacy.

I must have looked like a wreck because he dropped everything and came over to me. "What's wrong?"

"This is my fault. I should have checked her crib before I left the room."

"It was an accident. That damn bulb fell off your sweater. You didn't see it happen."

"I know, but I can't help feeling like if I'd just done something differently..."

"What are you talking about? You saved her life."

"Yes. But only because I was lucky enough to wake up when I did. I can't even imagine what today would be like if I hadn't."

"Don't think about that. God was with her. She's okay. She'll be okay. It wasn't your fault."

"I just can't help feeling like a horrible mother."

"Listen to me. Remember that night we stayed up talking at the beach house that first summer? You told me you felt like teaching wasn't what you were meant to do, that there was something else out there you'd be better at."

"Yes."

"I'll never forget this past summer when I came home unexpectedly to find you and Bea there. You were in that fucked-up state of disarray. I'd never witnessed anyone give of themself so fully for the good of another human being like that. There isn't one moment of any day when you don't put her first. You don't think about yourself, your own mental well-being, getting a break. I'd watch you feeding her sometimes and wish that I'd had a mother like you. Not so I could suck on your tits." He winked. "But because of how nurturing you are. When we were growing up, I always thought you were pretty amazing, but it doesn't even come close to how I see you now. So don't you dare. Don't you *dare* call yourself a horrible mother, Amelia Payne. That thing you were meant to do that you couldn't figure out? It was to be a mother to that little girl. That's your calling. And you're doing a damn good job."

I closed my eyes and took a deep breath, so thankful for his reassurance, which had just basically talked me off of a mental ledge. "Thank you."

He walked over to the bags and handed me a Dunkin' Donuts iced coffee along with a Chipotle burrito bowl. "Now, eat…before she wakes up."

After we finished our food, Justin plugged the small tree into an outlet in the corner of the room. This was as good as Christmas Eve was going to get under the circumstances.

When Bea finally woke up, we got a little Christmas miracle. Justin was looking down at her when she finally smiled for the first time since the choking incident. It was the best gift we could have ever asked for.

"Merry Christmas, Bumblebee," Justin said. I could feel the sense of relief in the air. It may have been one smile out of many, but it was an important one. To us, it meant she was going to be okay.

Justin pulled up Pandora on his phone and streamed Christmas music until it got late. The hospital brought in two cots that we set up on each side of Bea's bed.

It was past 11 p.m. Justin was exhausted from his trip and dozed off along with Bea, but I still wasn't able to relax enough to shut my eyes. I wouldn't be happy until we were home.

With both of them asleep, I played on my phone for a bit, going back to the text message chain between Justin and me to see exactly what I'd written him from the ambulance. I had been so stressed, I had no recollection of what I'd typed in those horrific moments.

That was when I noticed a message that had come in from him earlier that night, a text I hadn't noticed due to everything that had happened with Bea.

I don't like fighting with you. I love you. In case there was any doubt.

The time of the message was shortly before 4 a.m. That was almost exactly the time I had woken up right before Bea's wheezing had started. I had figured that my waking up out of the blue was random, but it must have been the text that had interrupted my slumber.

As I looked over at Justin sleeping peacefully, my heart felt like it was going to explode out of my chest. Not because he'd finally said those three words I'd longed to hear. It was the other realization. If it hadn't been for that text, I wouldn't have woken up.

I hadn't saved Bea's life.

Justin had.

CHAPTER 22

Bea was released from the hospital on Christmas Day. We were overjoyed to take her home after the doctors officially ruled out any brain injury. It had even started snowing on the ride back from Providence to Newport, making it truly a white Christmas.

Justin would be staying with us for a couple of days before meeting up with the tour in London for the start of the European leg. I wouldn't allow myself to get sad yet, since this was stolen time anyway.

Christmas night, we sat around the tree with Bea and helped her open her presents. I saved the small box from Justin to open last. When we finally got to it, Justin watched anxiously as I ripped open the tape and removed the generous amount of bubble wrap.

Inside was a small wooden guitar that sat vertically atop a cylindrical base. The bottom of the cylinder opened, and you could store small items inside of it. On top of the guitar was a hand-painted black and yellow bumblebee. It was made to look like the bee had just landed on the instrument.

Justin took it from me and wound the bottom. The guitar began to slowly spin around to a song I didn't recognize.

"I have a friend back in New York who designs custom music boxes," he said. "I asked him to make me one for her. The bee represents the fact that she's always with me no matter where I am."

So extremely touched, I paid special attention to the song, but after several seconds of listening, still didn't recognize it. "What song is that? It's beautiful."

"It's the melody of something I'm writing. This guy was able to program it into the box. I'm still working on the lyrics, though."

"That's so amazing. This is the most thoughtful gift you could have given her."

"It's just something to make me feel like I'm with her when I can't be." He looked down at Bea as she hypnotically watched the guitar spin round and round. He stared at her for a while before he said, "What do you get for someone you can never repay...for all she's taught you, all she's given you?"

"I think you taking on the responsibility of being her father is a pretty big gift."

He kissed Bea on the head. "That gift is all mine."

Smiling at the both of them, I asked a question I'd been wondering ever since he'd come home. "What changed?"

"What do you mean?"

"Before you left, it seemed like you were still unsure about what your role in her life was going to be. So what changed?"

He looked up at me. "My doubts were never about her, just whether I was worthy of her love. I didn't want to be a disappointment to someone who meant so much to me. But being away from her made me realize that she'd already become a part of me. My fear of inadequacy aside, she was already my daughter in every way that mattered. Stepping away helped me see that even more clearly."

Earlier, I'd explained to Justin my realization about the timing of his text. He'd refused to take responsibility for saving Bea's life, insisting I deserved all of the credit for that. I hadn't addressed the actual subject of his text until now.

I leaned my head against his shoulder, so grateful to have him home with us, even if just for a couple of days. "I love you, Justin. You know, I was so fixated on the fact that you hadn't used those three words toward me yet. By the time you finally did—in that text—it came as no surprise because, deep down, I already knew. You've taught me that love isn't about words. It's a series of actions. You've shown your love for me in how you look at me, how you treat me, and most of all, in how much you love my daughter as your own."

He leaned in to kiss me, then said, "I love you both very much. That night, I realized how foolish it was that I hadn't said those words. But the truth is, it almost felt unnatural to announce it because it's not like I just recently fell in love with you. It's something that's been there for years. There may have been times when I tried to hate you, but even then, I never stopped loving you."

"I never stopped loving you, either. It was wrong of me to assume that you didn't love me because you didn't say it."

He wriggled his brows. "You know what they say about assuming things…"

"You end up in a porno theater watching anal?" I chuckled.

"Good girl. That is correct." He winked.

Having gotten no sleep since Bea's ordeal began, I was quickly losing steam. The three of us turned in early for the night. But putting Bea back into the crib alone tonight was just not something I was ready for yet. Instead, she slept right

285

in between Justin and me—her parents. I could definitely get used to that.

We had one more day with him—the day after Christmas. Then, Justin would be leaving us again, flying out of New York to London.

———

It felt like a dream to wake up to the smell of Justin's coffee fusion brewing in the kitchen.

Bea was still sleeping when I went downstairs and snuck up behind him, looping my arms underneath his. My braless chest pressed through my nightgown into his broad back. We both gazed out at the frigid waves rolling through the wintry ocean. I was already pining for summer, not only because of the balmy weather, but because Justin would be home with us by then.

He turned around and covered my mouth with a hungry kiss. Now that my nerves had calmed down over Bea, my sexual desire was slowly escalating back to a normal level. Justin's hair was sticking up in all directions, and a small beard was growing out. As it scratched my face in a pleasurable way, I felt wetness between my legs. Pressing my body into his erection, I took a deep breath in, savoring his masculine smell mixed with the aroma of the percolating coffee.

I wanted him more than I wanted my morning cup of Joe, and that was saying something. Surviving the next few months without him wasn't going to be easy, but at least I knew now where things stood between us.

He stopped kissing me and caressed my face, looking like he had something on his mind.

"I have a couple of questions for you," he said.

"Okay…"

"I was thinking…I would love it if you and Bea could come to the last show in the spring. It'll be in New York, so it won't be too far for you to travel. I can book you a flight if you don't want to drive. Then, we can all come home together in my car. It would be nice if you could at least see me on the big stage once before it's over. What do you think? We could get noise-reducing headphones for her if it's too loud."

"I wouldn't miss it for the world. I've been thinking that I should try to see you on tour for one show. New York would be the perfect location."

"Good. I'll make all the arrangements."

"What's the other question?"

"What are the chances I could fuck you raw on that counter before she wakes up?"

I hesitated. My period had just come this morning, and I was never comfortable doing the deed on the heaviest day of my cycle. "I really want that right now, but…"

Disappointment flashed across his face. "What?"

"I stabbed myself…pretty heavily."

Shutting his eyes, he grumbled, "Shit. I need you so badly right now." He looked down at the ground, then up at me. "I don't mind…if you don't. I'll stab you so good myself, you won't even think about the other wound."

As much as I wanted to, I just couldn't. I pulled on the edge of his pants, taking a peek at the rock-hard erection inside. "I have a better idea."

"Oh yeah?"

Dropping to my knees, I slowly undid the string of his navy pajama pants.

Leaning his elbows against the counter, Justin bent his head back and surrendered without argument, except to laugh under his breath as he said, "Or…we could do this. Fuck. Yeah."

Admiring the cut V of his lower abs and the thin line of hair that ran down the middle, I said, "I've always wanted to go down on you. That time we left the porno theater, remember that? I couldn't have you back then, but I fantasized that whole night about sucking you off."

He massaged my hair. "I'll never forget that night. It was so damn hot to see you getting turned on during that movie. I wanted nothing more than to lift you on top of me and fuck that pretty pink pussy right in the little red theater. I wanted you so fucking badly that night, so much it hurt. Almost as much as I want you now."

His breath hitched when I took his cock out. I opened wide and wrapped my lips around it. He let out a hot, throaty sound and was already wet the moment my tongue took its first swirl around his crown.

"Holy shit," he hissed. "That's good. Your mouth on my cock, Amelia...nothing like it. This feels like a dream."

He tasted warm and salty as I sucked, rubbing my palm along his shaft. He gripped the back of my hair to guide my mouth as it bobbed up and down over his cock.

At one point, I began to take him as deeply as I could without choking. As I intentionally squeezed the back of my throat around his cock, I snuck a glance up at his reaction as he muttered, "Oh, you evil bitch. That is so fucking good."

I repeated the movement again and again. His eyes were closed so tightly that he looked like his mind had traveled to another dimension.

My own moans vibrated over his cock as he suddenly bucked his hips and came hard down my throat. Pulling my hair, he groaned, "Shit. Take it all, baby. Take it all," as I drank in the hot spurts of cum shooting down my throat.

I looked up at him seductively as I swallowed every last drop.

When there was nothing left but his panting, he said, "Fuck. You didn't hold back. I always knew you liked cream with your coffee, but damn. It was hot to see how much you enjoyed it too." He released a long breath as he adjusted his pants. "I already want to do it again. Is this a trick to get me to stay or something? Because it just might fucking work."

"Really? If that's the case, my mouth is ready."

"Oh, we *will* be doing that again before I leave. That... was mind-blowing. Where the hell did you learn to suck like that?" He shook his head fast. "Never mind. I don't really want to know." Wiping the corners of my mouth, he asked, "What the heck did I do to deserve that, anyway?"

"You saved my daughter's life. You deserved the blow job of *your* life."

He squeezed me close. "Quick, run out to the beach and jump in the choppy ocean."

I squinted my eyes. "Why?"

"That way I can save you. Maybe you'll let me take that ass later."

———

Justin spent a record amount of time that afternoon trying to get Bea to say "Dada."

She babbled a lot in general but hadn't used the letter D as much as the letters B or M. She also knew how to say "bye bye."

I watched the two of them from the kitchen as Justin sat with Bea on the couch, trying to get her to repeat his words.

"Say 'Dada.'" He pointed to himself. "I'm Dada."

"Baba," she said.

He repeated, "Dada."

"Baba."

"Dada."

She blew a raspberry and giggled.

"You silly girl. Say 'Dada.'"

Bea paused for a bit, then said, "Mama," before cracking up. Justin tickled her belly with his hair, and she fell into a laughing fit.

Wiping the kitchen counter, I was in stitches watching all of this go down. Either I was raising a Mama's girl, or she was one hell of a little comedian.

CHAPTER 23

The three months that followed Christmas dragged.

Bea started to walk right around the time she turned one on March fifteenth. Justin was pissed that he'd missed not only her birthday, but her first steps. He kept trying to get her to say "Dada" or "Daddy" during our Skype chats to no avail.

Those weeks were tough, but knowing with absolute certainty that he was coming home to us was what got me through. Getting to finally see him in concert at the end of it all would be the cherry on top.

The tour had finally made its way back to this side of the pond. The final shows were in Nova Scotia, Maine, and New York City.

It was finally the weekend of the long-awaited Manhattan show. Justin had purchased plane tickets for Bea and me to fly to New York. We would then immediately check into a hotel near the concert venue. Since the band's travel time back from Maine on Saturday afternoon would be cutting it close to showtime, we wouldn't have a chance to see Justin until after his performance that night.

Bea was great on the quick commuter flight from Providence to La Guardia. I'd packed one small carry-on for both of us and a polka dot umbrella stroller.

When we landed, Justin's manager, Steve, was nice enough to pick us up from the airport and drive us to the hotel. We had to pass through Times Square. Bea looked around in awe as she took in all of the flashing primary colors and commotion. It was definitely sensory overload, probably for both of us. I'd been homebound on the island for so long, I'd almost forgotten what city life was like.

The hotel was right around the corner from the venue. After the show, the three of us would spend the night here and linger in the city tomorrow before heading back home to the island.

After we checked into our hotel room, I had the jitters. Seeing Justin perform always made me so emotional, but seeing him perform for the first time on a big stage would surely be overwhelmingly poignant.

I lay down next to Bea in the plush hotel bed, trying to get her to nap since she'd be up way past her bedtime tonight. She managed to get an hour of sleeping in before we packed up and headed to the venue.

When we arrived at the concert hall, the line to get in was a mile long. Gazing at the illuminated sign gave me chills: *Calvin Sprockett, featuring Justin Banks*. We were able to pass through to the VIP line, and an usher escorted us to our seats in the center of the third row.

Bea looked so cute as she sat on my lap. Her noise-reducing headphones were huge. She looked like a little Martian in them. Thankfully, despite all of the crying she had done for the first three months of her life, she'd turned into a mild-mannered baby, so I banked on her being able to sit through the whole performance without interruption.

When the lights dimmed and the spotlight shined down onto Justin, my heart raced. The pitter-patter of excitement was all-consuming. Justin had told me that his view of the audience was always too dark to make out faces, but I could see him looking out into the vast crowd for a moment before the first song began. My body practically melted into my seat as I bowed down to the sheer power of his amplified voice. That very first note, the initial recognition of his deep, soulful sound was always so amazing.

Squeezing Bea tightly as we rocked back and forth, I listened to him sing song after song that I'd never heard before. I hadn't realized that he only performed original songs on this tour, no covers. It made me feel like I'd missed so much in never having heard most of these songs. I closed my eyes from time to time, enjoying the sound waves of his guitar strings vibrating through me as I deciphered the lyrics.

I sat there for that first forty minutes in awe of him: the way his fingers worked the instrument with speedy precision, the way his voice could change depending on the song, the way he could mesmerize hundreds of people with nothing but his smoky voice, a guitar, and a microphone.

Justin had mentioned that his opening act was only about forty-five minutes, so I knew we were nearing the end.

He spoke into the mic. "Tonight is special for several reasons, not only because this marks the end of our tour, but also because we're here in my second favorite place in the world, New York. This was my home up until recently. My new home is on an island with the love of my life and my daughter. After tonight, I get to go home after a long time away from them. But the biggest reason tonight is special is because my daughter is here. Bea, thank you for teaching me that sometimes the thing we fear more than anything is really what our soul craves the most. This last song is one I finally finished. It took me a while because of how important it was to me because I wrote it for her. It's called 'Bea-u-tiful Girl.'"

I immediately recognized the opening melody as the same song programmed inside of the music box he had given Bea.

Then, he started to sing, and I was a goner.

My soul was sick, but you were the cure.
Never before felt a love so pure.
That thing I once feared the most,
Now turns my heart to toast.

Bea-u-tiful Girl,
I didn't make you, but you were made for me.

Bea-u-tiful Girl,
Thank you for helping me see,
The way life was meant to be.

With every one of your cries,
A part of my heart dies.
But you'll smile at me and then,
Put it back together again.

Bea-u-tiful Girl,
I didn't make you, but you were made for me.

Bea-u-tiful Girl,
Thank you for helping me see,
The way life was meant to be.

An angel in disguise,
Is reflected in the eyes,
Of a little Bumblebee.
Thank you for choosing me.

Bea-u-tiful Girl,
I didn't make you, but you were made for me.

Bea-u-tiful Girl,
Thank you for helping me see,
The way life was meant to be.

When the song finished, Justin received a standing ovation. My eyes were stinging from tears of joy. Him writing that song for Bea touched me on so many levels. I wished so much that she could understand the words.

Justin disappeared from sight as they shut down the stage for a bit to set up for Calvin. My badge was supposed to give me backstage access, but we hadn't discussed logistics. I wasn't sure if I should try to go back there now or wait for a text from him, maybe watch some of Calvin's performance.

Anxious to see him and tell him how much I loved the song, I lifted myself and Bea out of the seat and made my way down the long center aisle to the entrance. An usher directed us to the backstage entrance. A large security guard greeted me there.

"Do you have a badge?"

Flashing it, I said, "Yes. I'm Justin Banks's girlfriend, and this is his daughter."

He examined the badge again more closely and stepped aside, gesturing behind him. "Right this way. He's in dressing room four."

The door was cracked open, and it shocked me to find that Justin wasn't alone. I immediately moved to the side so that I could avoid being seen while I listened to their conversation.

"I hope you don't mind me coming here," a woman's voice said. "When I heard you were playing in town, I just had to see you. I contacted Steve, and he gave me a backstage pass."

"Of course, I don't mind. It's really good to see you, Jade."

Even though a little bit of jealousy was creeping in, it wasn't anything like what it used to be. My confidence in Justin's feelings toward me now overrode that insecurity. Still, it was always going to be uncomfortable for me to think about him and Jade, given all of my memories of them together.

"I just need to talk to you, Justin," Jade went on. "Steve told me you were with Amelia now, and I just...to be honest, I'm shocked. And then the song you sang..."

"I'm sorry, Jade. I should've been the one to tell you the news. I didn't want to hurt you any more than I already had."

"So, apparently...you *did* want children. Just not mine?"

"I didn't expect to fall in love with that baby girl."

"But you did see falling in love with her mother coming a mile away. When we lived together, you made it seem like you hated her. It wasn't hate at all, was it? I should have known. No one acts like that toward someone unless they care *too much*."

"There was no way you could have known because I kept it inside. During those early days, I fought my feelings for her. I really did. I wanted things to work between you and me. I didn't think I'd end up with Amelia. But yes, the animosity toward her was a result of other deep-rooted feelings I couldn't control. It was very complicated."

There was a bit of awkward silence before I heard her ask, "Were you with her at any point when we were together?"

"No. Nothing happened until after we broke up. I didn't

want to hurt you, but apparently, I managed to anyway. For that, I'm so sorry. You're a beautiful person, inside and out. I will always look back happily at our time together. I hope you find someone who deserves you."

When I heard Jade start to cry, it made me uncomfortable, so I decided to leave and give them privacy to finish their conversation. My heart really did break for her, and I supposed the last person she wanted to see standing there when she left his dressing room was me.

Returning to the lobby, I texted him to let us know when we should come backstage. They were kindly holding Bea's stroller for me behind the ticket counter, so I retrieved it while we were waiting. From my corner spot, I saw Jade running across the lobby and out the revolving doors.

Almost immediately after, my phone chimed with a text from Justin.

Come backstage.

He didn't notice us at first. His back was facing us. I took a moment to admire his round, muscular ass. When Bea squealed in excitement, he turned around.

I took her out of the stroller and held on to her hands while she walked with wobbly legs toward him.

He knelt down to receive her with open arms. "Bumblebee! Oh my God, you're walking." He looked amused to see her in her noise-reducing headphones. I'd neglected to take them off. "Those things are bigger than your head!" He planted a messy kiss on her cheek before standing up to kiss me. I could tell from the desperate moan he let into my mouth that he was super horny. It made me a little wet thinking about what might happen later tonight after Bea fell asleep. I'd ordered a crib to be sent up to our room so that Justin and I could have the bed. I hoped it worked out.

"You were so amazing," I said. "That song—"

"You liked it?"

"I loved it." Examining his face, I asked, "Are you okay?"

"Jade was here. She saw the show, heard the song. Steve gave her a pass, and she caught me in here, confronted me about us." It pleased me that he felt the need to be honest with me.

"I know."

"You know?"

"Yeah. We were outside the door. I heard a little of the conversation, but then I left to give you some privacy."

"Wow."

"You don't need to explain anything. It is what it is. And I understand what she's going through. I know what it's like to love you and lose you. I'm just so thankful that I have you now." I hesitated. There was so much I needed to tell him. *Proud* didn't cover how seeing him perform tonight had made me feel. "Now that I've seen you on the big stage, it solidified more than ever how much you were meant to do this with your life. Not only are you so extremely talented, but people are naturally drawn to you. I don't ever want you to give up on this because you feel guilty. You'll never have to choose. We'll always be here for you."

He lifted Bea up and planted another kiss on my lips. "You're amazing for saying that because I know how hard me being away has been. I used to think it was the fame that I wanted, but this experience has taught me that, for me, it's about the music. I don't think I really want the rest of it long-term. I would never trade this experience, and if an opportunity falls at my feet, I'll consider it. But being away from

my family week after week is not okay. It's not what I want."
He paused, then cupped my face in his hands. "There is no
music without you. Music is an expression of the things you
live for...a reflection of the passion within your soul. I live
for you. You're my passion. You're my music...you and Bea."

"I love you so much."

He grabbed his jacket. "Let's get out of here."

"What? No wild after-party? What kind of rock star are you?"

"What do you mean? I'm wild." He winked. "I'm taking
two girls back to my hotel room."

EPILOGUE
JUSTIN

Never in a million fucking years had I expected my life to turn out like this.

I swear, if you would have asked my pussy-whipped fifteen-year-old self where he wanted to be in a decade, he would have probably said, "On an island somewhere with Patch."

I guess some things never change because that would be my exact answer today. While it would have seemed like an unattainable dream then, it was my reality now.

Watching Amelia playing with Bea down at the shoreline, I thought about the evolution of the roles she'd played in my life.

The mysterious girl with the eye patch.

The best friend.

The teenage fantasy.

The girl who'd stolen my heart then broken it and taken it with her when she'd run away.

The estranged friend.

The forbidden roommate.

The girlfriend.

The mother of my babies.

She'd never been sexier than now—with my baby inside of her. At four months along, Amelia was just starting to show, mostly in her tits and ass, which was just fine by me.

I had asked her to marry me a year ago on July twenty-sixth, a few months after getting home from the tour. I had planned to wait but had decided that I had to propose on that day and that we'd get married exactly a year later. That date meant everything because 0726 were the final numbers on my barcode tattoo and were supposed to represent the day she'd left me a decade earlier. I was determined to redefine the meaning of those numbers. Now, that date—today—would always be the day she became my wife.

We hadn't wanted a fancy wedding, just a private ceremony with the three of us at the beach. We would hang out by the water in the morning, and then we'd have a wedding on the beach at sunset, followed by a clam bake of Amelia's favorite: dirty snatch crabs, and lobster.

It turned out Roger next door had gotten himself ordained to perform a ceremony for a friend of his some years back, so we were going to let him marry us. Ironically, Roger Podger had become a pretty good friend of mine, even though I continued to bust his balls regularly.

A flock of seagulls dispersed as Bea came running toward me. Her dress was soaked as she handed me a seashell. "Daddy! Blue!"

"What do you have for me, Beatrice Banks?"

Amelia brushed sand off her skirt and explained, "We're trying to find something old, something new, something borrowed, and something blue for the ceremony later. We found this blue shell."

"That's perfect, Bumblebee," I said, handing it back to her as she beamed.

"We have to figure out the rest," Amelia said as she took something out of her pocket and handed it to Bea. "We have something new, but technically it's for you, not me. Bea, give it to Daddy."

My daughter handed me a tiny box. It had a guitar pick inside with the inscription, *Thank you for picking me.*

Squeezing her, I whispered in her ear, "Thank you for picking *me*, sweetie. I love this so much."

After the wedding, I'd be formally adopting Bea. She was two years old now and more attached to me than ever. Thankfully, that asswipe, Adam, had relinquished his parental rights without a fight.

Life was good. I was still working the software job and playing a few nights a week at Sandy's. I'd been offered another opportunity to tour with a different, lesser-known artist, but had turned it down. As exciting as it had been being a traveling musician, the downsides outweighed the benefits. I didn't want to miss any more precious moments with my family. I used to think music was my life; I had been wrong. My girls were my life.

"Okay, we have something new and something blue. Now, we just need something borrowed and something old," I said.

Amelia wrapped her arm around my neck. "I was thinking of looking through some of Nana's old things in the safe. I haven't gone through it since we moved in. I'm sure we could find something old in there."

I got up from my spot on the sand. "Let's do it."

The three of us walked back to the house. Amelia's simple white strapless dress was hanging off the mantle in the living room. It made me giddy just looking at it, knowing that tonight, she would officially become Amelia Banks. Although, the piece of paper didn't matter. She'd been mine for as long as I could remember.

I stared at her for a bit as she fumbled with the safe, which was located behind a picture in the wall of the kitchen. Her being pregnant with my baby did things to me. Admiring the voluptuous shape of her changing body and knowing that I was responsible for it ignited something primal in me. My sexual appetite was off the charts, but thankfully, so was hers. I couldn't wait until our wedding night tonight. Bea would be staying overnight for the first time with Susan and Roger. I planned to take full advantage of the empty house—and full advantage of Amelia.

Amelia finally managed to get the safe unlocked. I walked over to join her, and we examined the contents.

Inside was some paperwork, a few items of jewelry, and several photos.

I took an antique-looking rhinestone barrette and clipped it into Amelia's hair, tucking some strands behind her ear. "Beautiful. There's your something borrowed." For a moment, I could see the little girls I'd fallen in love with reflected in her face—both Bea and little Patch.

Amelia began to sift through the photos, some of which pictured her mother and grandfather. Her hand stilled at one point before she lifted a Polaroid. Nana had used to love to take pictures with old-fashioned cameras even in the digital age.

This particular photo was of Amelia and me at probably ten and eleven years old. We were sitting on Nana's steps, and the photo had been snapped from behind. I was holding my first guitar, and Amelia was leaning her head on my shoulder. Nana had written on the bottom in blue pen: *The way it was meant to be.*

I took the snapshot from her to examine it more closely. "Wow."

"This is proof, Justin. She gave us this house because she knew it would bring us back together. She knew we would find this photo and hoped it would remind us of how foolish our estrangement was. She probably didn't have faith that we would find our way back to each other on our own. She wanted to send us a message." She gazed at it. "Look at this. How precious. Think of all those years we wasted."

"It happened the way it was supposed to," I said.

"You think so?"

"Yes. Think about it. Without all of that pent-up frustration, we wouldn't have had as much angry sex." I smiled. "We might not have been able to create that little girl in your belly."

We'd found out the other day that our baby was a girl. We planned to name her Melody. I continued, "I know this is strange for me to say, seeing as I don't want to think about you and that asswipe, Adam, but if we hadn't separated, Bea wouldn't be here. So, no…I would never go back and change anything. Never."

I looked at the inscription on the photo again.

The Way it was Meant to Be.

I took a pencil from the counter and added a small letter "a" to the end of the sentence.

The Way it was Meant to Bea.

**WERE YOU WONDERING WHAT JUSTIN
WAS THINKING IN CERTAIN PARTS?**

Read on for two alternate
scenes from part one,
exclusively from Justin's point of view!

SCENE ONE
You Smell Like Vomit

One surefire way to guarantee you think about the wrong person while jerking off?

Try *not* to think about them.

Then you can bet she'll be the only person who pops into your head.

With both Amelia and Jade out of the house, I was hoping to relieve my stress in peace, ease some of the damn frustration that had been building ever since moving in with Amelia. For one afternoon, I wanted to forget about her. Instead, my brain chose to remind me just how messed up I was. With every pump of my cock, it was Amelia I kept seeing.

Visions of her taunted me in increments.

First, a hint of brown hair.

Followed by her big, seafoam-green eyes.

Then her whole face.

Her naked body—or what I imagined it to look like.

Sadly, my dick didn't seem to mind any of this, becoming harder with each flash of her that entered my awareness.

Closing my eyes tighter, I willed myself to conjure up someone else.

Think about Jade.

Think about Jade.

Think about Jade.

The images of Amelia only came in stronger.

Amelia's plump lips.

Amelia's huge tits.

Fuck. This was bad.

Finally, I gave up. I stopped fighting the thoughts and just let Amelia be there.

"Hey, Amelia. What's up? Stay awhile, you annoying pain in my ass," I muttered under my breath.

As if imaginary Amelia could hear what I'd said, she bent over, displaying her round, naked ass and looking ready to receive me.

Gritting my teeth, I pressed down on my balls with one hand while pumping harder with the other. My palm was covered in precum as my arousal intensified. Licking my bottom lip, I didn't even try to prolong the inevitable. The sooner this ended, the better, because it was wrong to be thinking about her this way. It was bad enough I'd been trying so hard to hate her lately. This was an entirely new level of fucked-up.

I jerked myself faster, feeling almost ready to come. My breathing intensified as my eyes rolled back. I finally let go, positioning the small towel next to me to catch the explosion of cum shooting out as I groaned loudly.

That was when I heard a sound—and it wasn't my damn echo.

My heard turned toward the door so fast I nearly gave myself whiplash.

What the fuck?

Am I hallucinating?

Unfortunately, I wasn't.

Amelia?

The *real* Amelia.

Before I could say anything, she ran off, practically leaving smoke in her wake.

Cleaning myself off as fast as possible, I pulled up my pants and ran downstairs, readying to—I didn't even know what— chastise her? Calmly ask her why the hell she'd been standing in my doorway watching me beat my meat? What the hell *was* I gonna say? I had no clue.

But it didn't matter. Because by the time I got downstairs, there was no sign of her.

"Amelia!" I called out to confirm she'd left.

No answer.

I panted, looking around the empty house.

Now what?

My face was burning up as I experienced a mix of shock, anger, and—sexual excitement. I'd try like hell not to analyze the latter.

Stepping outside for some air, I looked out toward the ocean, tempted to jump in, even in my clothes. Maybe that would help me forget what had just happened.

Turning to the left, I then saw what looked like Amelia's long, brown hair blowing in the wind. She was running up ahead on the sand.

Not just running.

Running *away*—fast.

I took off in her direction, determined to catch up and finally ask her why she'd been spying on me.

She stopped suddenly, hunching over to catch her breath.

309

I slowed my pace before coming to a halt, choosing to watch her from a distance before making a move. At one point, Amelia stumbled over to the water.

What the fuck is she doing?

Her hair covered her face as she lurched forward down by the shoreline. I couldn't see clearly from this far back, but it looked like she might've been…throwing up? I almost ran to her to make sure she was okay, but then she started walking normally again, making her way back over to the sand. Amelia plopped her ass down and just sat there, looking up at the sky.

Now was my chance to charge over and chastise her.

Come on Justin. Grow some balls.

Putting my guard up so damn high lately had taken a lot out of me. But it was the only way I could keep all of the old feelings for Amelia at bay. I'd vowed not to soften and didn't plan on starting now. For some reason, though, I couldn't get myself to make what was clearly already a bad situation for her worse at the moment. Even if I didn't understand exactly what she'd been thinking, I didn't want to kick her when she seemed down. Kicking her when she was up, though? That would be a different story. So, I'd give her a little time. *Just a little.*

After I stalked back to the house, I paced in the kitchen for a while in an attempt to figure out how I wanted to handle Amelia when she got back.

A few ideas came to mind.

One was to stick strategic notes around the house to mess with her but not actually say a single word about what had happened. That seemed like more fun than confronting her head on.

I grabbed a pen and sticky note from the kitchen drawer and wrote:

Does not saying a peep make you any less of a creep?

That cracked me up.

I opened the fridge and proceeded to stick it onto the orange juice container.

She'd see it the next time she went for a snack. Subtle but effective.

Deciding to take a shower, I couldn't help ruminating while under the water. I started to doubt whether leaving the note was the best way to handle things. Not only that, but I couldn't stop thinking of other, catchier lines.

Only the biggest perv will quietly observe.

Ugh. The orange juice idea sucked.

After I left the bathroom, I got dressed as fast as possible and raced downstairs to take the sticky note off the carton, hoping she hadn't already come home and seen it.

The second my feet hit the bottom of the stairs, I heard the door open.

Running over to the fridge just in time, I grabbed the carton, snatching the note and sticking it in my back pocket. I opened the orange juice and started downing it to seem nonchalant when she entered the kitchen.

Even though I wasn't looking at her, I sensed her nearness as she came up behind me. The hairs on the back of my neck rose as I thought about what might have been going through her head earlier while she had watched me—and what was going through her head now. I took a last gulp before closing the container and returning it to the refrigerator.

Given no choice, I finally turned to her.

Amelia looked exhausted. Her face was pale, her hair

disheveled. Moreover, her eyes seemed filled with fear. It was the expression of someone fully expecting to be humiliated.

I walked slowly toward her and inhaled deeply.

Several seconds of silence passed as I just stared at her before uttering the first thing that came to mind.

"You smell like vomit."

She really didn't. She just *looked* like she did.

With that, I cowered, deciding to say nothing else about what had happened today. Instead, I turned around and headed up the stairs to my room.

As I lay down on the bed, I let out a long breath and laughed to myself.

I spoke to the ceiling. "That went well."

After a couple of minutes, I tried to forget about the whole thing, reaching for my guitar and tooling around with some melodies. All of a sudden, these lyrics started coming to me.

> *She pretends to be a good girl,*
> *Quiet and refined.*
> *But Daddy always said,*
> *Those are the worst kind.*

Then it hit me: *exactly* how to handle Amelia's peeping. A one-liner would never be enough. Not in the least.
I'm gonna write her a fucking song.

SCENE TWO
Lick, Slam, Suck

As soon as I returned home to an empty house, I remembered Amelia mentioning she was meeting a friend for dinner in downtown Newport. Probably a good thing. I certainly didn't need to be alone with her again.

I was supposed to be performing at Sandy's, but when I'd arrived, I'd found out they'd had a kitchen fire and had to temporarily close down. So, there'd be no show tonight.

Amelia and I had been getting along lately, which was something I'd tried to avoid for a while. Getting along meant feeling all of the old feelings—both good and bad—again. And I didn't have the bandwidth to handle that, especially given that my time here on Aquidneck Island would be coming to an end soon.

I'd been keeping my distance from her ever since the night we'd stayed up talking. That had been the most time we'd spent together alone all summer. And I was still recovering mentally from that caffeine-fueled all-nighter. It was bad enough I'd accidentally taken her to an X-rated theater that evening. But the fact that she'd seemed *turned on* was something I was having trouble forgetting.

Tonight, I planned to take advantage of both Amelia's absence and my unexpected reprieve from performing. After going for a quick swim in the ocean, I took a shower, then got dressed. Had Amelia been home, I might've put on a shirt, but instead, I only threw on a pair of jeans. It seemed like the perfect night to head to the upper deck and smoke one of the Cuban cigars I'd been saving.

The water was calm with the perfect amount of ocean breeze. I took my hat off and enjoyed the feel of the air on my face as I sat down. Kicking my legs up on the ledge of the balcony, I'd just lit the cigar and taken my first puff when I heard steps.

I lowered my feet to the ground and turned to find Amelia standing there on the deck with a friend.

"What are you doing here?" she asked. "I thought you were playing at the restaurant."

I blew out some of the smoke. "I was supposed to be. But the place almost burned down."

"What?"

"There was a kitchen fire this afternoon. When I showed up, they told me they had to close to air out the entire restaurant. They won't be reopening for another week, at least. It doesn't look like I'll get to play there again before I leave."

"Holy shit. Did anyone get hurt?"

"No, but Salvatore was a fucking wreck." I looked over at her friend. "Who's this?"

"This is Tracy, a good friend from Providence and a teacher at my school. She came down to spend the day with me. She's gonna sleep over tonight."

My peaceful evening plans were apparently no more. I

314

reached for my hat and decided to give them some privacy, but not before introducing myself.

I held my hand out to her friend. "Nice to meet you."

"Likewise," she said, taking it.

Amelia frowned. "Wow. I can't believe that about the fire."

"I wasn't really in the mood to perform tonight, but I would have never wished that shit on Sal."

"Gosh. I wonder if I'll even be working there again myself before the end of summer," she said.

I took a puff of the cigar. "What are you ladies up to tonight?"

"We were gonna have some drinks and have a girls' night in," Amelia said.

"That sounds like a hot mess," I teased.

Tracy laughed. "It's not every night that I get away from my kids. So, this is about as wild as it gets for me."

I winked. "Well, I'll stay out of your way then."

"You don't have to," her friend said. "You should join us for a drink."

Yeah, right. The last thing I needed was to become inebriated with these two and let my guard down with Amelia any more than I already had lately.

"That's all right," I told her. "I'll pass."

They headed downstairs before I had a chance to leave the deck first. Breathing out a sigh of relief, I decided to resume my cigar time alone for a little while longer.

After I put out the stogie, I lingered on the deck for a while, avoiding having to make conversation with Amelia's friend again. But after the ocean wind picked up, it got cold as balls up there. So, I decided to make my way downstairs.

The first thing that I noticed was a bottle of tequila big enough to serve twenty people on the kitchen counter.

"Jesus Christ. Enough tequila?" I cracked.

Amelia, who'd been cutting up limes, turned to me. She pointed the knife toward her friend. "It was her idea. I've never done tequila shots before."

I narrowed my eyes. "You've never done a tequila shot?"

"Nope."

"Damn, Patch. What? Did they not know how to live it up in New Hampshire?"

"I never really drank at all until about a year ago. Actually, I've never drank more than I have this summer."

Ah. *I'd* driven her to drink. Made some sense, actually, given the tension in this house all summer.

I cocked a brow. "Can I take responsibility for that?"

"Maybe." She blushed.

My eyes lingered on Amelia's. I hadn't even realized her friend had left the room until she returned and announced, "I'm so sorry, Amelia, but Todd just called and said that Ava is sick and throwing up. He really needs me to head back home to Warwick."

Shit. She's leaving?

Amelia put down her knife. "Are you serious? I'm so sorry to hear that."

"I guess you two will have to enjoy the tequila without me. I'm just glad Todd called before I started drinking and couldn't drive myself home."

As they hugged and said goodbye to each other, I rubbed at the tension in the back of my neck.

Tracy turned to me. "It was nice meeting you, Justin."

I nodded and waved her off, feeling on edge that this woman was leaving me alone with Amelia and a bottle of tequila bigger than both our heads put together. It wasn't that I didn't trust myself with her. But I couldn't afford to lose my inhibitions when I'd already opened up too much recently. Complicating things further wasn't something I needed right before the end of my time here.

Crossing my arms, I leaned against the kitchen counter, feeling like I didn't know what to do with myself. It seemed rude to leave Amelia and head to my room now, even if that was probably what I should've done.

After her friend left, Amelia slowly made her way toward me, causing my pulse to react with every step closer. I needed to chill. Force myself to just lean into this night and stop trying so damn hard to resist being around her. Because, so far, resisting had only made my predicament worse.

"What are we gonna do with all this tequila?" I asked.

She flashed an impish grin. "I don't know."

Screw it.

"I think we should drink it," I suggested.

"I don't know how to do tequila shots. Tracy was gonna show me."

"Simple. Lick, slam, suck."

Her eyes widened. "Excuse me?"

"It's a four-step process. You wet your hand to salt it, lick the salt off, slam the glass down after drinking it, and then you suck the lime. Lick, slam, suck. I'll show you how to do it."

That sounded so wrong, and I tried to push away the dirty and inappropriate thoughts in my brain right now. *Licking* a line down Amelia's neck. *Slamming* her against the counter. *Sucking* on her—

Amelia's phone vibrated, interrupting my thoughts. I nosily looked down at the screen.

It was a text from her friend who'd just left. I lifted the phone to read it.

Justin totally wants you. You should fuck him
hard tonight.

I froze. *Are you kidding me?*

"Real fucking nice," I said as I handed it to her.

As Amelia turned several shades of red, my blood boiled.
That woman's assertion pissed me off. How the hell did
she know what I wanted? Had I given off a vibe that I was
unaware of? I'd barely even said anything.

The visual that the text had triggered in my brain, though?
Amelia fucking me hard? I wouldn't be able to get it out of
my mind now. And that really sucked when I wouldn't be
doing a damn thing about it.

Not with Amelia.

Never with Amelia.

I glared at her.

She started to laugh, but it didn't reach her eyes and seemed
forced. Amelia stumbled over her words as she attempted
damage control. "She's a jokester. She likes to bust balls. I'm
sorry."

Sure, she's joking. I somehow doubted that. I wondered
what fuckery Amelia had fed her when they were out to
dinner earlier that would've led Tracy to conclude that I
"wanted" Amelia.

I racked my brain. Had I done something to lead Amelia
on? It wasn't like she could read the inappropriate thoughts
in my head lately. Was it the other night at the porno theater?
Was it the song I'd written for her before that?

There was no way in hell I was going to encourage Amelia
to explain that text tonight, though. I needed to change the
subject, stat. *And* I needed alcohol.

"I really need that fucking drink," I announced.

"Me too." She exhaled.

Picking up the bottle, I took a look at the name on the label. "Did you pick out this tequila?"

"Yes."

"This brand sucks. It's cheap."

"I told you. I don't know anything about tequila."

"Actually, it's not the worst thing in the world, because we'll chug it down so fast, you won't even taste it. If it were the expensive stuff, then that would be a waste."

Still on edge, I was barely able to remember where anything was in this kitchen as I went in search of the salt. After I finally found it, I located two shot glasses in the cabinet.

I slid a glass over to her, then began to demonstrate by separating my thumb and index finger. "Put your hand like this, and do what I do." I licked between my fingers. Maybe this wasn't a good idea, because I suddenly felt my pants getting tighter. It was the way she'd watched me intently while I'd licked my hand.

Being horny and about to be drunk with a woman who was not my girlfriend was a hopeless situation. And if it wasn't bad enough, it became worse when Amelia mimicked me, licking between her fingers. My dick twitched before I attempted to assure myself that I couldn't be blamed for my body's reaction to things. It had a mind of its own.

I added some salt to my hand, then hers. "You're gonna lick the salt off real fast before drinking the tequila down in one shot. Don't stop. Drink it all down. Then, grab a lime and suck."

Again, my own words caused a rush of adrenaline. I could've stood to sound a little less demanding...even if the idea of ordering Amelia around was so damn arousing.

I cleared my throat. "Ready? We'll do it together. On the count of three. One... Two... Three."

We licked our hands at the same time before slamming the shots down.

Then, I picked up a lime and brought it to her mouth, keeping my hand there. "Quick. Suck on this. It will diffuse the taste."

I watched as she sucked the juice out, my fingers making contact with her lips. I was mesmerized for a few seconds, never having witnessed Amelia do anything so erotic.

As I took the lime away, I urged my dick to soften.

She wiped her mouth with the back of her hand. "God, that was strong. What do we do now? Another one?"

"Easy, drunk-ass. We should wait a bit. You're a light-weight."

Despite my vow that we'd pace ourselves, we ended up throwing down too many. Even though I'd never considered myself a lightweight, I was beginning to feel it. And Amelia? She was most definitely shitfaced.

When she nearly fell on her ass from loss of balance, I announced, "All right. That's it. I'm cutting you off."

Meanwhile, I did two more shots myself before calling it quits. But I'd convinced myself that I needed them to get through the rest of this night. At one point, Amelia and I just looked at each other and started laughing for no reason. Yep. Definitely drunk off our asses.

Her legs wobbled as she made her way over to the sofa. I sat down next to her and rested my head on the back of the couch. Closing my eyes, I ran a hand through my hair. When I opened them, the room definitely seemed to be moving.

I looked over at Amelia. Through my drunken haze, she looked so damn beautiful. Her cheeks red from the alcohol. Her lips extra plump. Her hair a tousled mess. She looked like…sex. And that was not good.

Then she did something that shocked the shit out of me. Amelia reached over to me and started to drag her fingers through my hair.

I closed my eyes and groaned.

Fuck.

I should've immediately pushed back, but I didn't. With each second that passed, I fell into a deeper state of relaxation, one laced with sexual arousal.

My breathing accelerated. While I didn't want her to stop, I was afraid for it to continue. I finally forced my eyes open and snapped, "What the fuck are you doing, Amelia?"

She moved her hand back suddenly. "I'm sorry. I...I got carried away."

"I see. Blame it on the alcohol?"

My own words caused me to wince. What a damn fool to try to chastise her when *I* was the one who'd sat there for at least a full minute, enjoying every second of it. Drunk or not, I was disgusted with how I'd reacted. Especially because, despite knowing how inappropriate that had been, I was still turned on—my body wanted more. It wanted her hands back on me. But to apologize would mean having to admit *why* I'd overreacted. Instead of doing the right thing, I stood up suddenly and walked to the other side of the living room. Yanking on my hair, I started to pace.

Then, my behavior got even more bizarre as I dropped to the floor and did push-ups. I continued this for a while, multiple sets, one after the other, praying that the movement worked to sober me up fast. Because drunk Justin had lost his damn mind tonight.

I kept pushing myself until I finally collapsed, lying on my back, sweating profusely. Almost as soon as I sat up, I noticed Amelia walking toward the stairs.

No way I could let her go to bed without at least *trying* to make things right.

"Don't go," I called after her.

She turned. "I think I really need to just go to sleep."

"Come here," I whispered, feeling myself coming unhinged—not physically, this time, but emotionally.

She hesitantly walked back over to the couch.

I pointed to the spot next to me on the floor. "I said come... here." I needed her close to me to be able to show her something. After she sat down, I turned my bare back toward her. My tone softened. "You asked me what this tattoo on my back meant. Look at the numbers in three sets of four under the barcode."

This was the closest she'd ever been to my tattoo; I doubted she'd ever been able to make out the small digits before.

After staring at the numbers for a while, she finally said, "That's December twenty-first, your birthday."

"Yeah."

I could feel her finger point to the numbers next to it. "What's that one?"

"March twenty-third, 2001," I answered.

"What's the significance of that date?"

I raised a brow. "You don't know?"

She shook her head. "No."

"That was the day we met."

"How on earth did you remember the exact date?"

"I just never forgot."

There was actually a bit more to it than that. At eleven years old, I'd jotted the date down in a notebook next to the lyrics of the song I'd written for her that day—"One Eyed Girl." Something back then had told me she'd end up being special to me and that I'd want to remember when we'd met. I still had that notebook too.

She went silent again, and I assumed she was trying to figure out the last set of digits: 0726.

"July twenty-sixth was the date I left Providence in 2006." She paused. "The barcode represents your birth and the beginning and end of our relationship."

She finally got it. And perhaps finally got just how damn much she meant to me, even if I'd been trying like hell this summer to make her think the opposite.

"Yeah. Defining moments of my life."

"When did you get this tattoo?"

"The night I got it, I was in Boston finishing my first and last semester at Berklee. I knew I wasn't going to be returning, because I couldn't afford it. I was depressed and missing you like hell that night. But I'd refused to speak to you when you'd tried to contact me the year before, and I wasn't going to budge. I was young and stubborn. I wanted to make you pay for running away. The only way I knew how to achieve that was to do to you what you did to me—disappear. I found a tattoo place near school and had this inked on me. It represented letting you go once and for all."

"Did it do the trick?"

Hell no.

"You know…after that day, I really followed through with my vow to move on. And every year, it did get easier to forget everything, especially after I moved to New York. Days and weeks would go by without thinking about you. I thought I'd put you in the past where you belonged."

"Until you couldn't avoid me anymore."

I nodded, turning back to her. "Coming here, I had no idea what to expect. When I laid eyes on you that first day in the kitchen, I quickly realized the feelings hadn't gone away at all. I'd just been suppressing them. Seeing you again as a grown woman…it was jarring. I didn't know how to handle it."

"Besides being mean."

That hurt to hear, even if it was the absolute truth.

"At first, I was still so fucking angry at you. I wanted you to be a bitch to me, so that at least the anger would be justified. But instead, you were sweet and full of regret. The object of my anger has slowly been shifting from you to myself…for wasting all those years in bitterness. So you know what this tattoo represents to me now?" It was hard to admit. "Fucking stupidity."

Her eyes watered. "I was the stupid one for ever leaving you. I—"

"Let me finish. I've got to get this out tonight."

"All right."

I felt like I needed to address the elephant in the room before I lost the balls to do it.

"We need to talk about our attraction to each other, Amelia."

She swallowed hard. "Okay."

"That text from your friend…she was right. I want to fuck you so badly right now that I'm practically shaking. My conscience is the only thing stopping me. It's wrong and so messed up."

I kept waiting for her to say something, but she just kept looking at me, her face getting redder by the second and her chest heaving. One of two things was happening: Either she was aroused or about to hurl in my face.

I went on. "Ever since that day I caught you watching me in my room…I haven't been able to get you out of my head."

"I shouldn't have done that."

"No, you shouldn't have. But the thing is…I couldn't

even be mad at you, because you watching me jerk off was just about the hottest fucking thing I've ever experienced in my life."

Her face turned even more crimson. "I figured you thought I was perverted."

I shook my head. "I would've done the same thing if I walked by your room and saw you touching yourself."

"You have a beautiful body, Justin. It was hard to look away."

That was the first time she'd ever complimented me in a sexual way. Amelia had never known how much I'd strived for her approval. How much, especially when we were younger, I'd wanted her to want me.

My voice was barely audible as shameless curiosity got the best of me. "What were you thinking about?"

"What do you mean?"

"When you were watching me. What were you thinking about?"

"I was imagining that I was with you," she said.

I inhaled suddenly, needing to turn away for a moment. Her answer only made my dilemma worse. How much of this edging could I possibly take? I knew I wasn't going to make a move on her. But even though my body was complying for the moment, my brain kept pushing.

I finally looked her in the eyes again. "Have you always been as attracted to me as you are now?"

"Yes. But even more so now. I know it's wrong, Justin."

"Right or wrong, we can't help who we're attracted to. I don't want to want you like this. Just sitting next to you right now is hard for me. But wanting someone and acting on it are two different things. That's why when you were touching my hair, I had to stop it."

"I really wasn't trying to sleep with you. I just missed touching your hair. That's all. It was selfish."

"Believe me, I understand. I'm not innocent in all of this. I've looked for excuses to touch you too. But I have a girlfriend. We have a good life in New York. There's no excuse. I'm starting to feel like my father, totally out of control with no concern for anyone else."

"You're not your father."

"My mother was just as bad."

"Well, you're not your parents."

I had a hard time believing that the apple didn't fall far from the tree.

"I don't want to hurt you either, Patch. I'm so fucking confused. This situation with sharing the house makes things very awkward." I closed my eyes for a moment, unsure of whether to propose something that felt like the only solution. "Maybe we should work out an arrangement next year."

Amelia narrowed her eyes. "Arrangement?"

"Yeah, like maybe we alternate months, so that we don't have to be here at the same time."

She moved back suddenly, as if I'd dealt her a physical blow. This proposal was an impulsive, desperate attempt at righting my wrongs tonight, a misguided belief that physical distance should be my punishment for a lack of self-control.

Amelia gritted her teeth, looking angrier than I'd ever seen her. "Let me get this straight. You can't trust yourself around me, so you don't want to physically see me ever again?"

Basically.

"That's not it."

"Then why else would you not want to be around me?"

"Do you really enjoy hearing me and Jade fucking?" I shouted.

"No. But—"

"Well, I don't want to hear you fucking anyone, either. I'm trying to protect both of us here."

Her voice shook. "So, you'd rather just not see me at all?"

"I didn't say that. But coming up with a schedule is something we should at least consider. I think that would be a smart option."

Smart, right. It was nothing more than running away from my feelings for her again. I hadn't thought my suggestion through, especially how she might react. Not to mention, physical distance had never been the answer to our unfinished business. It wasn't really what I wanted. But I'd made my bed now. And it had backfired in a big way.

Her watery eyes filled with rage. "As hard as this has been for me, I've never once considered that. That's the difference between us. I would deal with any amount of discomfort that it took in order to have you in my life again. I would never choose any option that involved pretending you didn't exist anymore. I would take any fragment of you over nothing at all. Clearly, you don't feel the same about me. So, you know what? Now that I know that…I'm perfectly good with a schedule." Tears streamed down her cheeks.

Now I've gone and gone and done it. I felt like absolute shit.

"Fuck, Patch. Don't cry."

"Please. Don't call me that name ever again."

I covered my face with my hands. "Fuck!"

Amelia ran over to the kitchen and started pouring more of the tequila.

She'd drunk way too much already. I snatched the bottle and closed it. "You're gonna make yourself sick."

"That would be none of your concern."

It felt like we'd boarded the hot mess express and couldn't

327

get off. No sooner than I'd had that thought, our messy night turned into a full-fledged nightmare when the door suddenly opened.

The sight of Jade entering nearly knocked the wind out of me.

My heart pounding a mile a minute, I forced a smile. "Jade!"

My girlfriend smiled back, looking so happy to see me as she ran to give me a hug. "I couldn't wait till tomorrow. I missed you so much."

When she kissed me, my entire body froze. Even though I knew it was impossible, it somehow felt like she'd be able to taste my sins. I also felt nauseous with Amelia standing right there.

Jade pulled back and said, "You smell like tequila."

Smell like it? I imagine at this point it has to be coming out of my pores.

I swallowed, the guilt nearly choking me. "Yeah. Her friend was here and brought it."

"Glad to see you two are still speaking to each other." She walked over to Amelia and gave her a hug. "I missed you too, Amelia."

What a clusterfuck.

Amelia clutched her stomach, looking ready to vomit. "I'm so glad you're back."

Jade squinted as she took a closer look at my drinking buddy, seeming to finally notice that something was off. "Your eyes look red. Are you okay?"

"Yes. I just drank too much. I'm not used to it."

"Tequila is rough." She glanced over at the bottle we'd destroyed. "Especially cheap crap like that."

Jade proceeded to ramble on to Amelia about her time in

New York. I kept glancing over at Amelia, trying to silently apologize with my eyes for my behavior tonight.

"Well, I'm exhausted. I'm gonna head upstairs," Amelia finally announced.

"Hope we don't disturb you too much tonight." Jade winked, then looked to me. "It's been a while."

A shooting pain blasted through my head. That was probably the worst thing she could've said. But what I really needed to ponder was why *my girlfriend* wanting to have sex with me was suddenly a bad thing. This was proof that my feelings for Amelia had officially crossed a line, since it now felt like I was betraying *both* of them.

"Don't worry about me. Go to town," Amelia said, her tone filled with bitterness.

My stomach was in knots. The idea that I'd be able to "not worry" about Amelia and forget about everything that happened was laughable. But there was no way to fix things tonight while Amelia was drunk and Jade looked ready to pounce.

As I followed Jade upstairs, I vowed to do better tomorrow, to come up with a plan of action that would result in neither Jade nor Amelia getting hurt. Maybe that meant walking away from both of them.

Until then? I'd be literally and figuratively fucked.

Acknowledgments

First and foremost, thank you to my husband for your love and patience throughout this writing journey.

To Vi: I cringe at the thought of never having found you. Who would I talk to? How would I do this alone? Thanks for everything…all day long!

To Julie: Thank you for always reminding me with your example that talent and integrity can go hand in hand.

To Erika: Thank you for always being there, for July get-togethers, and always spreading your sunshine.

To Luna: Te adoro mucho. Gracias para todo.

To Cheri: Thank you for never forgetting a Wednesday!

To Darlene: For always spoiling me with your friendship.

To my invaluable Facebook reader group, Penelope's Peeps: Love you all! Can't wait for more live chats.

To all the bloggers/influencers who help and support me: You are the reason for my success.

To Give Me Books: Thank you for handling my release promotions. You rock!

To my readers: None of this would be possible without you, and nothing makes me happier than knowing I've provided you with an escape from the daily stresses of life. That same escape was why I started writing. There is no greater joy in this business than to hear from you directly and to know that something I wrote touched you in some way.

To my parents: For inspiring me to follow my dreams from a very young age.

To Allison: For manifesting all of this, and to my besties, Angela, Tarah, and Sonia for your friendship. Last but not least, to my daughter and son: Mommy loves you. You are my motivation and inspiration!

About the Author

Penelope Ward is a *New York Times, USA Today,* and #1 *Wall Street Journal* bestselling author of contemporary romance.

She grew up in Boston with five older brothers and spent most of her twenties as a television news anchor. Penelope resides in Rhode Island with her husband, son, and beautiful daughter with autism.

With millions of books sold, she is a twenty-one-time *New York Times* bestseller and the author of over thirty books. Her novels have been translated into over a dozen languages and can be found in bookstores around the world.

Email Penelope at: penelopewardauthor@gmail.com
Newsletter Signup: bit.ly/1X725rj
Facebook Author Page: penelopewardauthor
Facebook Fan Group (Request to join!):
facebook.com/groups/PenelopesPeeps/
Instagram: @PenelopeWardAuthor
Website: penelopewardauthor.com